JESUS' SILENT YEARS

VOLUME 3

Journey

VANCE SHEPPERSON

ISBN's:
978-1-7344471-4-9 (softcover)
978-1-7344471-5-6 (e-book)
978-1-7344471-6-3 (audiobook)

Published by Carpenter's Son, Nashville, TN

Publisher's Note

This is a work of fiction. Names, characters, places, and incidents either are the product of the author's imagination or are used fictitiously, and any resemblance to actual persons, living or dead, events, or locales is entirely coincidental.

Printed in the United States of America.
Cover and interior illustrations by Dorine Deen

To my encourager and life companion, Bethyl Joy.

There are so many other things Jesus did. If they were all written down, each of them, one by one, I can't imagine a world big enough to hold such a library.

John 21:25

AUTHOR'S NOTE

Some studies report that the average person experiences about 60,000 thoughts a day and eighty per cent of them are negative in nature. *Journey*'s fictional stories, embedded in Jewish and Roman history, are intended to help flip your script inside a new angle on an old story. Listen with a fresh ear to Father's voice through the Spirit's power coming from Jesus' mouth.

The classic hero's journey is shaped like a 'check mark'—medium to low and high at the end. Stories in *Journey*, this third volume of four in *Jesus' Silent Years,* are at the bottom of the check mark. These stories are Jesus' roughest ride into adulthood. However, as in all character driven stories, suffering is the furnace that shapes us more than any other.

This book gives a new wrinkle to *Jesus' Silent Years.* Windy tells Jesus at one point, "Shame has silenced you, taken your voice." This part of Jesus' journey leaves him in a prolonged silence for a good, long while.

I primarily wrote this third book for people who've been marginalized—prisoners, the sexually abused, minorities, poor, orphans, and aliens. Jesus experiences all of this in *Journey*.

I'm convinced *all* of us need an Advocate who's been there, done that. I was pressured by some folks to leave this stuff out, sanitize the story. Bottom line? I wanted everyone to have a representative, a vulnerable, courageous, awkward Messiah who rose to overcome abuse of all sorts. Most will accept the idea that Jesus went through what we all go through. A nice idea. But they haven't taken their imagination for a walk into what this might have meant.

Spoiler alert—if you have a weak constitution, history of abuse, or otherwise don't want your imagination stretched in these ways, skip chapter nine, and move on. The scenes do not include gratuitous description, but the bare bones of a prison rape are plain. Further, as one of my reviewers has noted, I failed to provide a do-it-yourself appendectomy kit. So, save yourself the gut wrench. The chapters following the rape scene in prison (or after Slow's rape scene later in chapter 38) are kind, practical stories of how to seek comfort from God in the midst of hard times. You might want to move straight to comfort.

LIST OF MAJOR CHARACTERS IN JOURNEY

Caligula, Germanicus' younger son, one of Tiberius' lovers, 3rd emperor of Rome

Claudia, daughter to Tribune Gaius and Livena, granddaughter of Caesar Augustus

Crispus, Samaritan terrorist, demon-harassed, all-around bad guy

Deborah, Jesus' baby sister, the youngest sibling

El Roi, proprietor of Rahab's Rehab

Esmerelda, Zac's African wife, bought off a slaver's mule train

Esther, Rav Moshe's wife

Gaius, Roman tribune, father of the twins, Claudius and Claudia, husband to Livena

Gemellus, Drusus' grandson, Germanicus' oldest son, adopted by Tiberius.

Gomaria, sister to Leah, wife of Laz, name changed to Slow by Jesus

Ioanna, Greek wife to Giorgos, mother of Luke and Sophia

James, Jesus next youngest brother, three years younger

John, also called John the Baptist, Jesus' second cousin

Jesus, also called: Jesus bar Joseph, Messiah, Jesus of Nazareth

Jude, Jesus middle brother, after James, before Justus

Julilla, Augustus' granddaughter by his only biological child, Julia

Julius, Jesus' childhood friend from Egypt, son of Egyptian Prefect

Justus, Jesus' youngest brother

Laz, called Lazarus, Jesus' close friend, husband of Gomaria

Leah, daughter of Achan, sister to Gomaria, or Go; wife to Rabbus

Livia, wife to Caesar Augustus, also known as Augusta

Maltesa, known also as Maltie, husband to Rastus, rich merchantess in Jericho

Mary, wife to Ehud, daughter of Hez and Beta, sister to Martha and Laz

Mary, Jesus' mother, daughter of Eli, a scribe

Martha, wife to Mordi, daughter of Hez and Beta, sister to Mary and Laz

Mordi, Martha's husband; Laz's brother-in-law

Moshe, also called Rav; Jesus teacher from age eight to twenty-eight

Rabbus, Leah's husband, Tiberius' bodyguard

Rastus, healed murder-thief-leper, married to Maltesa, older half-brother to Zacchaeus

Slow, Laz's wife, example of a dissociative identity disordered person

Sophia, daughter of Greek physician Giorgos and sister to Luke

Tiberius, adopted son of Augustus, birth son of Augusta (or Livia), 2nd Roman emperor

Zacchaeus, tax collector in Jericho, husband to Esmeralda, younger half-brother to Rastus

TABLE OF CONTENTS

1

MARY

Jesus finished last. He brought up the end of Caesar Augustus' funeral parade, almost lost in the dust eddies blowing across the road. Thousands of Imperial troops had already passed. Senators, statesmen, royalty of all kinds had followed the golden casket and golden carriages. The parade had gone for miles on this hot August day.

I stood beneath our sixth-floor apartment on the corner, waiting for Jesus, feeling flaccid and thin-skinned as a popped soap bubble. This corner fountain, fed by an aqueduct, made the heat barely tolerable. James filled our drinking jugs time and again. Justice, Jude, and Miriam played with other children. Deborah, now four years old, mostly wanted me to hold her. She went from me to pulling on Gabe in Leah's arms. Leah, precious Leah, Rabbus' wife, had lost weight. She reminded me of a pale moon on the wane. When she wasn't holding her toddler, she gnawed her left thumb. Out of the corner of my eye, I saw her glancing at me as if I'd caught her finger in the worry till.

And also, there was cousin Elizabeth's son, John. I'd more or less adopted this earnest, eccentric, lovable nephew since Elizabeth and her husband, Zechariah, had died. He paced in circles, sweat popping out on his forehead. "Aunt Mary, I *have* to find Jesus! I have to prepare his path. *That's my* job. How can I do that at a standstill?"

"Why waste preparation time with movement, John? There's more going on between heaven and earth than either of us will ever know. Stand still, like warriors have done since time out of mind, waiting for God to work on their behalf.[1] Surround him with prayer, like a fortress wall."

He wasn't good at this whole "still-thing." He sighed, took Deborah from my arms, and raced around the fountain, dunking her time and again, to her delight. He would scream, "I baptize you, child, in your big brother's name!" She'd flop around, not having a clue what he meant, other than he loved her.

Now, finally, in the heat of the afternoon, here Jesus came. He clanked along barefoot, clad only in a loincloth and chains. He was the rag-tag tail end of all that pomp and circumstance. Half-trot, right leg trailing, behind the last beast of burden, covered in the dust of all who had gone before him.

I told John, "Please. Don't go to him now. Let me. You keep the other children here."

He must have seen my desperation. Yes, now was the time for action, but not his action. He clamped down resolve and nailed himself in place, nodding me toward my son. He must have known, certain as Windy's breath in his lungs; this was for me to do.

I raced across the street, pushed past the guards. "Have mercy. I'm his mother. I beg you, let me give him water."

One guard looked at Jesus, saw he was dragging. On his last leg. He took pity and let me pass. I knelt in front of Son and lifted a two-liter jug of cool water. He stood before me, hands on knees, panting. Under the layers of grime, a long scar ran down both his right arm and right leg—long, angry welts. Thin, black thread held his skin together.

So many questions, so many hugs—but now, none. The only thing the guard allowed was a drink from my gourd. Jesus tipped the jug back and drained it. After he drank, he fell to his knees, head bowed. When he looked up, tears had streaked their way through the mud on his face.

His voice scraped from him like a stick on jagged tin. He said, "Mother, Father's will has fallen on me. It is his pleasure for me to be brought low. It will also be his pleasure to raise me up in due time."

The guard prodded him with the sharp end of his spear, "No more talk. Move!"

Jesus rose, half-trotted, and was half-pulled by the pack mule in front of him. I longed to run after him, rescue him from such pain.

A stronger voice, one I knew well, the voice of my Heavenly Husband, rose in my heart. *Don't rescue him from his destiny. He's in my care. Your place is apart, in a quiet space. Cover your head. Be with me. Pray for him.*

Jesus didn't look back.

I didn't know then what I know now. That very night, after John had gone for a run in the hills, Rome's troops came for us in this fancy apartment Augustus had provided. They didn't knock. Instead, they knocked down the door, trashed the furniture, shredded the children's toys, and threw it all out through the windows to the ground below. We were herded down the steps, all six floors, to the street where a wagon waited for us. Between the door and the wagon, we crunched glass—broken windows, wine glasses, crystal ware, shattered windows. I remember it now with tears still in my eyes, this night of broken glass.[2]

We rattled down to the port on side roads, twenty miles or so, and were on the next ship back to Israel, leaving Jesus, Rabbus, Leah, and John behind in Rome. I wouldn't see Jesus again for almost a decade.

2

AUGUSTA

I sat in my gold-plated carriage at the very front of Tavius' funeral parade. Rome's next two emperors, blood of my blood, sat next to me. The Fates had smiled on me. Tiberius and Caligula, dear boys, both loved privilege and hated responsibility—a perfect marriage of my competence and their potential.

I patted Tibbie's hand and reminisced. My, my. Fifty-two years of marriage to Augustus. We'd started out with a bang. Love at first sight. He divorced his wife. I divorced my husband. We hopped into bed. Maybe not in that order.

Now that I think about it, our passion did last for a good long while. When did it start to fizzle? Maybe when Tavius left me more and more alone. Out there roaming the empire, glory-mongering, and bedding his consorts. My spies had dossiers on all of those trollops, one in every port across the empire. That wouldn't have been so bad. All those women were out there, and after he loved them, he left them for me. He always came home to me where I'd go over him with a fine-toothed comb, turn him inside out, rummage about. He'd regale me with his stories and be curious about mine.

But here's the thing. After some years, his curiosity about me waned. Like he'd taken a big eraser and gradually smudged me from sight. All he wanted were the financials, complicity in his conspiracy theories, and endless adoration. And yes, a blind eye to his affairs, particularly the local stable of broodmares he'd dolloped around town.

One more item. He loved his figs—the ones I had brought up from his orchards in Nola. So, as usual, I fell into line. I cooked up a consummate marriage of blind eye, conspiracy, and figs. Let it stew for years. Over time

I added a few special ingredients—hemlock, adder venom, bitters, and a bit of nightshade extract.

One glorious night, we'd invited the whole batch of those generals and senators, the *current* conspiracy cabal, to a gala dinner. Everyone showed up heavy in silk and diamonds, like they'd covered themselves with glue and rolled around in the trappings of wealth. After dinner, they all trolloped into the drawing-room, that leathery, ponderous, paunchy boys' room of congealed opulence. They'd all smoked cigars, drank brandy, oh'd and ah'd at Tavius' stories of conquest. Noses all becoming quite brown.

I waltzed in, flirty as you please, and served dessert on a platinum platter. Tavius went on about my special fig sauce with its secret recipe. They could hardly say no. One general in particular, a hobbied, gourmet chef, was curious. I fed him my most salacious smile. Told him the exact amounts of vanilla, maple syrup, and lemon bitters. Mentioned how important it was to marinate in a cool cellar. I might have forgotten a few ingredients. But I did stress how important it was to let everything simmer for some time. And, of course, froth well before serving.

He and our other guests gobbled down those delicious figs. Everyone frothed well, right before we carried them out, feet first, to the crematory—a very efficient evening.

That was years ago, a favorite memory. Long before Tavius' shaking sticks and fuzzy recall took him over some edge. At the end, on his birthday ten days ago, he pled, "Help me. Help me cross over. I'm tired. I've seen it all, done it all, want no more. I want to go home. Home to Nola, have a fig or two. Be done with it."

I obliged. There was a bit of drama in his maze at the end, but once he'd flopped over, I felt *so* relieved. And the delight of it all? I rid myself of that granddaughter *and* the Jew. Tavius liked both of them entirely too much. Thus the rope-a-dope, wrapped around lots of plausible deniability.

Truth was, I never could stand Tavius' daughter, Livena—the bastard daughter of an early dip in some Greek honeypot. Livena, dear girl, went bonkers after her son, Claud, died. Devolved into a true nutcase. But Claud's twin sister, Claudia, remained a threat.

Tavius had come home from roaming abroad one time too many asking for Claudia before he asked for me. I'd be in the executive suite, poring over my ledgers, plotting the next disinformation campaign, and they'd be twittering in the library. She'd sit on his lap, play with his beard, whisper local gossip in his ear. Conniving, wee bitch.

I confronted him. He'd argued back, "Everything *always* comes back to you!"

I replied, "Quite. And I have the very great advantage of having *me* on my side."

After I helped Tavius trot off to Paradise, my guards trussed the Jew and the bastard granddaughter like hogs to market. Jew in the Dungeon, Claudia in exile. Which island was it? Oh yes, Trimerus, the one where I'd smacked that other hot-pants granddaughter.

I roused myself from these pleasant memories. Caligula stroked Tiberius's arm, imbibed from his flask, and chattered on inanely. Boy this, girl that—a real omnivore. Unfortunately, he'd never learned to read properly. Got his letters all tangled up and ended up twittering endlessly about intrigues and bodies between the sheets.

Just then, Cal looked over his shoulder and waved at his sisters. Agrippina, Drusilla, and Livilla all sat straight and pretty in their carriage. Quite proper.

Cal said, "They're good entertainment, Uncle. When I have an urge, in they lather. Agrippina's *so* frisky compared to Dru and Liv. Only one problem with her—she's less than adoring. Just yesterday, she went on, 'Cal, Uncle Tibbie will dump you soon. He's so erudite, compared to you.'

"I disagreed and told her I was *totally* erudite. She said, 'you don't even know what that means.' I replied that if I *did* know, I'd certainly be that and more."

Tibbie tipped his head, amused. "She reply?"

"She agreed I was hard to out-argue. Changed the subject. 'Cal, your wig just slipped over your ear. You look like an unmade bed.' An unmade bed she's willing to crawl into, mind you. But tell me, how does one get a yapping mouth like hers to shut up?"

We approached Palatine Hill, near my apartments. A clutch of senators clucked about, straightening their toupees, sucking in their guts. I prodded my progeny. "Sit up and stop your chatter, boys. Rome is watching. Mind your manners and hide that flask. Mustn't let them see you both drunk.

And when we pass by those senators, remember the magic phrase, '*Memento mori.*' It's the law for emperors at state funerals. And, a good reminder—life is *so* brief."

I lifted my veil and glared at Tibbie. *Why are you so obtuse? Have you lost all discretion? Act your age. After all, you are in your fifties, and he's a pimply-faced teen.*

Tibbie stared back at me, blank-eyed. *That child always could outstare a corpse.* He signaled the driver, and our carriage creaked to a halt just short of where those cloying senators simpered. Son and grandson quit the carriage, surrounded by guards.

Tiberius' next words wounded me. "Mother. Read up on sows, the ones who eat their young. Might be instructive."

He nodded at the senators. "I no longer have to abide you or your soporific echo chambers. Further, I deserve relaxation at the bathhouse with a certain young thing." His voice positively hissed, "I do find it so challenging to steam you off me, Mother! Your presence lingers, like a cloud of wee beasties over tainted meat, gone off long ago."

He certainly did know how to hurt his loving mother. Such poisonous talk, and after all my years of training him in political culinaries. I'd return to my cookbooks. Revise my recipes.

3

TIBERIUS

The day after father's funeral, mother and I lounged in the sixth-floor dayroom on Palatine Hill. The late afternoon sun slanted through stained glass on our right. Marguerite, daisy, and marigold colors splashed over us and the oriental carpet. To my left, our shadows on the carpet looked like monsters.

Mother hunched over, bony as a desiccated bat, paps dangling beneath her silk blouse. Eggplants left too long in the sun. Her eyes sagged into the folds of her face. She picked at her sweetbreads—expressly taken, at her command, from an unblemished lamb. She was picky, using her tiny knife to cut out tiny bites for her prim mouth. Such pickiness had served her well. She'd waited for years, waited while she sliced and shaped me into tiny bits for her emperor decoupage—a male body to mask Her Majesty's presence behind the throne.

Her voice boomed in my ears. Every word thrummed from a set jaw she'd been grinding for decades. Painted eyebrows and glittering eyes accentuated her every word. "A quiet execution, son—chop-chop. No public hoo-hah. He's nothing but trouble. Throw him in the same dragnet that caught the others. No one will blink an eye."

A blood vessel in my nose popped. I wiped a dribble of red off my beard.

Mother sighed, whisked out her cream-colored, silk hanky. "Get that bloody snot off your emperor's robe. Am I the only one who makes you blow your cork?"

I looked out the window and longed for another battle campaign where I could kill someone. War and peace were no different. People relished killing each other in both arenas. But in war, I didn't have to pretend. I'd killed tons of Germanics and Illyrians while mother, at home, smiled and turned me to sweetbread.

She never ceased to amaze and confuse. How did she return me to diapers the moment I stepped into a room with her? I became a mental midget and elevated to emperor, all in her same stroke—a mongoloid toddler building an empire with bright-colored blocks.

"Trust me, Tibbie. I've run this empire for years. Tavius left me with it while he was out glory-mongering. He abandoned us both. The imperial succession was far more important to him than we were. He loved a good abstraction."

"Mother, he loved you."

I gazed out the window at a flower box overfilled with violet pansies, rippling in the breeze. A fat blue jay swooped down and snagged an unsuspecting gecko. She was now quite busy working it down her throat. The gecko's tail frantically thrashed back and forth as it disappeared into her gullet.

Mother allowed, "He did love me once. But take heed. He's gone. The wolves are loosed. This is how it goes for us Claudians—one kingpin shoves himself through the front door, and the last gets carried out the back door with an ice pick in his chest. Impossible to be too wary, Tibbie-tot."

"But mother, this Jew's done nothing wrong. In fact, one of his followers resurrected me, if you recall." *A four-year-old whining.*

She paused, examined her face in a small mirror. Licked a wild hair that had strayed, stuck it back into her gold and silver bun on top of her head. "Tibbie, stop sniveling. Listen to your mother. If he or his drones pull any more rabbits out of the hat, they might gain a following. And obviously, you weren't dead—just sleeping, dear boy. This isn't a play like *Psyche*. We're in the big leagues. Might is right and dead is dead."

Her black eyes, chipped obsidian, positively flashed from the deep shadow where she sat. "He fooled Tavius at the end. If Jeez-the-Jew could bamboozle the original Potentate of Paranoia, others could get pulled into his mystical razzle-dazzle. A few creaking senators leaping around, healed. One or two more casket pop-ups. Who knows where that kind of chicanery could go? Tavius won't be the last in this emperor parade to the charnel house, dear boy."

The Shade behind my throne sucked in silence and spat out darkness. "Yes, here's what we must do: exterminate the foxes while they're babies. If no chop-chop, they chomp-chomp. The whole vineyard, ruined."

Silver knitting needles flashed, stabbing the blood-red shawl in her lap.

I salvaged an inch of ground from the Dragon's lair. "Yes, Mother. Once the huff and puff of the funeral have settled down, I'll make my announcement—quietly, within the next year or two. Then it's off to the cross for that Jew."

Mother sniffed, turned her head aside. Her jaws did the grind-and-twitch dance, twitch left, grind right. Amazing she had any molars left at all. Left to her, the seer wouldn't have seen another sunrise.

She rose from her straight-back chair, grabbed and dabbed at my chin with stabbing motions, sopping up my ooze, fingers cold as an ice carving. "And one more thing, be discrete when you pump away with all those consorts and gigolos, particularly young Caligula. He's a consummate plotter, and at such a tender age. Mind you, don't quick-fill queenie's throne. Exiled Julia, your unfortunate bride, will take her own sweet time starving to death. And face it—you need up-skilling in this emperor business. Absolutely *no* distractions from a wannabe queen or gigolo wheedling his or her way under your covers, Tibbie-tot."

Two swordsmen jousted back of my eyes, stabbing here, slicing there.

"I'll be along, as usual, this evening for your backrub. You look like you have a teensy-weensy headache."

Just come right out and say it, Mother—let's get married, officially, in front of gods and senate. Suck the gossip mills dry.

Mother walked to the door, added an afterthought. "Clean Trimerus of anything edible—conniving Claudia and my other sweet granddaughter can starve quicker. Ha! Tavius' *daughter,* Julia, exiled in the Tyrrhenian, his granddaughter*s* in the Adriatic. Jackals can pick over Julia's bones, and the last granddaughter alive gets to feast on the other."

I wandered to my desk on the other side of the room and busied myself signing blank scrolls out of her view. *Look emperesque, Tiberius—not a gleeful toddler in romper room, holding up his arms to be held.*

She wouldn't let it rest. Added one final nail to the Jewish coffin. "If you let Teen-Wonder-Jew loiter, remember, it's not just him. He's not a mushroom that sprang up full- blown after a summer shower. He has family—and you *do* know how those creatures breed. Like rabbits. When you add in all his relations, there'll be more of these little Jesuses running around than stars in the sky. He has to be stopped here. Now."

4
JESUS

The place had a brackish stink, like salt swamp at low tide, permeated with the fear of all who had come before me. The guard's mustache was a black tusk mounted sideways over his mouth. His jaw clench might have been intended as a grin. He yelled at the ledger keeper, "Another Kike! What's the last Jew number we had?" *Mumble from around the corner.*

"What?" *More mumbling.* "So, that's 777?"

"Yo, Scalder; let'er rip."

"Be a good boy, Heebie. Up with your right sleeve." He held a white-hot branding iron in his right hand. I rolled up my tunic and turned my head the other way. Held my breath. Smell of meat roasting. Me. I screamed and couldn't seem to stop. Terror crowded my throat.

Rough hands pushed me down the hall. Now I was a no-name, but only a number, 777. We came to a double-wide cell door, crusted with rust and barnacles. Key clattered in the lock. Ceiling to floor bars creaked open—a hobnailed boot connected with my butt. I shot inwards like a cannonball.

"Don't let that door hit ya in the ass, kid."

Sound of door slamming shut behind me in this sub-basement, seven stories below the Imperial quarters on Palatine Hill. They called this place the Dungeon. More formally, the Dungeon of Indeterminate Emigrantes. Forty pairs of wary eyes here in DIE jerked my way. Six of those eyes belonged to three men playing dice on a top ledge in the far corner.

The dirt floor angled diagonally toward the sewer hole in the lowest corner. Sludge burped up from the sewers. Overlapping wavelets rippled toward me. I looked around for a spot to sit, trying to focus.

Top ledge space, taken. A few spaces remained along the wall toward this end, close to the sewer hole. I scuttled through floating turds and positioned myself between two other muddy men of indeterminate race. Men, like me. Sat in sludge between them. Both of them scratched their bleeding scabs, and I tried to pretend my arm wasn't on fire.

The guy to my right, "Name's Benno. Keep a sharp eye out for Goliath and dung beetles. They're bad, but rat bites can kill. All of 'em come up with the sewage when it rains. Eat you alive down here." He pointed to his crotch and legs.

I felt a sharp pain on my thigh and began to learn the fine art of scratching myself raw.

I felt like a furiously itchy fumarole, smoke mist, nothing more. Comfort was a distant idea, for other people. I drowsed, head tipping toward my chest, a vacant lot where some impressive temple used to stand. The vision fuzzed. I scratched a new bite. Time became a dung beetle laboring through sludge.

Metal spoon banging, banging back and forth along dungeon's bars. Must be the dinner bell. Got in the back of the line. Finally, my turn at the door. Shallow metal bowl got pushed through the bars. Something in that bowl looked like what I was sitting in, but I didn't argue. A floating carrot peel, a crust of a heel off a loaf of brown bread. I told Windy, *this looks like a crapshoot where the winner gets cholera. Safe me.*

Silence.

After dinner, shadows deepened. Men re-grouped along the sloping top ledge. The latest arrivals slept closest to the sewer, head of one man next to the feet of his mate. The three men at the top didn't leave their niche. They kept playing dice and looked up, time to time, to better survey their domain—emperors of the night.

I didn't sleep, except in snatches. *Slapping, crunching sounds.*

I rolled over. Benno, up-ledge from me, scooped a cockroach off the wall with a sideways slapping motion. Threw it in his mouth. One crunch, gone. *Ah, mystery solved.*

The next evening, Ahmed-the-Arabaa, down-ledge from me, made an even bigger score. *Lunge, squeal, and snapping sound.*

I rolled over and looked around. Ahmed grinned. A rat, the size of a gopher, flopped wildly in his mouth. He'd snapped the rat's neck, pulled off his head. Now he gorged himself on the still twitching body.

Words, garbled. "Keep quiet, and I'll give you some."

"Your secret's mine, Ahmed. None for me, thanks."

Those who had no family or friends, like Ahmed, or me, fought hardest to stay alive. It was the law of survival—eat or be eaten. Lice, crabs, and men were as hungry as the beetles and rats. All had appetites. All itched to take what was yours.

The power hierarchy was set. Any food, drink, drugs, smokes, or clothing—anything at all, really—was "taxed" by the Triad, the three guys at the top. Grippa, Pojak, and Putzi were strongest and fittest. They took the best, returned the rest. They searched a new arrival's stuff just yesterday and found a mouth organ. Ordered him to play his harmonica and dance for them. His music, a dirge, floated through the stink and wrapped 'round my ears while I sat in the corner closest to the sewer, head between my knees. Grippa took his organ once the song and dance were done. Lifted the man's chin, "Yep, yur mouth shaped just right for organs, now, ain't it?"

The Triad kept fit doing calisthenics when they weren't busy with cards or dice. One sadistic exercise they'd devised was to bench-press other inmates. This was a cruel way of exhibiting power at others' expense, because they could. For example, the day after the Harmonica man arrived, Pojak ordered, "Get over here Mouth Organ. Lay flat, face down, over Putzi and Grip. Stiffen up. Putzi's got your shoulders, and Grip's got your crotch. Fifty thrusts up and down—we all get our turn; you get your ups and downs. We plays nice, now, don't we?"

No one challenged their molestation routine for humiliating men into barbells. People who fought back, through carelessness or defiance, didn't fare well. For example, if you let your shadow fall on the Triad from a smudge torch in a wall scone, that same torch would be held under your hand till your skin bubbled and crisped. The rest of us grew into common-enemy friends. Wary distrust flowed down from Imperial guards to jailers to Triad to the rest of us in the cell.

One cup of gruel, one ragged piece of wormy bread, one cup of water. My skin grew closer to my bones. It erupted into open sores where maggots laid their eggs at night. Distrust also laid its eggs in my mind, like cholera or plague, spreading into fear or shame.

Where was my family? Where were my friends? Why had I been abandoned to die alone, fading in faith? Father knew faith in Him was the most important thing in my life. Why would he grind me to dust with His absence?

I called to Father, to Windy. No reply. I remembered the Israeli king God abandoned, so He would know all that was within his own heart.[3] Faith in Father's protection evaporated. Perhaps this was for a purpose. Maybe Father wanted to cut sloth from my body. But that still made me quivering meat, and him the vivisectionist, now, didn't it?

Nights, I heard other men's moans of terror or pleasure. Many nights I stifled my cries of fear, put a rag in my mouth, pressed close to the wall, knees drawn to my chest.

Ahmed made a mistake a few days after his night-time rat feast. Real bad mistake.

His wife had finally found him after searching for weeks. She'd stood outside Dungeon's gate. She did a hoppy, excited dance—her lost husband was found! The two of them held hands through the bars. She slipped him bread and cheese. He tore off a chunk of each for the prison guard and stuffed the rest in his mouth.

That night I roused out of a dead, dreamless sleep. *Frantic sounds of struggle.* The Triad had dragged Ahmed off the sleeping ledge, gagged him. Putzi held him face down in the mud. Each man in the Triad took turns exacting revenge for not getting their share at the door.

Ahmed flailed, got his head above sewage, spit out his gag, and started screaming for help. The guard, a new man, roused himself outside the iron bars. Grippa shoved Ahmed's head back down in the sewage, hard. Ahmed stopped flailing, stopped breathing, there below our ledge, a few feet away from me. The guard went back to sleep.

Grippa wiped the dead man's face clear of the mud and returned him to his pallet next to me. He searched his bedroll for anything worth keeping or trading. Filthy breath in my nose, "Squeal, Jew, and you're next."

No explanation to the dayshift guards was offered next morning. Pojak rattled the bars on the door, "You better check this guy—don't look like he's breathing too good." Guards dragged his body out to the burn pile. One less mouth to feed at Rome's expense.

I kept a low profile, challenged no one in the weeks and months that came and went. I entered sleep as if it were a sewage ditch subject to flooding. Something was wrong with my heart, wrong enough to make me think my blood was pumping backward. Every few hours, more blood seemed to drain from my head. Did this place hold me in the grip of a more powerful form of gravity? My head still felt unmoored from my neck, like I might catch sight of it floating by in the sewage.

Other inmates asked if I'd really killed the emperor. My tongue, a bag of dust, lay still.

Conversations with Windy and Father felt sketchy, even in the best of times. I had a sense of Windy blowing round the planet, watchful but distant. Mainly she left me alone to dance with wolves. Predators complained I was getting too light to bother with.

One of them, Putzi, must have learned Hebrew somewhere. Might have even been part Jewish. Don't know. But he knew the *asher yatzar*. One morning I squatted over the sewer grate, releasing my bowels, eyes closed, reciting the commanded blessing in Hebrew, "Blessed are You, Adonai, our God, King of the universe, who formed man with wisdom and created within him many openings and many hollow spaces. It is known before Your Seat of Honor that if even one of them would be opened, or if even one of them would be sealed, it would be impossible to survive even for one hour."

He said, "We'll make sure those holy hollows stay wide open, butt boy." He took even the pleasure of a good poo from me. Shivers rippled through my hollow soul. Time crawled by like a scarab in poo stew.

5

JOHN

Work finally ended for the day. I climbed out of the sewer and scraped chunks of poop off my toes. Walked a block to the Tiber River and dove in. Swam around, and my skin turned a shade or two lighter. I went home to my shanty in the slums and changed to my other camel hair tunic.

Today was the day. After two years, I'd finally be able to see Jesus. Leah and little Gabe met me at their front door. Rabbus, newly returned from the battlefront, came around the corner and greeted me.

He walked me through a series of hallways inside Palatine Hill, passing through at least four or five checkpoints on our way down from one level to the next of rough-cut stone walls and gates. We bottomed out. The dim hall dripped with ground weep.

Rabbus' voice was rough, like a cat's tongue. He said, "Never been inside the Dungeon. Greet him for me. I have to get to work upstairs." When he turned to go, even someone like me, a guy with no feelings, could feel his relief.

A guard called out a number, "777, visitor!" I stood outside the bars, shuffling my feet a bit in the brown stream that flowed around my sandals. Familiar smell.

A skeleton with skin approached, stood at an angle. My cousin was barely recognizable, all knobs and bone. But his eyes still had that old fire in them, but the fire had changed to what you might expect to see in a martyr being burned over green firewood.

I'd counted eighteen sets of forty days and nights. Chalk marks on a slate beneath my sleeping mat. Neat sets of white slash marks. Bundles of days. The days and months for me had gone quick—but for him? Must have been Italian water-torture. Drips on his forehead.

I passed a few things through after the guards had checked them—bread, cheese, a cluster of red grapes, and a homespun cloak. I knew his Elijah cloak was gone. A guy standing behind Jesus was wrapped in a blue cloak, just like what Jesus used to have. Scraps of burlap clung to Jesus' stick body—cheesecloth over baling wire.

Jesus asked me, "Day or night outside? Never can tell in here."

I said, "Afternoon. Just finished work, washed up, and checked at the guardhouse—as usual. Rules changed today. Rabbus is back. He's been with Tiberius on his latest campaign—two years in Gaul. One bunch of pagans killing another and feeling good about it, far as I can tell."

Blue Cloak had moved up. Stood next to Jesus after I'd handed him the stuff. Cloak broke off a small piece of cheese and bread and gave that back to Jesus. Took all but two grapes and wandered away, saying, "two tiny balls for the pint-sized Jew."

I wanted to slug the guy and get Jesus' stuff back, in that order.

Jesus said, "Chill, John. That's how it works here. People hate me for no good reason.[4] If you make trouble, it'll be worse for me."

He looked down, somber-like. "How's our family?"

"Long gone. Almost since the day you were thrown in here. I was rambling in the hills when they came. No warning—soldiers showed up with two carts, kicked our stuff into kindling. Miriam's painted doll, the one with the pink cheeks, remember that one? Shredded."

Jesus said, "Why am I surprised by such sadness? I've worked so hard not to remember. Forgetting's become my business. Family memories, phantom faces in a dream. They require too much upkeep. A good meal's also only to be had in memory, but I can daydream about food easier than family."

He paused, then asked, "What of you? What of you?"

I leaned in. On the other side of the iron grate, Jesus' face was crisscrossed shadows, a solitary oak in winter. Light cut to shreds.

I said, "I got lost easy—been doing that ever since I can remember. I live alone in the city's slums. Most of the city's fires happen there with all the oil-burning stoves. The Vigiles try to keep us from burning ourselves down, but my place has burned twice despite them. Pays to not have much stuff.

"I got a job shoveling shit. I go from one end of Rome to the other in a crew of immigrants, cleaning out sewer choke points that feed into the Cloaca Max. We keep the city from gettin' constipated."

Jesus said, "You've always had a nose for poop." He pointed to the long, brown turds bubbling up from the sewer on his side of the grate.

I felt my face twisting into something, maybe a frown. "If I had your mother's garden bench, maybe I'd know what to say. I'd make 'sorry' sounds. But I've forgotten all that. All I know to say is what I do."

Jesus regarded me solemnly.

"Every day after work, I clean up and head to the main synagogue. Forty people, more or less, from the Diaspora, each with bits and pieces of the Torah. They spend most of their time disagreeing about what to agree on."

"So, you bounce between sewer and synagogue?"

I nodded. "I'm the only one there who's memorized the whole Torah. When I get to the synagogue, they're ready to take dictation. We're into the poets now—love those Lamentations!"

Jesus reached through the bars and grabbed my wrist. "Your words are God's gift to Rome. You prepare them for *my* words if I ever get the chance to speak again. For now, silence suits me."

He took a sharp breath, eyes down, toward the sewer. His voice was ironwood scraping over a washboard. "I remember touching those holy words with a silver yad on inked parchment. Yeah, now they're faint word whorls, kites spinning in the clouds, dice clattering in my head."

He banged his head on the bars. "All I want is to scream, 'I hate this place! Get me out of here, Father!'"

Words welled up against the back of my teeth. I grabbed his hand. "Cousin, we're word hurlers. If we don't speak, God's spears set in a corner, un-blooded."

His face looked absent in a way, like he was listening to a distant explosion. He started to say something, but I interrupted. "When I recite scripture at synagogue, sometimes I'll say, 'stop writing.' I explain how the passage points to you—law, prophets, histories. Millions fall, forever forgotten. But their fingers stick out of the mud and point straight at you."

Jesus said, "You shovel shit and scripture. All I do is sit in what you shovel."

I whispered back, "Hold on to the promises. They're still there, down in that dark stone below the sewage, beneath your feet—ink's ecstasy—alive, pulsing. Each sentence, black on ivory, outlines the shape of the world as it was, is, and will be. Getting depressed is no excuse for getting lost."

Jesus rolled his eyes. "Stop it! Preaching doesn't help me now. Three points and a poem? *Really?* You think that means something to one like me, *here*? Sermons, homilies? Dust and ash, blown vapor."

"Jesus, you—you're the Word Master! Aren't you shaking hands with sacrilege?"

He said, "My *head* knows what's right and what's not. But all those words don't matter when loneliness grows fangs. People who stand *outside* the bars make me feel, what is it? Ah yes, *that's it*—like a fervent preacher who pokes table scraps of good advice through the bars and then walks away."

I asked myself what his mother would say. Spoke what sounded like thin gruel, even to me. "God doesn't change. He'll protect you."

"Yes and no. Love isn't always protection. Maximum love, minimum protection— that's the rule here. Father's character doesn't change, but his methods change all the time."

"So, how will we ever find Him?"

"He'll find you. Somewhere along the journey, He'll show up and find you. But for now, I've lost my bearings and my confidence."

I was empty of a quick scripture fix. I gripped his hand through the bars, gaze fixed on him, not knowing what to say, not having any idea at all how to join in his sadness.

He reached back with his eyes. He said, "Sermons in sandals, visits behind bars—those are the words that count. Ink and parchment crisp like branded skin." He rolled his sleeve up so I could see his new name, 777.

I skittered my eyes over that pain. "I won't let you die, even though you look like blown skin and bones. Yesterday, leaving work, I saw a pile of burnt feathers left over after someone ate the bird. You put me in mind of that."

His face was all hard planes, like Jerusalem limestone. "I look as flimsy as I feel, huh?"

I said, "Doesn't doing time drive you nuts?"

"Breathing no longer agrees with me. This is boot camp for scrappy living. Fleas, lice, rats, diarrhea, and hunger. All practice and no books—except lines already laid down in my head, and I can't even remember those, most of the time. Brain is on strike. Only a chance breeze of fresh air, the touch of your hand through the bars—those things, they make suffering almost livable."

I said, "I get panicky looking through the bars at you. I'd go whacko if we ever had to swap places."

"Who knows? For now, I'm in; you're out. We're each helpless to change our situation. But, now that I speak it out loud, helplessness has been a gift of sorts. It's pushed me, like a spear point, into the present moment. I take no thought for the future. I live one breath to the next, hanging on only at Father's will."

Something like butterfly wings tickled my tongue. "Helplessness the main pain? Or is there something else?"

"Ah, yeah, there's much more—I miss Claudia. When I see her face, hear her laugh, my missing is a physical thing. Gnaws at me. Shreds my heart."

I chewed my lip.

He said, 'You're not calling her a whore, for my sake. Your restraint grows."

"I'm trying to do tender, like when I told Aunt Mary about your abba's death. But nothing's there now. I remember Windy blowing through me in my Essene days with Uncle Zeb. Now Windy bangs on my door when I least expect him—then he disappears for weeks. Maybe he'll leave for good someday."

Jesus said, "Windy's wispy for me too. But, now that I think about it, can you bring me parchment, ink, and a quill? I'd like to write my thoughts down now you're allowed to visit. Maybe I could pass them through to you."

"You live inside a prickle of porcupines, Jeez. You think they're going to let you keep a quill?" I motioned to Blue Cloak with his two other buddies on a high ledge. They were chowing down my grapes and spitting out the seeds.

Jesus hesitated, ate one of my two grapes, grinding the seed up, swallowing. Offered me the other one. I refused.

He said, "My felt faith comes and goes. Right now, a wisp returned. Father's seeding me. Countless people-orchards will grow from what we seed here. Even though this still life feels one heartbeat away from stillbirth."

"I'll have to think about that one—too deep for me, cousin. My guess is no scrolls from you will ever leave this stinking dungeon."

I looked at him quiet-like, "If you'd known how hard this Messiah stuff would be, up there in heaven before your get-go in Bethlehem, chances are you'd never done it, huh?"

Jesus said, "I never knew what I would suffer. But I do know fish swim, pigs don't fly, and Father is good. Even in molar-grinding darkness, the unimportance of everything else is hard to underestimate."

6

CLAUDIA

I'd been exiled with cousin Julilla, Aunt Julia's daughter, for a wheel or two of seasons. Exile in our family was a multi-purpose tool. Any emperor in need of taking his power for a walk used exile as a walking stick. Need embarrassment relief from an errant royal? Exile. Need a playbill, advertising to the whole empire not to mess with Rome? Exile. Having an off day? Constipated? Exile the last person who'd walked out your door.

Pontii and the boys carted me away from grandpa's estate, three days journey to the Adriatic coast. I bounced around in that cart like a marble in a shoebox. From Vasto, a seaport village, Pontii tossed me in a galley the size of a thimble for the voyage to Trimerus. I lay tangled in my ropes on the floorboards, eying Pontii like a fish circling a net. His mouth was narrow, wet, and red. He kept it stamped to his face directly over a salt 'n pepper goatee. He smelled like seaweed soaked in brine.

He said, "Your grandma wouldn't be unhappy if our boat capsized by accident, and you went to join your brother at the bottom of the sea." He rocked the boat, almost flipping me overboard, barked out a laugh.

I shrugged. Sounded like grandma. She'd probably walked into grandpa's throne room one time too many, caught him laughing with the granddaughter of his consort. Face it. I wasn't her blood; I was just her reminder.

Finally, we beached in a cove. Pontii dragged me over the keel and dumped me on the beach. He untied my bonds and sloshed back to the galley, wordless. Threw a burlap bag overboard on his way out. That was it, gone. His silhouette shrank into a dot.

I retrieved the bag and examined the contents—not a single diamond necklace included. How thoughtless, grandma. I sat in the shallows, froth lapping my ankles, stinging but soothing my raw skin, all at once. I daydreamed of Jesus—he was over there somewhere. Was he thinking of me too? *Taste of tears on my lips.*

A voice behind me. "I'm *so* glad you came, cousin. How lucky! We can die together and not be lonesome."

Julilla. She and her cotton singlet were so thin you could read the time of day through them. *More than a decade older than me and slammed on this stinking rock for seven years.*

I stood and hugged her. She buried her face in my shoulder and sobbed like a rainstorm. Once she'd finished embarrassing me, I said, "You're right, Julie. We're the luckiest women in the world. Let's party."

We sat on a flat rock, and she poked through the stuff in my bag. "He left you fishing line, hooks, and a bag of seeds! They just threw us on the sand. Didn't kit us out like this.

"I remember, now, Pontii looking at Paullus. He said, 'Kill that whoring wife of yours, Paulie. Whack Silanus' baby, that bump she's carrying. The emperor might recall you—if you serve justice.'"

"So, it was true, your affair?"

Julie nodded. "Mother had told me, 'When marriage is absent love, find love absent marriage. Life without love, too empty.' She honey-coated her poison pill with a hug so it would slip down a thirteen-year-old's throat easier."

"I didn't know your mother was that wise."

"At that age, she was my idea of wisdom. I'd pinned it on her like a badge, regardless of who she was. I lived out her "wisdom," lost contact with Paullus and our daughter, Aemilia. Wandered from one man to another. Became a party animal; became pregnant."

"Grandfather caught wind of this. Rounded up Paullus and me from opposite sides of town, dumped us here. We scrabbled out a hand-to-mouth existence. He fished. I gardened. He stayed in that hut over there, on the far cliff. I stayed in the one up there." She vaguely gestured over her head, her wrist circling in the wind.

"He forgave me my affairs, or so he said. But when my time came to give birth, he disappeared. I dropped the baby alone, all alone. Screamed my guts out when Julian crowned. I thought he'd killed me, but I was doomed to live."

Tears streamed down her face. "Paullus took my baby to that bluff up there. Left him naked on the rocks. Julian's wailing was so piteous. Hawks and turkey vultures ate him alive. My punishment for cheating on him, you know."

I snorted. "Men! What happened then?"

"Pontii came back, maybe a year or so later. I can't remember. I said to myself, 'Get ready to die.'"

"But you still live."

"Paullus doesn't. Pontii walked up to both of us. Stood in front of my hut. He drew out a scroll with Tavius' seal on it. Paullus' execution orders for his supposed role in plotting a revolt—but really, Tavius wanted him dead because he hadn't killed me."

I asked, "And then, what happened next?"

"Pontii and Paullus had been friends since boyhood. Pontii drew out a sword and stabbed it in the earth.

"He said, 'One of us has to use this on you, friend. Now. You choose.'

Paullus took the sword. He knelt in front of me, asked me to forgive him for all he had done to hurt me. I stared at him, undone. Remembered Julian. He lowered his eyes. Then he put the tip under his heart, in that hollow, and went about his business."

My eyes widened, and I leaned forward. I always liked the bloody details, unless it had to do with me and my blood.

She finished the story. "He whispered the name of our son, our together son, who'd died in infancy back in Rome, cried in a loud voice, "Marcus, I come to you.' Slumped on Pontii's sword."

"Did his dying take long?" *It had taken Postie such a long time to die once I'd skewered him with his mother's poison arrow.*

"The sword worked its way straight through his chest. Got stuck inside somewhere. He groaned and pushed down harder. The sword came out beside his backbone. He flopped around on the ground. I watched, down to his last gasp."

"I guess death had its day."

"I suppose. I can still see it like it was yesterday. I threw up. My puke barely missed his head."

"Then you really were alone."

She nodded, eyes vacant. "Pontii and his men took Paullus' body, weighted it with rocks inside a canvas, wrapped it tight with ropes.

He said, 'We'll drop him off on the way to Vasto.' Like they were stopping by a corner market."

"After they left, I lived on my garden." Shook her head. "Fishing scared me. I feared whatever I caught would catch me. Eat me. I used my small net to catch minnows in the shallows where I swam in this inlet, where my feet can touch sand."

"You live on minnows?"

"I'd dry them on the rocks. Pretend they were caviar. Eat them with a few vegetables, roots, berries, grass, dried seaweed. It was barely enough. For sure, not enough for the two of us. Then there's my garden. I got water from a brook I named Kerith. Watered each plant by hand. This year, no rain. Kerith died.[5]"

Julie said, "Past feels more present than the present. Even the future hurries into history. Paullus and Julian's corpses rise to meet me every day—the rock where the ravens ate my son, the ground that drank my husband's blood. Some days my grief is a whining dog, caged; other times, a wolf howling at the moon."

"Julie, grandma's killed enough. Let's stay alive, just to piss her off. I'll learn to yank stuff out of the sea. We *have* to live."

"The gods sent you to me, Claudia. You were always such a spitfire, even as a little girl. You make me want to try. But I fear I'll not live much longer. Mind-fog most of the time. I know I'm starving—not even hungry anymore."

Buoyed by such optimism, I walked with her up a snaky Z-path to the bluff above the inlet. Two stone huts were opposite each other on the finger of a promontory. One faced east toward Illyria; the other, west toward the boot of Italy. On a clear day, like today, land was a smudge, both east and west, but the Italian coastline was clearer than the Illyrian. Julie had chosen the hut facing Rome, and home.

A worn bench made of lava sat outside her hut. "Here's where I sit most times, listening to the white caps on the rocks. They and the wind have their conversation. I don't butt in."

"You always had a nice voice, Julie. Join the song. What time of day do you to sit to feel the sun's warmth?"

"Afternoons. The sun's light is like melted butter. Soothes me. I lean against that black wall-stone next to the door, the one that matches my princess bench."

I was impressed with her throne room, but not her menu. "The sun will warm your bones soon enough, bleach you chalky white. But you can't eat it. Let's live before we die."

7
WINDY

The two ex-palace girls settled into a routine. They grubbed together on hands and knees, working the garden Julie had staked out between the two cottages. The rest of the hilltop was volcanic rock, different shades of black and grey from earlier and later lava flows.

Each used a sharp stone to break big clods into itty-bitty dirtballs, even as I was using exile's blunt edge to break up their stony hearts. Julie spilled her dirt-ball memories at the same time, smacking her lips over chewed-up pain of childbirth, croup, diarrhea, dumping, and being dumped by lovers.

Claudia had a poor idea of how to listen but no idea at all of how to garden. She also had not one notion of what was in these seeds—could have been pumpkins or poppies or blow-up emperor dolls for all she knew.

She consulted her cousin. "How far do we put this seed down, a little bit or a bunch?"

Julie guessed, "Last year, I put them all down a squidge. About half popped up. That tiny black one looks like lettuce to me."

"A squidge, huh? Such expert knowledge comforts me. Let' pray for rain, Julie."

"Who's the god of rain?"

"I have a God-man friend, son of some Father who bosses around lesser gods."

"Well, what do we do—cut ourselves, dance in circles, bark at the moon? I don't have energy for all that."

"Nope. I'll do it. Look up, now. Fold your hands real nice. Here goes, 'Jesus' Pop. You know we need rain if we're gonna live. So, if you want us to stay kickin', make it happen.'

"That's it. Oops, forgot something. Jesus says, 'amen,' like a secret handshake or something."

'So, for Jesus' sake. Amen.'"

They stopped praying and kept working. Claudia, the storyteller, made up stories for Julie, "Once upon a time a little princess appeared as a mysterious seed in a crack in the lava flow, burped up from the center of the world in an eruption long ago. The little seed had been trapped in a lava gas bubble for eons. Time had worn down the lava, and at last she was released to the elements." She paused, waggled her eyebrows, "Little did she know that she was destined to join the world's greatest love story…."

Julie looked up, now and again, sat back on her haunches, and offered suggestions for how such a triumph could be a tragedy in disguise. Claudia tired of tragic trajectories, saying, "Julie, can we serve up our love without such a topping of pain?"

Julie shrugged, "It's all I know. I've always fed my fires with pieces of my broken heart. That's *my* destiny, Miss Volcano Seed."

Claudia dropped this mutual storytelling and became a solo actress in a musical. She sang to her seeds. She danced and wailed, put on a show for Julie —a piteous show that encouraged seed-break in the dark with the promise of lettuce to come. Julie laughed, once.

Their only container was a leaky tin pitcher. Two holes, one here, one there. They walked to the dried-up brook, holy pitcher in hand. Claudia was thrilled to see a trickle appear from out of sheer rock, like magic. She said, "Go figure. No rain, but here comes water from a half-ass spring, a hundred yards along a rocky path."

She blessed each seed while picturing Jesus' face, "Fall apart and grow, you little farts. Amen."

A few weeks passed like this. When Claudia wasn't watering seeds or sharing Julie's litany of grief, she explored. One day, on her way from the miracle spring I'd provided for them, she noticed a tiny green shoot poking up along the path. She stopped and held her can in front of her, staring at the plant. A drip hit her toe.

She thought, *Hmm. I've been watering seeds I didn't know existed.* Before long a whole row of buried seeds, from years gone by, sprouted along the path.

I popped a thought in her head. She mused, *my mouth, another leaky pot. Should be more careful what I dribble from that pot.* For now, she was happy with daisies, verbena, and sunflowers—blue dancing between the yellows.

Claudia learned to savor human silence for the first time in her life. Wind whipped waves against rocks, a non-stop conversation. She and Mr. Leak cruised the rock listening to the ocean talk to the rocks. She scraped up handfuls of any soil that looked vaguely grow-worthy and dumped them in Mr. Leak.

I woke Claudia that night on her cot. They slept far enough apart, she and Julie, to put their bare feet, with their chipped toenails, on dirt when they got up to pee. Claudia listened to a new kind of chatter in the night wind. What was that?

Soft patter of rain.

Together my two exiles danced naked in the warm shower, shedding stink, soaking in midnight hope, under a hint of silvery moon.

Arms up, palms out, head back, Claudia said, "Jesus' Father—maybe you'd like to hear thanks. You get a gut full of my whining. Thanks for seeding me and this ground, turning us, troweling us, growing a crop outta my rock."

She added, "Jesus, one more thing. I'd like to hear your voice again and feel your touch. That's all. Let it be soon. I miss you so much." Tears spilled out of her eyes under pressure from what felt like an iron band tightening around her skull.

Their pips fell apart at the speed of seed. Took their own sweet time. Bones took up more space; fat, less in each of their bodies. Julie was weakening—and Claudia too. The younger exile ventured out while the older one rested. Took her bit of fishing line and picked her way around inlets, coves, and bays. Waves talked to rocks, seagulls talked to each other; she talked to no one except me.

And then, around a hidden corner, she discovered a new cove I'd been saving just for her, one I'd shielded from the breakers by a tongue of rock. She gazed down, saw stuff moving in the deep and deeper shades of blue from her overhang. Shadows with meat on them.

She learned to fish by making mistakes. I taught her that learning without using muscles was only a rumor that had no substance.

She laid down on her stomach and hung out on the rock, edged her upper torso over the water, watched movement under that water. She unwrapped her line from a bit of knobby tree branch and put a slimy bit of seaweed over her hook.

She prayed to her Boyfriend-Gone-Missing, "Jesus, help me stay alive! I need a fish for Julie, and one for me. Today."

I decided to preview her dinner with an opening act. She didn't see it coming. I cracked lightning and thunder right over her head. I whipped around her, up one side and down the other. She stayed on her perch, rolled over, held her mouth open for a drink.

She prayed, *Ok, Jesus, you answered the request for rain. Now, what about food?*

Her line remained lifeless. She pulled it up. Seaweed gone, hook bare. Repeat. Wrap the hook differently. Same result. Repeat, repeat, repeat.

Two impatient hours blew by, sun and squall, bait gone missing over and over again. One strand of slime remained.

Shadows were lengthening when she returned to their hut. She poked her head in the door's archway. Julie slept on her pallet, exhausted from doing nothing and nothing doing her.

Claudia flopped two big fish from her burlap bag on Julie's head and danced like a mad hatter around the thoroughly awake Julie. She picked dinner off the dirt floor, one entree in each hand, and looked them in the eye.

Neither one ate her. She decided not to return the favor. Claudia held both Julie's shoulders, looked her in the eye, and breathed out my words from her mouth. "Today, the squall beat survival into me. I'm leaking it onto you, out my two eye holes. We get to choose our destinies that God chose for us. Got it?"

Julie took in her resolve and my mystery. Glimmer of hope trickled back out her eyes, a dim mirror.

They went to the fire pit outside the front door. Julie took her knife, her only knife, and gutted the fish. Claudia's fresh interest in fish guts was longer and straighter than Julie's blade. When handed a double handful of fish guts, Claudia didn't shrink away from this new, excellent bait. She dumped 'em all in Mr. Leak.

Julie struck rock and flint together. A faint spark didn't catch. She bit down on her lower lip, concentrated. Claudia sat cross-legged in front of her, hands shielding her spark, their spark, while I swirled around and over their hilltop hut. Three tries and a feeble flame grew out of thin air.

Once the sticks of wood had burned down to white-hot coal, they watched fish sizzle and crisp. In palace days, this would have interested Claudia as much as watching paint dry. Now she drooled, a primate slathering over fresh kill.

One of the mystery seeds from their garden had come up as parsley. Bits of that over juicy white-meat fish never tasted so good. They sucked the fish off all the tiny bones. Julie ground the bones between two rocks, sprinkled them over their garden patch. Wasted nothing.

Months passed in this new life. Claudia grew stubborn gladness. Julie's face brightened. Her storyline evolved, became sharp enough to hook memories of good times. Suffering edged toward upbeat resignation with only a dollop of despair.

One day, after a few more seasons had passed, Claudia busied her crowded calendar with cloud watching. I skittered a zillion colors of blue and white and grey over sky and ocean. I trundled clouds over their island in ranks—puffy rows of cumulus, sheets of stratus, a squidge of cirrus smeared against a ceiling of dark blue—my magician's bowl under Father's sun. I added a vision in her mind of a worm-woman becoming a thresher, harrowing the hills into a loamy field full of harvests.[6]

Around mid-morning, a familiar galley beached itself below their hut. Pontii and two guards climbed the snake path. Their eyes flicked up, then down, on the zigzagging trail.

Julie hid. Claudia walked up to Pontii, a foot away from him, face to face. Feet splayed, hands on hips. "You got execution orders for us like you did for Paullus? If you do, I'm not falling on any sword, not for Grandma, not for you. Run me through yourself."

He looked her up and down. She wore my cotton pantaloons and thin blouse like a legionnaire's uniform. Long time since they'd seen each other. His hair was thinning, and his sideburns greying. She'd slimmed down, browned by the sun. Very much alive, thank you.

Pontii said, "Still full of brass, aren't you? I've no orders today for execution, but I can do the job if you want. No harm to me."

Claudia laughed in his face. "When I'm restored to my position back in Rome, I may well do that job on you."

He looked at her, his expression wry. "Fortunes rise and fall, for sure, exile princess. For now, I'm in; you're out. Even so, you look stronger. Dowager Mother will *not* be pleased. Other plotters in your cabal sneak over here to feed you?"

She held up her hands, palms open. "Who you see is what you get, buster. We're surviving together, without any imaginary plotters to help us. Unless you mean Jesus. When I don't know what to do, he counsels me in my dreams, a voice in my ear behind me, saying, 'walk this way, lay down on this ledge. Drop your line here.' He even sends rain to grow our seeds into salads and flowers."

Pontii ordered his men back to the beach. As they marched away, around the first of the switchbacks, Pontii hung back. He said, out of earshot from Julie, "Augusta left a garrote for me to bring here. I'll be back in six months. Save me the work. Polish off Julie, and then figure a way to die on your own."

Pontii made his way down-trail with his men and disappeared from view beneath a rock crag before reappearing on the beach. He pushed his boat out into the shallows. The three of them shoved into the breakers. Pontii manned the rudder but couldn't get his ship's prow into the surf. A wave capsized them, ass over teakettle.

Both Julie and Claudia hee-hawed. Knee-slapping theatre, courtesy of Rome. The three men came up from under the keel of their boat, sputtering and cursing.

When they had gone, Julie napped and Claudia wandered down the trail to her fishing hole. She poked her head under the promontory where Pontii had disappeared, rooted around. A bag was tucked in between two rocks. In it, more seed, fishing line, hooks, another knife, grandma's garrote, and two cotton singlets.

8

RABBUS

We sat on our horses, the Emperor and I, overlooking the Rhine river and the forests east of it. Fingers of fog swirled around us and through the valley below, exposing and then hiding each other and the ongoing battle.

It had been a bloody year, fighting alongside Tiberius. He'd decided to decamp from Rome shortly after Jesus was imprisoned. He took me with him to battle more safely, he said; foreigners, not family.

We'd arrived on Rome's blood-soaked northern boundary. Any one patch of ground could belong to Rome one day and Arminius' German legions the next. Dead soldiers marked the ever-shifting boundaries—wormfood, returning to dust.

Tiberius said, "Swords clang in the fog there below us. We look into light opaque as tinplate."

He still lapsed into word fuzz now and again. Like now.

Emperor Augustus had never recovered from the loss of General Varus and his three legions eight years earlier. The German commander, Arminius, dispatched General Varus's head back to Rome in a bag. Augustus held the head, ordered the messenger's head sent back to Arminius, and wept over his lost legions.

Now we were back in the same forest, same battleground, same opponent, hoping for a different outcome. Tiberius had brought five legions of heavy infantry, two legions of cavalrymen and archers—7,000 men in all to restore Rome's honor. Rome wore forest greens and browns, not brilliant red. The other warriors, the "bad guys," wore similar colors. Hard to tell good guys from bad ones.

The passing Wind blew a crazy thought my way. *God doesn't take sides. He wants to take over. He wants the allegiance of foot soldiers, generals, and emperors; even you, Rabbus—and he's using this battle to sort out his soldiers.*

This thought flickered and faded. I listened to the river beneath us somewhere. The snaky Rhine fascinated me. This river, and the mountains around her, didn't respect others' boundaries. They *were* the boundary, unmoved, even while moving. One flowed, the other trickled. River surged and waned. Mountain peaks cracked off slow streams of cooling pebbles each night, rock tear-trickle.

My attention returned to the battle. "Sire, I could melt into the woods, and no one could tell whose side I was on. I could pick Arminius off with a slinger stone. He'd never know what hit him."

Tiberius said, "Good idea, Rabbus. But high risk. That border between safety and danger is always moving."

The mist opened up long enough for me to see him clean out some ear wax with his right pinky. "My brother, Drusus, thought he was so safe, galloping over that field of gopher holes. Then, his horse's leg snapped. A triumphant general, one moment; the next, a dying man whose horse had rolled over him. Snapped his legs, crushed his ribs. Gone within two days. I've carried my life more carefully since then."

The fog socked us both back into itself.

Tiberius continued musing, "The edge between armies isn't so different than the one between the living and the dead. These borders all shift in the fog, don't they? An arrow or stone could fly out of the fog and kill you or me before I finish speaking."

At that moment, the Wind nested truth in my ears. *You've become Tiberius' lost brother.*

He said, "Boys disappear in these boundaries here. The return rate is poor—especially for fog-boys who want to become solid men."

His voice drifted. "I've never made it through those boy-man woods—got lost in loss."

This naked statement would never have happened if either of us could have seen the other's face. I ventured a suggestion, "Ever chat with my Jewish friend, Jesus? Though young, he's more a man than any I've met."

"I've forgotten who he is."

"He's the exact expression of their Jewish God, come to show us how to live."

"Now that you speak of him, I remember Mother wanted him killed, quietly. I exercised my right to forget and hoped she would forget too—but her memory's elephantine. She remembers how to run the empire while I play army games. He's been right there, all along, under her nose—and, believe me, that provides for a lot of shade."

I thought, *a lot of death hides inside her shade.*

Tiberius kept rambling in this odd, intimate, fog-driven fashion. "Being with you, bodyguard, gives me a fresh wind. I'm thinking of acting the emperor instead of living like a throw-away general on the edge of things. But that border crossing, from general to emperor, requires coins I've not yet minted."

"Emperor, speak with the Jew, if he lives. Augustus valued his words. Perhaps he could help in your own border crossings."

Even as the words left my mouth, I was unsure what he'd heard. After all, our ears were curved differently.

9

JESUS

The sewage levels had risen all day. I couldn't sit in my spot by the sewer hole without being waist-deep in wastewater. I felt like someone had poured sewage in a hole in my skull. I'd moved to the only dry ground that was available—a few yards from the triad's dice-playing niche. I sat there in the only clothing I owned, my filthy loincloth.

I moved in slow motion. If I wanted to rub my nose, I spoke brain's command to hand—*move!* My hand obeyed grudgingly, but only after a long lag. A moan, involuntary, came from my throat. I clamped my lips shut, trying to shut myself up, but sound still escaped me.

Putzi's voice. "Think our Jew might be hungry for some down-and-dirty? He's moaning with desire."

Grippa rolled the dice. "Could be. Been a while."

I pried open one eye. Putzi looked me up and down. The thunder wasn't yet rain, but a storm was coming.

A familiar demon voice from that disastrous day in Shechem. *Ready? I told you to wait for Rome, didn't I?*

The day inched by. Pain crept from the back of my eyes along the top of my head. Clusters of tiny spikes in there chattering, *what can we nail into?*

The jailors, hours earlier, had clanked open the iron gate with our one daily feed. We all trooped by the door. Watered-down gruel hit my shallow tin cup, stale piece of bread crawling with weevils. Turnip shred floating in gruel. I tried to pull flavor from the turnip but gave up after one chew and swallowed.

Meal now long finished. The food here didn't keep you alive so much as extending your dying. Maybe that's why they called the place DIE.

I sloshed through sewage fifteen paces to the sleeping ledge, lay down, rocked back and forth. Fever and chills waged a tug of war. A band of bad boys sledgehammered both my temples. I listed to one side, then startled awake, pulled the thin blanket over my head. Tried to doze. Woke up disoriented. Black silence all around me. Where was I? Oh yeah, right, the Dungeon. Night felt strong enough to crawl down my throat and tie my lungs in a knot.

Sound of men snoring all around me. Faint word in my ears. "Breathe, Son. Focus on Father now. Despise the shame."

Sound of slippery feet sloshing through dark slime. Stifled laughs punctuated snores.

"Father, Windy, please, protect me, help." I surrendered, waited in the dark, hands to my side, submissive not to men but Father alone.

Satan's voice floated through the pounding headache. *Ain't hell fun, junior?*

That was the only voice that I heard for a long time. Rough hands dragged me down on the cobbled floor, stripped off my loincloth, held my face down. I held my breath, gritted my teeth, and remembered Ahmed. My heart, a snared bird, beat against the cage of my chest, desperate for release.

I was not rescued. No angels, Father, or Windy put protection in place. I prayed, first with words. *You said I would suffer what all people experience, uniting me with those I came to save. You have kept your promise.*

I suffered through this humiliation as long as I could. When my body had felt enough, more than enough, my prayer left light and language far behind me. Body detached, mind-images only—*secret caves, ancient bones, catacombed stones, dead leaves whipped by summer storm, fast-paced tango, Father-Windy hugs, wandering Eden, skipping galaxies, world not born, flicker-blinking bright lights, fade to black.*

Grippa slapped me back into consciousness. "Talk to *anyone,* and we won't be so generous next time. Might just keep your pathetic head down in the turd soup." They left, chuckling.

I cleaned out my ears and eyes with my fingers. Skin prickled under a heavy wash of shame. Snoring all-around had stopped. Thirty-five men had listened to this gang rape and done nothing. I crawled back to my pallet, fell into a fetal position. Bled. Rocked myself. Shame stupor, like a thick, yellow fog, choked me. Alone, all alone, surrounded by wolves.

10

SLOW

It was a hot summer night. I lay in bed with my husband and our toddler son, Michael. Jericho's east wind howled and banged our shutters about. The shanties outside these city walls seemed tired of fighting it. Most simply sagged. Some blew over, and people roped their cloth walls back into place once the wind died down.

I rocked baby Michael to sleep. If I pretended sleep, maybe my husband would turn over and leave me alone. Why did God give me such an oversexed man and put our apartment beneath a whorehouse? Was this Jewish-God humor?

On this night, I wasn't all here. Mostly I felt like a kid, remembering early snatches of my childhood. One memory was not my own, but what my mother told me. I wasn't yet born. Moab's king saw mother alone, buying vegetables on the market's edge in Moab's capital city, Dhiban. She was Jewish, from a poor family, barely twelve years old, and in a newly arranged marriage to an Amalekite tradesman.

Eglon-the-Seventh waddled over and said, "Young woman, you are beautiful! You now have a new life. I've chosen you to be one of Moab's elite! Welcome to my harem."

Ma told me King Eglon was shaped like a pear with two twigs for legs. He was draped with so much gold jewelry you could have gotten several idols out of him if he was melted down, with enough left over for a kneeling stool so others could worship comfortably.

My fate was sealed as well as hers in that one moment. She was conscripted into palace life, learned the arts, and was trained to pleasure a man. Every Shabbat, she got a pass for the day. When she went to temple, the chief rabbi soon conscripted her into servicing him before the worship service. Once she came home, more of the same with her husband.

Then, next morning, back to the palace where she did the king's bidding. Somewhere in those years, she got pregnant with me. Once I was born, I got maybe an hour a week with my mother. Wet nurses and her husband filled in when she was gone. The night of my eighth birthday, her husband, Achan-the-Amalekite, had me do for him what mother did for the king.

It was all too much of him, too little of her, and too quick for a girl too little.

I know now that my father could have been any of mother's sex partners. The father-hole-in-my-soul became a dead sea of longing. This unknown man, this mystery father who never claimed me, became a hand around my throat or maybe a chunk of furniture too big to get rid of. Yeah, that fits best. The furniture one. I can see it now. A king-sized marble bed dropped off the city wall as I passed beneath. The bed and me, splintered to bits.

There's an old Moabite saying, "Grow through what you go through." Even now, I know the words, but I can't dance to the music. Instead, my me-splinters became leftover junk in a muddy river bed. Neither mother nor Mystery Abba taught my-me's anything useful, like how to float a friendship. We feel the pull and use of friends, but don't know how to make or keep them. That's for normal people.

I got out of bed, opened our eastern window. A whisper came. *You're not alone. I'm your Friend.* I asked Whisper, *if you're my friend, teach me normal. Make me a worthy friend.*

I clasped both arms around my breasts and faced a bent-over tree. A dead patch of water beyond, at the bottom of the world, framed the tree. The hot desert wind blew so hard that the tamarisk tree had taken its shape.

Laz, from behind, put his arms around me and molded me to his shape. "Hey, baby Mike's out of it. How's about me getting into it, baby?"

"Not in the mood, husband. Got a crowd in my head, and I don't need to crowd the other end. Achan memories are getting free rent between my ears right now."

"You married to that dead pervert or me, Slow?"

"I was claimed before you came, Laz. I'm damaged goods with no desire on tap for tonight. None. You know what's more evil than the Devil and more powerful than God? It's the same as what I feel for sex right now. Nothing."

He looked a bit confused. "Since God's all-powerful, let's ask him to throw out your ghosts. If Jesus were here, he'd do that for us. I've seen him toss demons to the wind. But he's gone now, and it's just us to figure things out. I do know that whatever love I take is the love I make. Let's make some right now, woman."

This was all quite beyond a woman possessed of nothing. I took my clothes off, laid down, and thought about broken furniture. He was very quick tonight. After, I got up, cleaned up. When I came back to bed, he was already snoring.

Laz, you know how to go slow. If you'd done that tonight, maybe I'd have come around. As it was, all my-me's had gone. Hope you had fun, cause I didn't.

In moments like this, I got so mad! In better times, I knew that there was a streak of something kind etched through his core. Like he was maybe good enough to be a rough place on God's chin. What he'd done tonight wasn't right. And what I thought wasn't right. Tonight, two wrongs raped a right.

11

WINDY

A new worker showed up at Rahab's. Roy assigned Slow to train her, even though she told him, "I don't like this new girl. Sarah's too much like me—good looks, stinking of fear."

He said, "Check her out, Slow. She survived a stoning."

This got Slow's attention. First day, Roy assigned these two women to take all the trash from Rahab's inn, synagogue, workshops, and brothel to the dump. Halfway there, pulling the trash cart together, Sarah pulled up short to wipe a dribble of sweat off her face.

She burst into an unexpected speech, "I heard about your parents, Slow. Both stoned. You prob'ly wanna know how I survived a stoning, right?"

I nodded.

"No one expected me to run that morning. Men, led by my husband, bound my hands behind me, dragged me outside the city limits. My tender, lovin' husband dragged me by my hair. You might say he was pretty steamed, finding me in bed with his best friend. He cussed me up one side and down the other. I felt like doin' the same to him, but there weren't no fence in between us, and besides, he was a-busy yanking me bald-headed."

"Right as the stoning pit came into view, I started frothing at the mouth, yanked my head out of his hands, and rolled around in the dirt. Husband got so disgusted with my little show that he picked up a stone and threw it at me right there. Knocked me flat."

I whispered, *keep your mouth shut, Slow. Let her talk.*

Slow looked surprised, hearing my voice. She thought to herself, *Wind must be teaching me how to be a friend.*

Sarah kept talking. "Just then, horses came clip-cloppin' down the road. Roman legionnaires. The local stoners hesitated. Their not-knowing turned into my gettin'-going. I bolted to my feet and ran towards Rome, fast as I could. Even with both hands bound, I was faster than the men running after me. Men chasing ya with murder in their eyes? That'll speed a girl right along."

"I got to the Romans maybe twenty paces ahead of them. One of those legionnaires, man named Titus, swung me up behind him in the saddle. Soldiers formed a circle around us. Waited for the stoners to catch up, and they didn't have to wait long.

"Words were exchanged, angry words—particularly with my husband. Titus looked at him, then at me, in the middle of all that arguing. I put on my best smile, my fragile smile, the kind that makes a man feel like a man."

Slow thought, *all's fair in this kind of war. Sarah's Harlot had her version of Fragile and Escape. I guess Cutter's an optional add-on, courtesy of Shame.*

Sarah continued, "Titus patted my thigh, wheeled his horse toward the south. There I was, with the least scary enemy, moving away from all I'd ever known. I got this case of wild, un-worried recklessness—a blast of no-name nothing. I gotta tell ya, it felt gorgeous! Vowed then and there not to keep a thing from yesterday. Clipped my whole life clean, there to tomorrow, left it back of me."

Slow thought, *Ok, we're on the same page, sister. My past got lighter the moment Leah told me Achan had been stoned in Nazareth.*

Sarah checked Slow's eyes to see if she was listening. "I hugged Titus close as I could. Told myself, 'you're alive, girl, alive!'."

I whispered to Slow, *keep nodding. Ask about her.*

Slow said, "Tell me more."

"We stopped at an oasis that night, middle of nowhere, but right beside a stream and a hillside covered with lamb's ear, sedge shoots, and curly dock. I knew what was coming, and it weren't me. He and his legionnaire friends, all ten of them, got paid. One after the other. They weren't mean, but I owed 'em, so why argue? Fair's fair. They saved my ass and wanted a piece of it."

Slow said, "First time I've thought of gang rape as fair trade."

"Don't ya know? Hope they didn't knock me up. My baby-making time of the month."

The two women kept walking, quiet-like, to the edge of the dump. Relieved worry washed over Slow. She inquired of me, *is this what normal feels like?* I hugged her with a soft breeze and sense of surety.

She said, "Sarah, ever think about the strange world we live in? Here you are feeling grateful for gang rape by foreign soldiers 'cause it saved you gettin' murdered by family and friends."

The irony must have settled in. She smiled.

"So, Slow," she said. "Ready to go back? We dumped our trash."

Slow thought, *you dumped your trash, but now we have other work to do.*

Slow said, "Let's look for broken stuff. Raw material for the potter's wheel. The more shattered, the better. Keep away from the fancy glazed stuff where you can see your face. Get whatever's broken and plain enough to be useful."

She started on the side of the trash dump furthest from Sarah.

I advised her. *Meet in the middle. That's how most friendships work—two people roam on a crooked line through trash, not knowing it's a straight line to friendship.*

They ranged from one side of the dump to the other, kicked through all the things no one wanted anymore.

I said, *find something good to say about what she's found or how she's gone about it. Mean what you say.*

Slow told her she didn't think Sarah was doin' too bad, for a trashy whore. Sarah allowed that Slow wasn't so bad for a snotty bitch. They hugged and trudged back to Rahab's, like mules, hauling their loot behind them.

Once home at the whorehouse, I said, *clean her feet.* Slow knelt on the courtyard threshing floor, poured water. Wiped dirt and poop from between Sarah's toes.

Sarah took all this in quietly. She said, "turnabout's fair," and did the same for Slow. Then Slow showed Sarah what Roy had shown her. Smashin' and a-breakin' and a-grinding something into nothing.

Roy came out of the pottery workshop. He still had on that smock he wore when working the wheel. He saw them kneeling and hammering shards into bits. He came over, squatted down on his haunches. They sat eye to eye. His eyes were red. He'd been crying.

He said, "You know, the words *kneel* and *bless* are the same in Hebrew—*barach*. Both point to the coming Messiah. He lowers himself—kneels and blesses—joins our distress. He chooses to mingle his suffering with our sin."

El Roi was quiet, looked at each of them a long moment, eyes flowing with tears. Slow thought, looks like he's grieving something beyond bad, something we can't see, but he can. Roy got up and started to walk over to the synagogue; all bowed over.

I said, *don't let him go alone, without showing you care.*

Slow pulled Sarah to her feet and dragged her over to Roy. Caught up with him. They put their arms around him from either side and rocked together in my wind.

She said, "Roy, you see what you see, and grind it into bread so we can eat. I wanted to say thanks."

Roy nodded, kept moving. Slow and Sarah went back to their work. I popped a strange vision into Slow's head—*Jesus pushed to his knees in a dark and stinky place.* I let the vision dance around long enough, so she knew it was real. Then I shredded it into nothing.

Slow prayed, *Wind, bless Jesus, Sarah, and me. Bless all of us who're trying to turn garbage into friendship.*

12

TIBERIUS

Jesus-the-Jew stood before Rome after almost two years in the Dungeon. Guards had marched him barefoot across the throne room, chains clinking on the marble floor. This was my courtroom, Rome's final court, the court without appeal.

Jesus had been shorn of hair and beard. He stood before me in his simple wool tunic, looking thin as a flea on a flagpole. Blue blood vessels pulsed in his temples; his skin so waxy it was almost transparent.

Rabbus stood slightly behind me. Caligula, my brother Drusus' grandson and my part-time lover, sat to my right. His elevated stool, with a satin seat, put his head at about my waistline. He kept his head slightly tipped back and squinted. He'd been nearsighted ever since I could remember. But he had such a lovely, lean body—autumn's new lease on spring.

Mother, like a lioness in winter, sat to my left, glowering. Her expression was corrosive enough to eat a cement block for breakfast. She raised an eyebrow to the Imperial Guard, who stood behind Jesus. He kicked the prisoner in the back of his knees. Jesus, obligingly, knelt.

Only the six of us were in the room—two rulers, an emperor in training, two guards, and one, what shall I call him—killer, saint, or shorn sheep?

I blessed the kneeled one with a direct inquiry. "You've been given time to consider the error of your ways. You were the last person with my father before he collapsed. Correct?

Sheep didn't bleat a word.

"You were touching him when he breathed his last. What do you have to say in your defense?"

Sheep remained head-down, kneeling, silent, looking for all the world skinnier, more shorn than before I voiced my question. I doubted he would have the strength to kill lice. His hands were on the floor by his sides, palms were up and turned out like he was relishing his fate.

I glanced at mother. Her right hand twitched like an over-strung bow. She delicately picked at a long nail on her left hand. She said, "You took my husband of 52 years from me, Jew. Poisoned him. Do you deny this?"

Jesus remained silent.

She said, "Speak, or you will not live out this day."

He said, "I come as a witness of the truth. Only those who live from love have ears to hear such plain speaking."

Mother cracked an icy retort. "Love and facts are mutually exclusive. The man I loved was poisoned. That is a fact. And the figs were there at your right hand."

I interrupted, tentatively, with the merest trace of a whine, "Mother, let him speak."

I turned to Jesus. "Try your brand of factual plain-speaking with me, Seer."

Jesus regarded me from his kneeling posture. He was five feet below me and an equal distance in front of me. *Why did I feel as if I was looking up to him, not him to me? And why was it I felt as if truth dawned in his eyes, without him speaking a word? Most curious.*

The Shorn Sheep said, "In his last moments, Augustus gained a toe hold on love. Fear and love had raced toward the finish line in his maze. Love won, helped him pass through death's door to where my Father welcomed him."

Mother said, "Your 'facts' smolder in mystic vapor."

Caligula stroked my knee, nodding vigorous agreement.

Jesus said, "The figs you fed us in the Cavern of Lights were truly delicious, Madame Dowager. One of the two figs you left at the center of the maze also smelled delicious."

Mother opened her mouth as if to speak. Shut up and turned her head away at a quarter angle. I noticed she didn't deny his words, though she teetered on edge.

Jesus continued, "Your husband said to Claudia and me, 'Livia followed our plans exactly. She let me choose life or death.' His palsied hand went straight for the one poisoned fig. He was grateful for your assist in his suicide, Madame Dowager."

Mother's face turned a mottled purple. No one ever spoke so directly to her, not even me. If Sheep could stop her breathing, with such a simple statement, I might elevate him to status of senior magician.

Mother expelled a violent, deep breath. Stomped her foot. "Garrote him, Cal! And you, Captain Rabbus, bury him in an unmarked grave! Leave no trace behind."

Jesus knelt before her, gazing placidly at her. One eyelid trembled.

She stood, chin up, shoulders racked back, a fierce imperator. She whipped a garrote out of her gown and threw it to Caligula. "Kill him now while I watch!"

Caligula grabbed it and walked back of Jesus, one handle in each hand and a strip of razor wire in the middle. Jesus bowed his head, immobile.

This was my moment. Her rage served to witness Sheep's truth, even if she was a hostile witness. It was my time to move across some border—boy to man, general to emperor, or another? I couldn't tell.

I looked at young Caligula and held up my hand, stopping him. Caligula looked downcast—a young lion denied his kill. I'd soothe his frayed nerves later.

I pulled Rabbus to me by his sleeve, whispered in his ear. "Take him away. Keep him alive. I'll tell her later when the time is ripe."

My move left me stuck in the borderlands between who I was and who I wanted to be. But I conciliated. Reasoned with myself. This land of the liminal is long, a province in itself, full of mist and bogs. There's plenty of time.

This was the last I saw of Sheep for about a year—his back, as he was led out of my sight and memory. Mother Vesuvius stood, invective rising through her vent holes, tiny teeth glistening.

I held up my hand in her face. "Enough."

I turned to Cal, "Come, nephew, this woman's waxing apoplectic. She must have swallowed a bottle of vinegar, the way it flows so freely from her tongue. We must save her from further embarrassment. Besides, you appear quite ripe for your next tutorial in governmental affairs."

Cal and I strolled arm in arm out a side door into the morning's mist.

13

CLAUDIA

Julie and I had settled into a simple, plodding routine. Life as exiles on our isle was now survivable. We had figured out a few ways to fix fish and greens, greens and fish, boiled fish and no greens. Greens without fish. Minnow pâté. Cousin's Grill, exclusive clientele.

She told her stories. I told mine—same stories freshened up for a new audience. On an island charged with human silence, any conversation between people was creamy and covered with honey swirls. My Jesus' memories, in particular, were soft, golden, luscious – a butter cake layered with lemon pudding, memories that melted in my mouth, sticky as desire, so sugary it made my teeth hurt.

Julie's memories were not so sweet. She said, "I couldn't believe how vindictive Grandpa was. Our new home in Rome had just been completed when he came to visit. Paullus and I were so proud, but Grandpa didn't like it—'way too grand,' he said."

"He was always careful, at least in Rome, Julie. Wanted to appear *less than*." I pushed air down with both hands.

"I didn't know how much fear he carried. The day after his visit, a wrecking crew tore down our house. A sign was posted on our gate. 'Orders of the Emperor.'"

"Hmm. Clear message, huh? This is the first I've heard of this. We were in Sepphoris about then. What did you do?"

"I went to him straight-off. 'Grandpa, why did you tear down our new house?'

"He said, 'Envy kills. The whole city would become envious. I'll have them build you something smaller on the edge of town and away from Silanus' neighborhood.' That was the only time he mentioned my affair.

Grandpa was like that, as good at innuendo as he was at tearing down and killing."

We finished our talk on the way down the Z-path. Julie then gave me another swimming lesson. We had all-access passes to a specially constructed saltwater pool—the inlet where Pontii and the Doo-Dah's rolled their skiff. This sugar sand beach was our safe, swimmable nook, the corner of the Adriatic with our name on it. We'd strip naked, and I'd stand waist-deep in the lapping water, lay on her arms like a baby. Slowly, I moved my arms, practiced my breathing, kicked my feet, and tamed my terror of the sea. At first, I looked to see if *Ouroboros* was beneath me, ready to pounce, drag me to the bottom where Claud would be waving at me atop grandpa's gold.

I let my body figure out how to stay afloat. Julie's coaching was a faint murmur in my ears. I'd flap around and sink, stand up, and watch her do the crawl, backstroke, and breaststroke. I followed suit. Swimming became more than not dying in the water.

I started even to like it—a teensy bit. Jesus swam. Why shouldn't I? When swimming, I thought of him, longed for him. Galilee, Adriatic, bathing together in Unknown God's fountain back in Rome—hey, water was water.

Four more seasons passed. The wheel turned. Boring tasks like seeding and weeding strung days together, moment by moment. Every day my heart sucked Jesus-juice out of each memory, one by one. *The bones of his jaw and cheek sculpted into fine lines, nose long and fluted, eyes clear, lips firm and full. Laughing out loud, rolling around in the mud with him, smearing cow poo in his hair after Postie teetered off, hugging vendors' stalls like a drunk. The night that viper spooked us—hmm, so close we were to doing it. That embarrassing moment in the cornfield where he smelled mother's stupid perfume a mile away. The times he came to my theatre auditions in Rome and stood in the back row, clapping.*

These memories were double-edged. Life-giving but wrapped in painful absence. I tried, really tried, to blur his memory and dull the pain. Examined memories sideways, as through a thin layer of water, all wavy. I made his face fade; amber eyes, gold-flecked, closed and slipped away.

None of this helped. He felt so present, like I could wheel around and hug him like I felt him hugging me. I tried it a few times. Nothing there but the Wind. Jesus' vacancy was the hole left by a pulled tooth, all aching and empty.

When I wanted a walk on the wild side, I'd ramble to the other side of the island with fish guts in my pail and a fishing line in the other hand. This was the side of the island where faster currents ripped along into a vast ocean, seeming without end.

When I walked to this side, I was put in mind of Jesus more than usual—such a wild Presence. I talked to myself, *he took you apart, dismantled you down to bare bone and, face it, self, you've not recovered.* So, me and myself, the two of us, wandered skinless across the island, fish-gut bait, jiggling in his pail. We could barely hold us in.

Cousin Julie, this exiled one with austere, luminous eyes, had gained some weight and hope— almost against her will. When I fished, she tended the garden and gazed out to sea, each in turn. Her blue-grey eyes held a distance in them that I didn't belong to, that didn't belong to me. The empty grey-blue sky was the constant companion that most mirrored her life. It stretched toward land but never arrived, never joined her to home, just to those now lost from her world, a festival of friends living their lives without her.

She would trudge to the spring trickling out of the limestone hillside, sit and fill her holey bucket. Trudge back to the garden. Sit on her three-legged stool and pull weeds, water each plant from this leaking tin. I decided then and there that leaky containers weren't so bad, but only if you knew what to leak on.

She leaked around the base of each plant, water and words. Stroked little leaves, shed a tear for the plant when she had to harvest it, thanked the plant for sacrificing its life for hers. I could handle only bits of this too-much-tenderness before I had to leave, fish, and think about ways to get off this rock.

On this particular day, I wandered to the windblown side of the island, dressed only in my thin fisherwoman's toga, sash at the waist, calluses for footwear. Auburn hair now was waist long with sun-streaks and split ends. Hot winds blew it straight back.

I crested the hilltop of the wild, west coastline. Lava formations popped up and out at odd angles from the granite, like gnomes playing peek-a-boo.

I hung onto one's nose as I slipped through a tight crevice, one I called Fat Woman's Agony.

My scree path came 'round a granite bluff that grew out of a sediment base. This slippery red shale reminded me of the rosy cliff on the way to Apollo's temple, the cliff with the false, falling face. I leaned back into the heat of the cliff, slipping sideways along the narrow ledge with a sharp drop off into a deep canyon. After twenty paces or so in the searing sun, it opened out to a flat red rock with a forty-foot drop into the wide-open sea.

I cut off a section of fish guts with my paring knife and stuck the knife back in my sash; baited my hook with yesterday's guts, slung it into the sea—into any mouth that would find it. I prayed it would be a big fish. I was hungry. I wrapped the excess line 'round and 'round my wrist—didn't want to lose a lifeline that connected me to food. I propped myself on an elbow, looking down, daydreaming about revenge on grandma—and father's killer. Jesus would call this talking with Father. I called it screaming at Neptune to lob his trident at Grandma, pin her to the ocean floor for killing Grandpa. She'd probably glorified herself into some weird version of Artesemia, that ancient Roman matron who ate her husband's ashes so she could be his casket.[7] It wasn't enough to coast on his living genius. No, Grandma had to keep doing it after his death.

Ocean turquoise blue faded through five shades of deepening color. The dramatic sea-sky line beyond was crisp, clear. The light blue sky was painted with wispy, ladder-back clouds. Silver enough to be bankable.

I grew calmer. The sky's broad expanse, placid, placating, refused me my rage.

I lowered my gaze into the deep. I'd noticed different sorts of fish here, bigger ones, sweeping in and out with the currents. I remembered my version of a prayer Jesus taught me—*God, give me this day my daily fish. Forgive my debts even though I don't forgive my debtors. And overlook my little slip there, huh, okay?—for Jesus' sake, amen.*

I laid on my ledge, sunning myself in late morning brilliance. My toes gripped the rock behind me and freed my arms to haul in any fish I might catch. I kept the coils of line tight around my wrist. Didn't want to miss a tug.

A school of smaller fish swarmed, zigged and zagged, so close to my baited hook. They jittered in the midst of unsure shadows. Never mind, just a little closer now.

I jiggled my hook. My bait danced a little samba—*look at me, take my bit, just a nip!*

My mind wandered. I missed my father. His *memory* was probably wildly different from the man who raised me. I remembered him as logical, cool, lustful, detached, powerful. A man proud of me, a man who ignored me, a man I never knew.

He took up more space in my mind now that he was dead than when he was alive. Not fair, that. But, still, I wanted to know how he died, who had killed him, and how I could avenge his death. *Ah, mystery father, given and ghosted, where are you now?*

Sound of scree crumbling. I turned my head. My eyes rested on a pair of hobnail boots, about three feet away. This usually indicated the bottom end of a Roman soldier. A voice, Pontii's voice, further scared the bejesus into me, "Catching anything?"

"How did you find me here?" My stomach butter-flied, heart did a backflip into my guts, and toes tightened on the rock. Didn't look at his face.

"Julie said you'd wandered off this way, fisherwoman." His voice had changed, lost its clawing rasp, morphed into a purring growl, like the staked-out lion at Grandpa's garden party, like my memory of father watching me dance before King Herod.

Dawning glimmer. I might be hauling in the biggest catch of my life. I shouldn't let him off my hook. I slipped a smile on my face whilst still turned away from him, wiggled my butt a bare shimmy. Rolled over to get a good look at this big fish.

All decked out in his usual Roman red. The hardness of his face had softened to humanoid. A calculating smile twitched in the corners of that hole where he kept his teeth.

Jerk on my wrist. I pulled back, hard, setting the hook. Whatever was on the other end gave an enormous yank that blew me off my slippery slope. Suspended me in mid-air, momentarily. Then I dropped forty feet, hit the water, and headed to the bottom, pulled by something way stronger than me.

14

JESUS

"I know just the place for you, Jesus. Follow me." Rabbus and two other Imperial Guards under his command escorted me to the other side of Palatine Hill. We rounded a few corners before he unlocked my chains and looped them over his neck. We walked together from that point, muted chains clinking.

Rabbus said, "There are several huts down over here, no longer used. They once belonged to Romulus and Remus, the twins that founded Rome seven hundred fifty years ago.[8] What remains, ruined stumps. Several other huts, built in the last century, serve as guardhouses. The original ruins, yours. Stockade on three sides—sharp drop-off on the fourth side. You'll have to dig your own pit toilet.

Rabbus kept talking. "I returned a couple of days ago from Germania. Tiberius ordered me to check on you now, regular-like. He wants to preserve your magician skills—thought you might serve him well in certain areas. Leah and I'll bring you food and clothing, writing pen, and parchment. You're going to be Tiberius' best-kept secret if I have anything to say about it."

"You came just in time, Rabbus. I'm not sure how much longer I'd have survived the Dungeon. I couldn't have taken much more fever, chills, starvation, and rape."

Rabbus' head snapped toward me, "What did you say?"

"They didn't know what they were doing, Rabbus. None of the Triad there knew my Father or me. Revenge produces folks like Jonah, but twice over."

Rabbus looked confused. "Uh, we get eaten by big fish?"

I said, "Something like that, but only after we're chewed up a bit. Revenge has big teeth."

"No hatred in your Father's kingdom, huh?"

"We're to return good for evil. Father judges and executes."

"And that second thing?"

"When we refuse to forgive, we don't get forgiven. Every teaspoon of resentment we store will be served back to us. We become the hot end of a branding iron." I fingered the branding scar on my arm, the one they said would fade over time to nothing at all.

Rabbus said, "Might work for you, but I punish people who hurt me."

Our peaceful bodies walked arm in arm. Our spirits battled. Windy squeezed a few streaks of light past a cloud and across the cobbles, bounced 'em off his face. She blew streams of mercy his way, wrapping and working him, undoing his armor without damaging his heart. But my words and Windy's work couldn't clean what he packed inside and refused to deal with. God's love has limits. Father, Windy, and I—none of Us can bandage a person who admits no wounds.

We rounded a bend past a cluster of shacks and lean-to's, walked toward a wooden stockade. The supervising sergeant, Rimulus, a man with leathery, lined skin, let us pass. We walked past the wooden gates and a few huts where the guards lived. The guards stared hard at me as I passed, eyes shaded and unflinching. Then, at a distance from the others, a scattering of stone ruins with a small stream running quietly through them.

Rabbus said, "There's your palace, carpenter." Here's a small bottle of oil that Leah gave me. He opened it, poured a little in his cupped hand, and turned his hand upside down on my head. "She said to do this for you, for some reason. Beats me, but now you have an oily, shaved head."

I took his words in silently. We walked to the remnants. Knee-high stone walls, clumped here and there. Dandelion fluff blew between stones worn smooth by wind and rain. Doorposts, long gone, left posthole indents in the stony ground. My sleeping pallet and a bag of supplies lay next to the chunks of these stones and beside the stream. A couple of mangy sheep grazed next to the far fence. A rod and staff lay on the ground beside the other supplies.

Rabbus' feet were bouncy—enough energy to burn a hole in the rock. I picked up all his nervous energy, and it wore me out. I stared around me blankly, feeling his heat, watching the staked-out sheep, listening to the quiet brook. Far below, the Tiber River flowed—a thin ribbon of hammered silver glinting in sun's last blaze of glory.

Rabbus said, "Workmen'll bring you more supplies tomorrow. Your job? Restore and rebuild Rome's foundations. And the sheep? Move 'em around, so they keep the grass down; let 'em drink from the still part of that stream."

His grim grin flashed like an executioner's ax. He turned on his heel and left me standing in what would be my new home for the next year. Dark fell, and quickly; a right-now thing. Night sucked all sight into its stone quiet.

I laid down on my pallet and tried to feel safe, but beds no longer felt comforting, like when I was a boy. Sleep and sleeping pallets and beds felt like places where bad things happen to good people, places where many women die in childbirth, places where many languish in sickness or sadness, places where most people die.

I prayed to my Partners for safety, but they'd gone quiet again. I heard only the wind whistling through the stockade's gates and the guards' huts. Every shift in the wind, or creak in the gates, woke me with a start. I couldn't stop my hands from shaking, even when one held the other.

I, like King David, my hero, was in the presence of my enemies. I grabbed hold of goodness and mercy only by faith in Father because what I *felt* wasn't anything remotely like safety, goodness, or mercy.

Two days passed. I had dug two post-holes deeper and stuck posts in them, tamped 'em down with concrete and strung a line between them. That morning I'd scrubbed my white shirt and singlets on a washboard in the stream. Now they flapped in the wind and looked like headless angels dancing dirges. My iron frying pan, on a cooking grate, stared at me with its round, black eye.

I'd prepared fast bread for breakfast but wasn't hungry enough to eat it. The bread sat on a table beside the skillet with the morning's hot ash blowing over it. My tin cup lay in the stream, on edge, overflowing. I watched the water fill and flow, running downstream over the cliff, waterfalling its way to the Tiber far below.

I kept swinging my pick-ax under the pouring-down sun, working in my loincloth, sweat pouring down my face and chest. Slow, sparky work, cracking rocks open, digging footings, while headless angels flopped about, a frying pan stared me down, and my cup overflowed.[9]

Sergeant Rimulus came over. He said, "Interesting news. Remember your last home, the Dungeon? Three prisoners, the supposed Triad, got whacked last night on their sleeping ledge. Throats cut, ear to ear." I stared at him and saw Rabbus' face.

15
WINDY

Leah met her for the first time while carrying Gabe. The young mother was returning to her two-room apartment on lower Palatine Hill and stopped to rest at the Unknown God fountain. She sat on fountain's edge, watching Gabe-the-babe do his happy toddler gurgle and splash.

She looked at the blue bougainvillea blossoms to the fountain's left. Noticed a glistening. A spider had rolled a struggling something into her silken, glutinous web. She was busily gorging herself. At this moment, another woman came into the courtyard from within the royal quarters. A protege trailed behind her, tablet in hand, ready to take further notes. The larger figure in her silk gown padded, predaceous, on velvet slippers. Her shadow preceded her, thick as tar.

She and he saw Leah laughing with her son in the shadow of the Unknown. The larger woman licked a question mark off her curved lips and flattened her features into a mask. She came within three feet of the younger woman who was playing with her child.

"At last I meet the Resurrection Queen."

Leah turned to look, immediately stood, and bowed from the waist. "Perhaps you mistake me for another, Madame Dowager. I'm a simple, immigrant housewife to your son's bodyguard. And also, as you see, a mother like you."

Augusta paused—a lioness toying with her prey. "Examine her, grandson. She is anything but simple; in fact, she's convinced our Tibbie that she raised him from the dead. We both know, don't we, that he was probably drugged by some witchy potion she fed him."

Protégé Caligula nodded vigorously. He squinted and took a note in a loopy script, *witchy potion*. He got the order of the words mixed up and spelled them, *poshun wishy*.

"Even so, your uncle remains deluded, poor boy. He sees Rabbus as bodyguard and wife as soul guard. What a coup for these muddy, middle easterners who seek to pick through royals like us as if we're a bone heap, all the while hoping to ransack our treasury."

Caligula's eyes narrowed, malignant insight dawning. This woman, indeed, was a threat. She could distract, dilute, subvert. Maybe misplace his lover's affections.

Leah didn't know what to say, so wisely, she said nothing. I caused Gabe to slip and fall in the water. He started crying. Leah sat back down, using the time to recoup comfort for the child within her and the one on her lap.

I said to her, *these two in front of you need resurrecting. Both are dead but don't know it. Together we will be an opposing spirit of liveliness. Let's invade their darkness with kind words. This is so much fun.*

Augusta continued, "You parade around Palatine with the footloose insouciance of a practiced sorceress. Keep dipping that mousy Sibyl's head of yours into my affairs, and I'll hand it back to your husband on a silver platter."

Night over-spilled her eyes' orbits, pouring into Leah.

Leah trembled. *Windy, kind words, now?*

I said, *sit straight, breathe. Her fear infects you. Intolerable vulnerability riddles this woman, and she flees into her illusions of power. Caligula is her student; you are mine. Stay alert.*

Leah obeyed. I exhaled words through her lungs, "Madame Dowager, your desire to protect your son and grandson is fierce, even admirable. But whether your son was dead or asleep, I do not know. And I do not resurrect anyone. I do nothing good by myself. It is God who spins, measures, and snips our thread."

She paused, stared intently at both the rulers who towered over her. "He also raises people from unconsciousness, birthing them into light."

Augusta latched onto the least of Leah's words. "Ah, so you also believe in those three sisters, the Fates, who manage the threads of our lives?"[10]

"I believe, Madame, only in one God. But my God goes by many names."

Dowager's face dripped contempt, "The Fates have nothing to do with your grubby pagan idol. They are glorious. I have fashioned my life after them."

"Dowager, you are, as they say, Rome's *doyenne*. Women across the empire admire and model themselves after you. However, in this matter of deity, I beg to differ. Your own workmen honored our God in this fountain. And Jesus of Nazareth is this Unknown God in human flesh."

"The assassin I had executed?"

"The power of life and death belongs to God, not you, Madame Dowager. Jesus one day will execute judgment on both royalty and peasants like me—not either of us on him."

Lioness turned to her cub-in-training. "Listen to this brazen hussy, dripping with insolence. She obviously views me as a fusty, desiccated dragon, guarding my gold."

She turned back to face Leah. "This pathetic Jesus is pushing up weeds in some unmarked grave. Augustus' name and my fame will last for centuries."

Leah hesitated, played with her son in the fountain for a few moments, fought off fear, and listened to me. Then she stood, eye to eye, and screwed her courage to the sticking place. "I'm but a simple child, soon forgotten. But Jesus' name and fame? That, Dowager, will far outlast yours; indeed, all will bow before him, including the two of you. You can willingly choose now, or later another will bow your knees for you."

Augusta suddenly grew rigid, her face reddening. Caligula's saucered eyes were glued to her face. She ratcheted her head toward Leah, a catapult ready to launch.

Leah clutched Gabe to her breast. *Windy, murder is in her eyes.*

I said, *I am God, not her, not Caligula. See the scared bullies they've become. Only kindness will bring them to repentance.*

An urgent voice from within the building called, "Dowager, come quickly. Gemellus and his armies in Illyria are being attacked. Their messenger requires your immediate reply."

Augusta, distracted by the courier I'd sent, gathered rage about her like a dark cloak. She strode away, robes roiling behind her. Caligula trailed after her, looking over his shoulder at Leah, eyes all-a-squint.

16

CLAUDIA

The big fish that I'd prayed to get, got me. I became Julie's nightmare. I grabbed a deep breath as I fell, right before I smacked into the chop—about the same height as the fall from Grandpa's sinking ship, but this one didn't knock me out. A lightning bolt had attached itself to me, and I couldn't let go. Blue water, darkening, flashed by me. I didn't need the downdraft of grandpa's doomed ship to pull me down. Neptune's own chariot was taking me down.

My ears started to scream. I fished the handle of my knife from my sash, fumbled it, lost my grip. Stabbed for knife again with left hand. Grabbed the blade, frantic, and sliced my palm.

I heard a Voice, soft but clear. *You're hooked to vengeance. Cut that cord, and you won't drown in it.*

I sliced the line.

Once freed, I kicked hard toward the light. Jesus had told me he'd kicked and prayed, kicked and pulled up. Somewhere in his crawl up, he got another breath from inside. My turn now. *Stroke, kick, stroke, kick. Jesus' Father, help!*

Air, one breath, swooped into my lungs. *Thanks, Spirit, thanks for this one, small, conscious breath.*

I popped up, sucked in all the free air I could hold. Turned in a full circle to see land, legs kicking beneath me. There, over there, land floating by. Current had dragged me further from land. Pontii was a tiny dot on the clifftop.

I didn't want to think of other company, sharp-toothed company from below, looking to hook up, have a lunch date. Me. I flailed, terrified. Refused to put my head down in the water and look. *Nope, not gonna do that.* I took a deep breath, rolled on my side, and started a steady crawl, heading for the shore.

A current far stronger than me had something else in mind. It folded me into itself and tugged me further out to sea. I kicked against the current with all my strength, but all my effort got me was further and further from shore. I flipped on my back and went with the flow. Current swept me down the coastline, a strand of seaweed in a tsunami.

Slick voice from within. *Shark food. Yum. A shiver of 'em, on their way, looking to feast on you. Here they come!*

Then Jesus' kind eyes and voice, *Look at me, Claudia. Look at me! Keep your eyes on me, not on Satan.*

I turned my eyes on Jesus. Tuned my ears to his voice.

I did that Jesus-gaze-listening-thing for about 2 seconds. Tapped out. Shark fears ate me again. I zoomed down the coastline. *Help! Jesus, help me.*

Coached myself, or Spirit coached me. Not sure. Either way, *eyes on Jesus, Claudia. See him see you. Hear him hear you.*

Another two seconds of relief.

Satan's voice again, *Give up, bitch. Grandma won. See that black dorsal fin cutting toward you? Right over there, closing the gap.*

I screamed, "Damn you, Satan!" I flipped over, back-stroked. Started singing out loud, drowning out his voice. No song came, so I made up nonsense words and threw them into the wind. Let Jesus' Father figure 'em out. I'd have plugged both ears with my thumbs, but my arms were needed elsewhere.

When I'd schemed for ways off the rock, this route hadn't occurred to me. Now a one- sentence prayer came to me. *Jesus, don't leave me alone.*

Jesus' face flip-flop-flashed with a shark's open jaws angling for my legs. I screamed, or Spirit screamed within me, "Stop it, Claudia! Live! Not for you, live for Jesus!"

The coastline of my exile passed me by, effortless. At the end of the island, the water changed temperature, warmed. Current slowed but didn't stop. No sharks anywhere. I started swimming again, using my best crawl, swimming for shore at an oblique angle. Going directly against Nature didn't seem to work. Maybe a slight angle of opposition might work better.

Our cove came into view around the precipice. *Help-Jesus-father-amen. Help, stroke, help, breath, help, swim… yes, thanks, help, thanks.*

I passed the cliff, into the lee side of the island, into the shade of the towering cliff, no current fighting me. No strength to fight it, even if the current was there. Arms and legs wobbly, boiled pasta. But un-shark-eaten.

Jesus, keep praying for me a little while more. I'm all washed up, not much left.

I breast stroked into the cove under a warm, grey drizzle of rain. There, around a corner, scrambling down the rabbit trail, Pontii. He fell on the slick path, picked himself up, ran into the surf, and swam toward me.

What was going on? He reached where I was, a hundred yards out, turned around, and swam next to me. Not a word, but company nonetheless. Human company. I felt sand beneath my feet. Leaned my head back into the water and swooshed my hair back off my face. Smoothed it down my back. Crawled onto sugar sand. Stopped to suck the blood from off my right palm where my knife had sliced it. Flopped onto the warm sand and let the rain wash off sea salt.

I laid flat out, thin cotton tunic plastered to my skin, eyes closed—exhilarated in exile, back in prison, lying beside an executioner under a light rain, overcast sky, clouds in clumps, and streaks of sunbeam arrows poking out from behind them.

Pontii rolled on his side and looked at me closely like he was inspecting an exotic creature from a distant constellation—maybe a Nyad or Hydra, the wild goddess from the sea.

He said, "Will you marry me?"

I stared at him so hard my look could have pulled the skin off his face. A fishy thought swam by. Marriage might be just the catapult to sling me off this rock.

I said, "So, you still want to kill me. Only now, it's death by marriage."

Pontii laughed, "This might work. Marriage would get you off this island alive. I'd get into the royal family. Tiberius might give me a posting as Pilate somewhere in the provinces, maybe Israel—like where your father served. He'd get us out from under Augusta's eye—out of sight, out of mind. We'd go up the ladder together. If one tires of the other, we'll divorce. Simple. It's the Roman road."

"Grandma will look the other way?"

"Something like that. Tiberius is flexing his muscles, standing up to her more, even if at a distance—sometimes from his villa on Rhodes or the one on Capri."

"Is Julie part of this deal? I just can't leave her alone. She'd die."

"I'll ask Tiberius to send another prisoner here. Exiles are a stable Italian export."

He paused, eyes flipped inward, "But one more thing, Claudia. That Jew. You have to drop your infatuation with him. It's him or me."

A half-truth wasn't a whole lie, like Jesus said. If Pontii thought my smile was the real deal, that was his problem. But even if Jesus *was* right, this didn't feel remotely right. If I married Pontii, I'd be doing the wrong thing for the right Roman reasons—like power, position, or politics.

I hadn't needed to ask Jesus, *please marry me*. My whole life was that question. Jesus was the right guy at the right time who'd shown me how to do right. But did three rights, not in sight, outweigh this wrong? *God-man, zip across the waters and rescue me, will you?*

I heard Jesus' voice, clear as day. *Claudia, didn't I come to you on the waters? Now, right now, look at me, not the shark within you or the one in front of you.*

Ok, I'll trust you, Jesus. No lie.

I kept my focus and promise for maybe another two seconds. Then I turned away from Jesus and back toward Pontii, the man lying beside me. We were both skilled liars, each leaning in on one elbow toward the other, studying the other's face. But I didn't need to lie here; just evade the need for it. Put on my face of pure water and let her lie for me. She was a wonderful liar.

I slipped a tiny smile into place on that face. Underneath-armor snicked—*click-click-click*—into the space beneath my thin, wet tunic and trembling breastbone.

17
LEAH

Rabbus took Gabe and I to the stockade. This was the first week of Jesus' imprisonment in this new place. Rabbus marched through the gates, wearing his Captain's uniform. He nodded toward our son and me, gave orders for the guards to let us visit as long and often as we wished. The guards saluted, shuffled their feet. This was the first time that the Emperor's bodyguard had come to visit. Rabbus returned to his duties and left us to visit the prisoner.

Jesus looked thin, pale, and listless. He slumped in a hollowed-out stone chair. Even so, hollowed out like the chair he sat on, he still asked after our lives. I shared some stories about Gabe and a few things we'd heard from family and friends in Israel. He seemed far away, eyes glazed. His hands shuffled the seed packets I'd brought for his garden.

I said, "Jesus, I don't remember you ever being *this* sad. You were plenty sad in the past—with Slow, me, our abbas' deaths. But not exactly like this. What happened?"

"The Dungeon happened, Leah. Stuff like Slow went through in Sepphoris."

I was shaken. Rabbus had said nothing of this to me. I fetched a basin, filled it with stream water. Got a washcloth and knelt in front of him, sitting back on my heels. I washed his feet and dried them. Jesus went quiet, closed his eyes, and seemed lost in some inner tangle.

I felt the vial of perfume hanging around my neck, hanging on its little cord, the place I'd kept it every day for the past two years. This was Slow's wedding present from Laz's mother.

She'd said, "This perfume is expensive—a one-off use. Once you crack it open, use it all. I know it's not for you or me. But you'll know better than me when, where, and who. Trust yourself."

I cracked it open, mixed it with olive oil from a flask in Jesus' simple kitchen. Together they made a lovely massage oil. The sweet fragrance filled the air.

My silent foot massage took all the time that Gabe needed for his afternoon nap, about an hour. Jesus seemed to take in my warmth, my touch, even when he could not take in my words. He held Gabe in his arms, gazed over the Tiber river valley.

I came back every day during Gabe's afternoon nap time. Same wordless foot massage with oil; same sleeping child; same wounded, silent friend. I never asked about what he'd told me. One day, though, I told him, "I keep getting this picture in my head—a dark, empty room; just you there, alone. After a long time, Windy comes and tugs you through a knothole in the wall. He goes invisible, feels absent. You now sit in a slightly bigger, dark, empty room."

Jesus glanced up, nodded once. Someone had understood him, someone who didn't beat the air with too many words.

On one particular day, my marketing day, I brought honey, flour, speckled brown eggs, a small packet of yeast, and fresh cow's milk. When I put the groceries on his table from my shoulder satchel, an egg slipped and went splat on the stone floor.

I put hands on hips and said, "Ah yes, what a good day for angel food cake."

I scooped up the egg with a knife, picked out the bits of shell and grit, mixed it with the other stuff I'd brought. Put it all in a pan and placed the cake in his oven over live coals.

I shared a memory. "This reminds me of my mother, shortly before she died. She'd used her time at home from the king's harem to make an apple pie for the two of us girls. It smelled so good, fresh from the oven. Pa came in, unexpected. Scared her. She dropped the pie in the middle of our kitchen floor. Splat."

"Pa cussed and stomped around. Ma gentled him. Got out four spoons. We all sat on the floor and scooped up warm apple pie.

"Ma talked through a big mouthful, 'Girls, your life will sometimes be a dropped pie. In those times, four things—

"'Sit. Find another to sit with you. Get spoons. Take nourishment.'"

Windy's love wafted through my words. Not preachy, but warm and filling. Her gentle reminiscence wandered along, looking for a place to land.

Gabe slept on Jesus' lap while the cake baked, and I rubbed Jesus' feet. When I was done with the foot massage, it was time to leave. Rabbus liked his supper on time.

Gabe kept hugging Jesus' neck with both arms and saying, "Love Jesus, mommy, love Jesus…." I pried Gabe off his chest, and he toddled along beside me, past the guard shack, and out of the stockade, looking back and waving the whole time.

Jesus raised his hand, a faint goodbye.

I pushed through the shopping crowds and talked with God. *I can't help myself, Windy. Jesus' face is the first I look for, the first I see in a crowd, even when he's not there. And you know, it's not that he's all that gorgeous; it's more that he's too genuine to counterfeit— compressed real. Like a teaspoon of him would weigh more than all Italy. Amazing he doesn't drop straight through the earth and come out the other side.*

Windy laughed and swirled around me in a breezy beam of sunlight.

18

WINDY

Our Son had been a prisoner in the stockade for yet another year. The time had passed more safely than the years before. He was slowly recovering from branding, starvation, beatings, and sexual violence.

Now, for the past few days, a storm brooded over Rome. A steady grey o'erwhelmed the day, and drizzle socked the city. Hours struggled by for Jesus like trapped flies in sticky syrup.

The bottom dropped out of the clouds, and sheets of lightning forked. Jesus sat in the driving rain on his ancient, hollowed-out stone chair. He kept tumbling Leah's seed packets over and over in his hand. No energy to plant them.

Here's the thing about Son. He faced his storms like he faced his pain. He refused to run away. Instead, he endured till both he and the storm were done with each other.

He said, *Some days, Father, I feel like the storm. Other days, the rocks—beaten by breakers. Today I'm the lighthouse, all alone, burning.*

Toward late afternoon, Father and I walked through the garrison gate, hand in hand. We stood quietly for a while, watching Son frame an outhouse over a pit toilet. He was screwing a privacy latch into the door when he turned and saw us. He took off his carpenter's apron, approached, and fell at Father's feet to worship.

Father knelt to bless him, and I gave him a hug. I said, "Take a break from rebuilding Rome's ruins, Son. Time to take care of your own garden." We walked to a patch of rocky soil, full of weeds, near the cliff.

I got two trowels from the guard's shack. He and I got down on our hands and knees. He fumbled around, trying to open a pack of seeds.

I put out my hand, palm forward, a stop sign. "Son, weeds before seeds. Pull, then plant."

Dirt whirled out of my weedy holes.[11] He watched. His face matched the weather, cloudy and full of rain, mired in goo glum. I moved over and stood behind him, put my hands over his, and moved his trowel with my energy. I hummed as I went, massaging life into his skin, the same as I had done with Leah's hands on his feet. Together we tore weeds out, down to the root, and put them in the burn pile.

While we weeded, Father worked. He worked the perimeter of the garden, close to where the two sheep were grazing. He stuck sticks in the ground with cross-pieces holding them all together—a picket fence of white crosses against the backdrop of Rome's Seven Hills. He wept while he worked.

Jesus and I turned our eyes on him, time to time. Watched him pounding out his stake-holding. We sifted rubble from good earth—one pile for burning, the other for growing his garden.

Around eleven o'clock, Jesus curled up in the middle of the drizzle and mud. He was wrung out. Mud dripped from his head, arms, and hands back into the earth. I sat cross-legged next to him in the mud, put his head in my lap. I said, "Son, you've been Father's word mule, plowing parables into dry ground. Now, rest here, on me, in the rain."

I rocked him, sang lullabies to my boy. After a good while, I laid my hand on his shoulder and said, "Ok, back to work now. Let's learn the unforced rhythms of grace, you and me, together. Let's push a little longer, dig a little deeper. Remember the root word of 'blessing' is 'wounding.' Dig into Father's blessing long enough, deep enough, and you'll find a wound. Today, we'll leave your wounds to bless others. Remember, *all* parents wound their children, most especially Father."

He sighed, kept digging, his muscles trembling, working the edge of exhaustion. Almost immediately, he hit something solid. He laid the trowel aside and moved the earth with his fingers. Two old idols, tangled together, presented themselves to him. He called to Father. Father put down his hammer and walked over. Took a knee beside our Son.

I let my trowel drop. "Centuries-old, those. Replicas of the Roman god, *Fascinus*."

One was an erect stone penis ejaculating onto an evil eye. A spider sat on top of the eye. The other was a *bás relief* of two erect phallus gods mirroring each other while they sawed an enormous eyeball in half.

Before Jesus knew what hit him, he vomited violently over both idols—a hot stream of stomach acid. Between heaves, he made gagging sounds, hands over his own throat. I pulled him to me. Began to hold and rock him again.

Father sat beside us, stroking Son's head. Once Son had quieted down, Father held the vomity idols in Son's view. "*Fascinus* and his pack of demons are in charge of Satan's sex trafficking, Son. They make good appear to be evil; evil appear to be good. See this saw, the one cutting that eyeball in half? Satan multiplies his evil eye, like a fertilized egg dividing again and again. But he's got it wrong; sees only back to the beginning of time and forward to the end of time. Short-sighted."

Jesus said, "Okay. But in this world, here, now, he…." His voice trembled. "He penetrates private, hollow spaces."

I drew him to me, hugged hard. "Yes, my love. Lucifer *is* defined by emptiness, not fullness. His darkness is Light's absence. His lies, Truth's absence. His hatred, love's absence."

Son didn't take my words in, not consciously. He'd remember them later, but for now, the idols had triggered flashbacks of sexual abuse.

He squinched his eyes shut and began to scream.

He pulled his knees to his chest and squished his butt deeper in the safety of the earth. I sat behind him, surrounded him with my arms and legs. Let him lean into me. Father scooted up to Jesus' front, his long legs open on either side of Son's clenched knees, encircling us both. We made a Son sandwich.

Son screamed protests, cursing the day he was born on this wretched planet, calling on Father to strike all those who had hurt him, listing them by name.

He cried out, "They sawed *me* in two, not that eye. My butt still hurts when I go over to that outhouse."

I soothed silently, encouraging his protest. Father also sat quietly, a vast Enfolder. Anyone who hurts Son hurts Father, hurts Me. We each wrapped the Others in our essence.

Son complained. "Father, you knew! For that matter, both of you did. Neither of you did anything to stop it. You did nothing! Even though I asked you to help, you didn't stop them. Windy, all you said was, 'Get ready.' How do you get ready for rape, Windy?"

"You don't. You set your mind on the joy before you, Son. And you did that. You despised the shame by filling your mind with Us, not emptiness."

Son slumped on His shoulder, somber, exhausted.

"Son, people will continue to make bad choices. Satan will continue to strut for yet a little while. In the midst of all that, you show people how to press into us for comfort."

Son's eyes and ears didn't seem to be working. Father's words were all good and true, but Son hurt. We'd left him to twist in the dark.

He prayed, *why didn't you care enough to put a fence around me in the Dungeon? Easy enough to put up a fence here, Father. Why no Trinity fence from the Triad when I needed it? Prison life left me feeling like a sack of scraps filled with stray parts. I no longer feel bold, only old and boneless.*

Neither Father nor I said a word to our Word. We listened carefully to his day and night rumblings. Let his pain wrap into our Being. We, the I AM's, were. We were what he needed us to be in the moment. Son lost track of time.

In the fullness of time, I began to sing. Father joined my melody. We sang our parts, wove them together. Something deep within Son rumbled, colors coalesced. His throat let slip a hacking sound, a cawing-sucking sound. Rasping inhale, ragged exhale. This noise grew into a wail, bleak and beaten as a bloody drum, rocking a rhythm of remembrance out of his chest.

I wove his chaos into my lament. Son had no head or heart space for his own song, so I sang him. I dove him into down-depths and then soared back up high and higher, far beyond where he was able to go. Father harmonized Son's wailing and my melodies with a rhythmic *swoooosh*, folding Son's pain into His vast, cosmic heartbeat.

Trinity's threnody.

Father smudged time from Son's mind. Son remembered only the ending and high points of his pain.[12] We smoothed his rage, regret, and betrayal into these peak moments.

In the midst of this smoothing and soothing, Father mingled pain into Son's frame with a litany of names. I continued this naming in Son's inner ear. I added faint, strobe-lit images into the mix—added story upon story, nuanced, complex interweaving storylines.

Son asked, *who are these people, each with a name, each with stories?*

In One voice, Father and I said, "These are the molested. All who have been and will be. Together we carry your grief *and* theirs. Their history, their feelings, their faces. We're readying you for the cross."

The depth of depravity on this earth sank into him. Corkscrewed into all his openings. He squirmed, keened a naked rawness that Father and I both caught and held, another night, another day. None of us spoke or ate. The names and faces and stories kept flashing, non-stop, in each of our together minds and hearts.

The storm blew and raged around us. Six more days and nights. Finally, at the end of this season of suffering, Father and I looked at each other and Son. He looked back at us.

We said together, "We're done.[13] Let's eat."

I produced a warm loaf of fresh bread. Gave it to Son. He broke it into three pieces. Gave one to me. Kept one for himself. Gave Father the final piece. He said, "Take, eat, this is my Body—broken for many."

Father teared up at Son's obedience—his willingness to join with all broken people in his creation. Father produced a cup of wine, red as blood. We fed each other the broken bread. We drank from the cup. Rested from our work.

It was the seventh day.

19
JESUS

Windy had found some coffee beans in my half-finished house, beans that Leah had brought. She put them in a hollow mortar and crushed them with a stone pestle, making a *chocka-chocka-chukka* sound. I sat at a little distance from her, facing out toward the valley below. I tipped my head, tuned my ears, and took in her snappy tune. Felt a change in my soul's weather.

She souped-up her Bean Crush Samba into fast-paced soul music. She moved her feet and hips in a syncopated rhythm, bobbed and weaved her head, circled the mortar, looking for all the world like a ballerina barista in swirling silver. She blew over and around me, pounded out her *chocka-chukka-chocka*. Smell of crushed beans floated my way, and then the smell of coffee beans brewing.

Windy breezed over, dipped her finger in the brew, and handed me a mug of sweet coffee. She murmured, "It's so *yum*, sweetheart, getting all caffeinated."

Father brought breakfast. Windy joined us in our triangle of stone thrones, and we began to eat.

Satan misted up from between two graves, constellated into flesh, and wafted our way. Our communion had entered a new chapter. Satan's shape-shifting form aped the idol, *Fascinus*—lean, muscular arms; abs precisely ridged, body oiled, complete with a proud erection under a brief loincloth.

He grinned. "Well, well, well—howdy-doodie! Here's the Perfect Trifecta—Geezer, Ghost, and Grump."

He turned at a quarter angle to the sun, flexed like a bodybuilder. "Please overlook my lack of a grand entry, but since this *is* my domain, I'll enter *whoever* I please."

He gave me a wicked wink. "But let's see. Something's not quite right here."

He moved into our triangle. Effortless sideways swipe of his foot. My stone chair flew from under me. I toppled sideways on the ground. He plopped down on that stone throne, positioned his sleek buttocks atop an emerald velvet cushion he'd summoned from thin air.

"There," he said, "much better, I'm comfy now, and oops! Almost forgot. I had someone bring goodies for our festive gathering. You domestics must be starved; all this gardening and kitchen work wears a body out, now doesn't it?"

He did a whirly-gig whirl with one hand. *Voila!* My dear mother showed up carrying my favorite foods.

She said, "Oh Jesus, you look so sad. Let me feed you, son." She came over, eye to eye, the soul of concern. I looked into the yellow-flecked heartwood of her brown eyes, smelled her fresh, aromatic bread, buttered like I liked it, with a side of honey.

I looked at Father and Windy. They looked back at me. It was my turn in the wheelhouse—my school, my exam.

Strength surged into me. I got up, yanked Satan's arm, and dragged him right through the apparition that was my mother. She and her platter of false food vaporized. I stormed along with him among the ancient graves moldering on cliff's edge. I walked with him to my right, cliff's edge on my left.

Satan gave me a sharp hip bump. I teetered, on edge, then a strong wind blew me back on course. The abyss was six inches to my left. The Tiber, far below, glinted like a burnished sword in the morning sun.

Satan cajoled, "Oops, almost slip? Here, let me help you. Such a virtuoso in forgiveness, me, in spite of your naughty display of temper back there, Junior." He lifted his arm to hold me close to him. I brushed him off.

He glanced over the edge of the abyss, "Now, how should I interpret your rudeness? Borders on being uppity. You know, me being Ruler of this world. I'll excuse your bad manners this once, my sweet, skinny butt-boy."

His voice slithered into syrup. "Poor boy-toy. Putzi put his fingers into squidgy, private spaces during his big-boy workout? And that night of consensual sex among consenting flirts? Has your teeny-weeny head juiced a false memory from that? Even called it rape? Victim mentality is *such* fun. Get a lot of sympathy that way, don't we, little glory hole?"

"Shut up, Satan. You put them up to it."

"Did I now, or was that you? Dressed real sexy, with your skimpy loincloth? Got what you needed—a little attention, a lot of touching. The four of you—normal men, normal desires. But you did egg them on, now, didn't you?"

I kept walking. He kept pace.

He said, "Your own scriptures say you're to bow before those in authority. Like me. Being as I was given this domain to do with as I please. Wouldn't want to stiff your scriptures, now would you?" He snorted with merriment, a stand-up comic, a real knee spanker.

I was silent for a few steps, considering my response. "Satan, you're a junior prince who controls a dust mote. And your control center? A paper-mâche ´ desk inside a furnace."

Satan flipped a response my way, a droll look plastered on his face. "Better to reign in Hell than serve Papa-Razzi in Heaven. All that praise music, droning on and on. A bit much. I got bored after the first million years or so.

"Personally, Junior, just between us boys, I doubt the Geezer would care if you knelt before me. Consider this—He didn't do anything to save your little sister or your abba. He didn't stop you from falling into the mountain chute when I collapsed your shale bridge. He didn't rescue you from my loving gang of three. Why should he do anything now?"

My eyes leaked hot tears as I remembered those falls, those losses. I wiped my tears away with the back of my hand, said nothing. Kept walking through this private hell—not gonna stop now, no sir. My fingers began snapping back and forth, picking up Windy's tune that I could still faintly hear. Her energy, my tears, mending soul tears, one stitch at a time.

Satan picked up my rhythm, mimicked it. He styled down Cemetery Boulevard, jinking and-a jiving to Windy's soul music. Adapted it to his purposes. Sashayed a syncopated song, in a gorgeous baritone, with lots of vibrato, "Turn back, Jack. Admire my stack. Join Team Black."

Vultures circled over our heads. Rain misted my eyes from within. I stifled a gag.

Brief memory flicker of me 'n Satan—a lovely friendship once upon a before-time—fun together, laughter ringing down timeless corridors. Somewhere in those eons, he'd gone off. Worms of sedition had nested larvae in his spirit—a frothy mix of envy and rage, dressed in needlessness. He gathered like-minded dissidents.

He and I walked next to ancient headstones in a jagged line along the cliff's edge. I stalked these doubtful dead—people who had doubted Father and trusted in idols. Graves had swallowed their bodies whole and turned them to dust. Their spirits wandered elsewhere.

Now was my turn to do something with doubt, other than puke grief of what had been done to me, mixed with fear of my future. Now was the time to act. One step to the left into the dizzying void and my clock-time would be done. I could skip the exquisite pain of crucifixion.

I turned my head to the right and looked at my walking companion from the corner of my eye. The left half of Satan's face smiled, secure in self-lit splendor. His profile was a study in pristine deity—confidence, cast in runic angles.

Ma had always challenged me, kindly, to view family and friends in profile from their good side. But Satan didn't pass muster. Something wasn't right. I stepped in front of him, stopped, and faced him full-on. He'd lost half his face. A seething mass of maggots moved in and out of his eyehole and down his cheeks. They stripped skin, nerve, and muscle down to the bone, leaving a sticky tangle of half-eaten sinew.

Windy's voice whispered, *he doesn't know what's eating him. Half-sighted, remember?*

Satan joked, "Ruling with me will be a promotion, junior. You get to be one of two, not the minor third of Three."

Father turned, looked our way over his shoulder, went back to work on his fence.

Satan levitated off the ground, morphing into a serpent. This hooded cobra rose, thick as my wrist, fangs dripping venom. He worked his mouth open, unhinged himself, ready to slot me into his mouth, ready to snare any like me who trafficked in his realm. He towered above me, shade flowing over me—a cool, dark current. I took a deep breath, raking my gaze from his bottom to top.

I spoke with an edge. "Lucifer, exhale. Come to ground. Save your writhing pomp 'n puff for the gullible."

He let out his air and dropped back to the graveyard, resuming human form.

I looked squarely at both halves of his face. "I'm the exact expression of Life on your dusty leasehold. You're the exact expression of Death. You mist in and out of graves easily. I claw into the hardness of human life and loss. Lucifer, turn to Father. His love dwarfs even *your* evil."

Satan's half-lit face turned granite-hard. "I will *never* bow my knee to Him again."

I replied, "You school yourself and others in the art of saving face, but you're too clever by half. I'm putting you on notice—the courage to lose face will one day save the human race."

He regained his fluff, tossed his head. His eye de-focused for a moment while he swiped an annoying itch off the bridge of his nose. Maggots crawled about in the hairs of his right armpit.

He replied, "Way too late for that, Junior. My power is real. And believe me, I enjoy it."

Roar of a Judah lion rose within me. I cut through his posturing with the sword of Windy's spirit. "Your refusals are your undoing."

He leered, rubbed his crotch. "I'm totally wowed. Your *huff* is *so hot*. One last chance to take a knee, Lover Bro, before I unleash Gog and Magog from the Four Corners.[14] Boy, that's gonna be a real screamer!"

I held in my left hand the erect, seven-inch-long stone phallus I'd unearthed—the *Fascinus'* idol ejaculating on the evil eye. I held it between Satan and me at eye level on his right side. He couldn't see it. Our faces were so close our beards tangled.

I said, "Father's gift is at hand, already unleashed."

I thrust the stone penis in his right eye, right up to the hilt. It sizzled and stuck on the back of his skull. I tried to jerk it out with a reverse thrust, but it stuck halfway, caught in some devilish machination. I yanked again, and it came out slimy with crawling maggots, in frontal view. Only then, in my mirror, could Satan truly see what was within his mind.

His penetrated façade shriveled. *Fascinus'* face fell, pride gone bad. Lucifer tore open the sky and zipped through in a nick, leaving one shinny green-red maggot caught in the crease, quivering in mid-air. Slight shimmer in the tenuous, sheer air, and the maggot sucked through to the other side.

The still, stone idol in my hand briefly flared; turned to ash. I was not burned in that fire. The empty space he'd occupied smoked with the stench of death.

I walked back to my Partners. Father and Windy were doing their work when I returned, just as I had done the work assigned to me. Father leaned on his sledgehammer and looked over at me. "Lucifer took his leave, did he?"

Your eyes, your strength, Father. Windy, you blew me back to firm footing. We all did that deal together. Exercising power over Satan—was that part of my recovery?

Father smiled in a most serious way. *New mastery skills are part of your healing.*

I continued, now out loud, "I fear Satan simmered me in his doubt-pot."

Windy interrupted the weeding in front of her to deal with the Work-in-Process beside her. Her voice emanated from beside Father, the two of them swirling in stereo. "Your felt shame joined you with the experience of millions. Shame had squashed you into silence. *Your silent years.*

I said, "Like Abraham silently grieved all the way to Mt Moriah with his son, Isaac?"

Father replied, "Yes. He was willing to sacrifice his son. Now you, like Abraham, emerge from this rite of passage—with your own voice and Our message."

I looked at what had been done to me, to all the molested, depressed, imprisoned, and abused. She thought-flashed back to me, *our invitation is come-as-you-are. Not stay-as-you-are. We love people too much to leave you alone.*

She pulled me into Father's truth, weeded free of fear. De-shamed. I collected myself afresh, became more than I had been.

She troweled out another gut weed. "Grieving is an alien art for the self-sufficient, but grief and just-doing are highways to healing for the humble. You can't heal what you can't feel. Satan knows grieving is the healing feeling, so he splinters whole grief into jagged shards of rage, bitterness, and grumbling."

I said, "Like Shame shattered Slow into Cutter, Escape, Fragile, and the rest?"

She nodded. "We each have our mix to deal with. What we choose to do with our parts is up to us. Slow is learning to love all those parts of her. Lucifer refuses love. He's such a suffering creature beneath his blowhard bravado—but that doesn't mean he's loving. In his case, suffering went in, and viciousness came out."

"Father, you make usable containers for grief, like Leah and Rabbus' vase. You breathe life into hope gone dead, Windy. And me? I sit and grieve, a moth in the flame."

Father responded, "We're all God. Three in One, One in three. Your job for this flicker of earth time is God-man. You do for people what Windy and I can't. You've become their journey—just like you're their road, truth, and life—the way to Us.[15] We make you known nightly in dreams, visions by day, nature all around, and the written word for those few with access to Scripture."

I felt myself settle and strengthen, my spirit relieved of undigested mourning. I went to the pit toilet, secured the latch, and also relieved my body. I said the *asher yatzar blessing* and found pleasure in pooing without pain.

Together, we three seeded my weeded patch. The sheep grazed peacefully beyond Father's picket fence of white crosses that surrounded us. The harvest from this garden would feed many.

20

JOHN

Sunset was a bloody riot. I cleaned up after work and walked over to the stockade. Depending on the gatekeeper's mood, I was allowed entry. Today I brought fresh sea bass for the keeper of the watch.

Jesus and I watched the sky go to flames. Cloud tendrils drifted through elbows in the hills, lazy like, catching color and then bleeding it off. My thoughts were mainly murky. Jesus might call them feelings. Once crimson faded to grey-black, we walked back to his stone cooking circle, and I blew life into his coals. I put our portion of sea bass on the grill. Fresh okra, bell peppers, each waited their turn.

"Jesus, today I discovered that Augusta knows you live. I told Rabbus before coming here. He says Augusta has her private crew of assassins, people Tiberius doesn't know."

I looked over my shoulder and lowered my voice. "Rabbus said she had made a guard change today. Put one of her men inside this stockade—over there, in that hut. I think it's the one with bristly hair down to his eyebrows."

Jesus added kindling to the white-hot coals. He blew; they burst into flame. He added a few twigs, built a steady crackle. Sound of fire and wind circled our silence.

A cool ground fog formed, twisted through our feet, and gathered against the side of his stone hut. I said, "Jesus, I'm ready to go home. Wild, open spaces look and smell good compared to sewers. Some can live without the wild and not go wild. I'm not one of them.

"Rabbus said he would ask Tiberius' permission. We could head north toward Gaul, then back to Palestine overland. Or go south to the bottom of the boot. Take a ferry over to Greece and walk east. Your call, our calling."

"Let me check Father's mind. And then, I'll mind *his* checks."

The words were barely out of his mouth when the guard with hair like a thorn bush approached. His lips were twitchy, his hand on his sword. He said, "Prisoner, the Dowager requires your presence. Get ready, one hour."

A tiny chill prickled the back of my neck, like goose feet scrabbling over a fresh grave.

21

CLAUDIA

I lay on the beach, stunned, next to the man who'd just proposed to me. Pontii lay beside his armor. I'd grown my own. He and his dirty grey under-tunic were sopping wet. Seaweed was wrapped around his neck and shoulder. He lay back on his elbows, eyes closed.

I'd felt closer to some distant constellations on cloudy nights. I said, "Pontii, your proposal sounds like a business deal. I've always thought my marriage would be a love match."

"We could jen up a good spate of love, if needed. But marriage works better among contracted equals with differing superiorities. Each one see-saws the other up to ascendency. Love might grow from that. Familiarity doesn't *have* to breed contempt—it might breed children, for example, or perhaps a dynasty.

I pulled my sopping cotton singlet down to mid-thigh, raised handfuls of sand on either side and pounded the sand back to ground. Felt good to pound sand. It meant I wasn't drifting on the ocean floor, being eaten by sharks.

I dodged his proposal. "Wanna hear a dream, Pontii?"

He looked confused. What does *this* have to do with marriage?

"I was fishing—layers of blue, with waves breaking around me, over me, beneath me. I caught a big fish about my size, and then things switched, and the hook was in my mouth. We took turns reeling the other in. Neither of us was particularly happy with the other—the outcome, uncertain. I woke up. Or am I still in the middle of that dream?"

Pontii was used to hooks of iron, not ones spun from dream-fiber. In spite of his metallic bent, he didn't blow me off. He opened his eyes and discovered the strands of seaweed that had drooped over his shoulder. An epaulet from Neptune. He rolled over on his left elbow and delicately reeled it from around his neck, winding it around his hand in precise, tidy circles.

He said, "I like a dreamy woman, like you. I might be open to your dreams if they don't turn into nightmares."

I kept my eyes closed, speaking into the wind. "Most of my dreams *are* nightmares. Being fished, burned alive, or dangled in the mouth of a giant grandma spider. Those occupy my night hours. These nightmares have grown on me, and now I've become a nightmare myself most of the time. Welcome to my world of dark mourning, oh white knight. Still want to rescue this fair maiden?"

He shrugged and flopped back down on the sand. "Only if you rescue me from the plebian mid-ranks of Rome's muling military."

Fortune's wild winds swept across the rocky beach and whispered warnings about his unspoken agendas. I ignored them and kept the conversation going, "You're another uncertainty in my dream-catcher net. A voice inside warns me, "don't leave mourning for knight."

"Oh, please, Claudia. My proposal, business or not, fishy or not, is no nightmare. It's a win-win for us. If marriage turns out to be a dead fish on a dry rock, it doesn't matter who caught whom. Unhook, move on. Hey, let's do it."

My soul, if I had such a vapor, had temporarily blown elsewhere to conduct business. I mustered my best fishy smile and unhooked heart from body.

Just then, Julie shouted to us from the rocks overhead. "Yoo-hoo, down there! Hey, you okay, Claudia?"

You just saved me from myself and the devil, Julie.

I jerked my head toward higher ground. "Better than I was a second ago."

Pontii's expression remained frozen, caught in an unanswered proposal. His profile against the sun looked like something I'd seen in Jerusalem once, the bronze bust of a cruel ruler.

22

TIBERIUS

Mother and I had just finished a little spat. She left me, stomped across the bedroom to the water closet, and slammed shut the door to her private throne room. I turned on my heel and climbed to the roof. Mother relished a quotidian life where she could bully the obsequious, all those approaching her with foreheads almost touching the ground. That life left me feeling like a wet weekend. Up here, with the wind blowing, perhaps I could fall into the life I was meant to live. I looked over the parapets at the empire that had been handed to me on a platinum platter. Yes, indeed, I felt more alive in mother's absence and Rabbus' presence.

Discreet knock. Rabbus stood at the door. *Could he read my mind?*

Rabbus approached in a half-circle, giving me a wide view of him in sunlight now faded to the color of pale butter.

He observed protocol. When approaching the emperor, be seen, move slow, hands on opposite forearms.

"Sire, I need help. Whisperings amongst the Guards tell me your mother has sent for Jesus. The word is he will not survive the walk to her office. Is this your wish?"

Rabbus stood with the hills behind him. I mused, Rabbus *is so earthy that he seems a mountain impersonating a human. His spies ferret secrets out of shadows.*

I said, "Mother wants to cleanse what's left of her guilt from Tavius' death by scapegoating Jesus. She claims he's an insurrection waiting to happen, a sun that will pale my candle."

Rabbus' mouth stayed shut.

I kept speaking. "Are Jesus' kingship claims worthy of frisson or insipid rumors without substance?"

Rabbus studied the setting sun's fading color. "His kingdom is out of this world, sire. He is a sun, for sure. But in the light of this Sun, we are all warmed and nourished. Kill this Sun, succeed in suicide."

"What should I do?"

"Guard yourself from anyone who would diminish liveliness, Emperor."

"When's this assassination to happen?"

"Within the hour, sire."

"Surround him with a platoon of your own chosen men. I'll be at mother's office upon his arrival." Rabbus bowed his head and left to do my bidding.

A great horned owl, fat as a feather pillow, floated past me on reaching wings. I took him as an omen of good things to come and summoned my better self. *Life is all about confidence, and the only way there is to take a step or two beyond some unknown border.* That voice seemed to come from Athena-the-Owl, or maybe my wish-fulfilling self.

I roused myself to deal with Mother. Better for me to cross this borderland at middle age than not at all. Perhaps the Seer could guide me down and through this mother maze.

23

JESUS

John and I sat in my garden. Green stalks flexed their stems and shook off the sun's beating. We'd shared his fish, vegetables, and my salad greens. Washed it down with water from the stream. John lay on his side, snoozing by the still glowing coals of our cooking fire.

We'd both prayed for courage. John also prayed for Father to awaken us to his presence but had fallen asleep in mid-sentence. He groaned, time to time. Could he not watch with me? Strange, viscous sweat, like blood, oozed from my forehead. I hugged myself, feeling soul-skint. Acid burned in my gorge.

Three loud knocks rang on the stockade door. A guard pointed legionnaires toward me. Burly, no-nonsense men strode my way. I gave John a swift kick in the ribs and became his answered prayer for awakening to God's presence.

Their leader asked, "Which of you is the man, Jesus?"

I said, "I'm the man," and approached my assassin, hands open. The leader drew his short sword and strode toward me.

In a twinkling, all these men fell backward. Knocked down. They stumbled back to their feet slowly, eyes wide with fear, codpieces wetted. The sergeant with the drawn sword swayed drunkenly, sword by his feet.

I looked behind me. Michael, my archangel, towered over me. Ah, yes, fall-down terror, a reasonable option.

Over my shoulder, I murmured to Michael, "Could you diminish your magnitude? I try to avoid humiliating others in my presence."

His blaze of brilliance shrank marginally. "Your time is not yet. Father sent me."

I said to the men and John, "Don't be afraid. Let's go."

They all followed me out the gate and into the open. The night continued to unfold surprises, like this memory. My fuzzy past came into focus. When Father trotted all his newly imagined creatures before Adam for naming., he'd waited to see what Adam would do. At one point, after yet another creature lumbered off the naming ground, the fledgling botanist had looked at Father, seeking reassurance. Father kindly said, "Ah yes, hippopotamus—just so! What a lovely name!"

I smiled at this memory fragment, given and ghosted. Gained calm. Archangels help with that whole calming thing.

I asked the lead killer, "Which turn here? Which gateway there?"

He'd not recovered sufficient to speak. He pointed and checked over his shoulder to see if Michael was about to incinerate him. Somewhere along the moonlit cobblestones, at a lonely juncture suitable for assassination, Rabbus and a platoon of men double-timed toward us. The gibbous moon reflected on Rabbus' drawn sword, sliced open a wedge of night.

I said, "Rabbus, could you take charge here? These men need some assurance they will survive this night passage."

"My concern was that *you* would not survive."

I looked 'round about. John stood behind me, absent Michael. Rabbus dismissed Augusta's soldiers back to their quarters. He carried a clay oil lamp with his left hand, sword in his right hand.

We entered the mound of power. Palatine Hill's snaky corridors ramped down, each turn swallowing light, pulsing, like a Dragon's intestine pushing food along to its ending. John's shoulders hunched, his head swiveling back and forth.

We came to an anonymous door, one of many, along these walls that reminded me of stories, tales of Leviathan.[16] Rabbus stopped, knocked. A single torch, hung from the wall, pooled an ulcer of light on the floor. Darkness swallowed the rest. I caught a movement and looked up from my feet—the writhing hall's walls seemed to pulse. I imagined they easily digested the thin-skinned. John stood in a hollow between the wall's folds.

I said, "John, wait and pray. Where I go now, you are not able to come."[17]

Tiberius' muffled voice, "Enter."

24
WINDY

Tiberius walked into his mother's office a few minutes before Jesus, without knocking. Caligula, acolyte-ruler in training, hovered beside his mother, scroll and pen in hand. Augusta had arranged herself behind a massive mahogany desk, her command center. She reminded him of an elegant clothes rack constructed entirely of brittle bones and topped with a twist of silver gold. She blew the steam off a cup of tea and stared at him as he entered. A row of candles inside amber glass flumes flared splashes of light over her desk.

The Emperor motioned for his mother to stand. He led her out from behind her barricade to a lowered, burnt umber couch, set at a precise right angle to her desk. He pointed. She sank into the soft leather cushions. Augusta, in this dim corner, became more of who she was—an intersection of shadows. Some shadows, like riptides, appeared to come from within her. Others melted into her.

Tiberius towered over her. "I'll take charge of what is about to happen here. Listen and do not speak. Understood?"

Almost imperceptible nod. Caligula scribbled, "taak charj."

Tiberius nodded to Caligula. He spoke prophetically but without insight. "Come closer, nephew. Watch the kingdom at work."

Caligula shoved a few scrolls off a straight-backed chair and slouched into it. An aura passed before his eyes like a scarlet fog. This aura, one of many possible colors, usually preceded a seizure. The poor lad closed his eyes and rolled his neck, hoping not to demonstrate his "falling down sickness" in this situation. Frothing on the floor would be most inopportune.

Rabbus ushered Jesus into the room. The meek Jew took in his surroundings. Smelled the bitter tea. Saw the lively shadows floating in and out of the Dowager. Sensed the Old Enemy lurking in her shade.

Tiberius spoke. "Sit, Jew."

Jesus ran his fingers over the carved edges of the tufted, mahogany antique chair, easily three hundred years old, imported from Macedonia. It was one of a matched pair, placed opposite the desk Tavius had given Livia as a present. Jesus bent from the waist and admired how the chairs' legs had been recently sawed short, beveled, fine-sanded, and shellacked, like those of the couch. He sat.

The emperor poured cups of black tea from his mother's ornate, silver pot, one for him, his nephew, and Jesus. Added two lumps of sugar to each and scratched his crotch.

"We haven't seen one another for a long time."

"As you say, Emperor." Jesus stirred his tea, sipped.

At that moment, I inserted an image in Tiberius' mind. An edgy thresher working the windrows of a field ripe for harvest. Sharp teeth chewed up boys, spat out men. Jesus operated the thresher—radiant, pellucid. On the far side of this field, past the thresher, stood the ruler Tiberius hoped to become.

I gave the emperor time to recover from this vision before I created another moving picture for his viewing pleasure. He raked his eyes across Jesus' frame and saw *a lamb with his throat cut. Seven horns spouted out of his head. Seven eyes surrounded his skull, and the lamb held a golden scroll—instead of a teacup.18*

Tiberius closed his eyes and rubbed his forehead. *My imagination's a lunatic, living rent-free in my attic.*

Caligula took this moment to puke a spectacular tidal wave of multi-colored vomit all over the floor. Some of it landed on Jesus' sandaled feet. Jesus moved out of his chair and dropped to his knees where Caligula lay frothing, eyes rolled up in his head, chewing on his tongue. Tiberius called for servants to clean the floor.

While the bucket brigade did their job, Jesus put his hand on Cal's head, murmured soft words. Cal blinked and sat up, clear-minded. He pushed away from Jesus and looked at his uncle. "What's that awful smell? Did that Jew puke on you, Uncle?"

Tiberius told Cal to sit back and try not to throw up again. Tiberius then closed his eyes, screwed a knuckle into his orbitals, and prayed to any available god on tap. *Please, when I open my eyes, let me see a person—not a sheep with a cut-throat.*

The young Jew sat before him in the sawed-off chair, looking quite serene.

Ah-ha, sanity's shred, returned.

He said, "Seer, what just happened with Cal? Some might say he was healed."

Augusta broke in, "Others would see witchery. Cal, do you quite feel your loving self?"

Cal discovered a bit of vomit on his tunic. He kept his mouth tightly clamped shut, nodded furiously toward the corner crammed with shadows.

Tiberius tried to get the interrogation back on track. "Mother's spies bring whisperings of insurrection that you are fueling from within the stockade. True, Jew, or tempests in a teacup?"

Jesus went sideways. "I'm not interested in earthly empires, sire. Father's kingdom encompasses many worlds far greater than this one. But in every world, the young must journey through my thresher to become mature. Journey takes charge, but only as you pry your fingers off the reins. He ventures below the limen, onto ground never before walked."

Tiberius jolted. *He also saw my thresher vision!*

He asked another question, "What is central to your Father's kingdom?"

I breathed these words out of Jesus' mouth, "Not what, who. A lamb. A lamb willingly led to the slaughter. The horn of power and the eye of clear vision are both bound together in this sacrificial lamb."

The emperor was astounded. *This is why they call him the Seer. He climbs in your head and watches your weirdness with you.* He said, "Really, true?"

Jesus nodded. "Yes, truth told slant, like in a parable or poem. But if this truth is to nourish you, first you must learn to thresh chaff from wheat."

The Dowager vomited words across the darkened room. "Remarkable nonsense."

Tiberius said, "Mother, be quiet. Read his *intention*. His ideas are ones of reason, not slip-knot treason."

Augusta looked into her teacup, stirring what remained. "Read tea leaves of effect, not intention. His mystic mutterings are poison."

Jesus sipped his tea, "Plenty of nourishment in those leaves, Madame Dowager, when steeped in Father's kindness."

Anger smoked from Augusta's eyes. She looked at her son, and no light emerged from her dark fire. She said, "Steep his ass in the royal incinerator. Dump what's left in the Tiber. No strength in those ashes."

Tiberius said, "Mother, you and I are twice fools—we're tempted to believe what's *not* true about the Jew." He paused, pregnant with portent. "And we refuse to believe what *is* true about us."

Augusta shot a sticky, spider stare at her son.

Tiberius could not stand his mother's look, so he sat. "*This* man is not tempted by jewels or honors. Tavius left you one-third of his fortune, two-thirds to me. We are one-way pipes—all affluence, no effluence. We're stoppered and bulging."

He added a secret thought that I only overheard. *And I've not gone round the flaming twist, buggered by a wild hair up my butt. I'm not nuts, just someone who's not yet got the bloody hang of being a grown-up.*

He spoke aloud now to his mother. "I just made a decision. I'll first see what I can unlearn from you—wariness of nature, isolation framed as safety, the shrinkage of trust. Soon all that remains are surfaces. For example, a face shriveled as a testicle."

He turned his eyes to Jesus. "Then I'll see what I can learn from you. We, you and I, are going on a trip to visit Gemellus. Have a bit of adventure."

He looked back at Augusta, not unkindly. "Besides, Mother, a coming-of-age emperor like me must do his best to make his mother hate him. That way, she won't miss him when he leaves."

25

SLOW

It was time for me to teach in the potter's workshop—my turn at the wheel. I bumped Laz with his son, handed him off, and made my way toward the pottery workshop.

Sarah waited for me at the workshop door, tapping her foot and cracking her knuckles. Roy was inside, working on a free-form table sculpture. He looked up, called us over.

Sarah leaned forward, distracted, and fanned her loose cotton shift, breezing it away from her armpits. "Today's gonna be a scorcher, Roy. And it's only eight in the morning. Temperature's already edging from hot to very hot."

He smiled at her. "Girl, can't take the heat, get out of the kitchen."

She said, "Great idea. Slow, let's go from low to high, Jericho to Mt. Hermon. We could set up a cool mountain resort for whores."

Roy commented, "You want to keep whoring, Sarah? Pottery's your exit from that life."

Her eyes skittered from him to me—eyes doing a glaze and go. "I'm stuck. I want to stop all this sexing, but I'm not able. Screwing men gives me power. At least one man, for one moment, enjoys me. But after, when I look back, I feel terrible."

Roy sat back, scratched his beard. "You remind me of another woman who looked back. She gets a lot of bad press, but, you know, I don't blame her. I'm sculpting her."

We both looked at what was emerging from El Roi's hands, still incomplete, but someone he could clearly see.

He said, "We'd likely have done the same thing as her. There she was, her whole life going up in flames—friends and neighbors, house of worship, coffee klatch, sewing circle—all burning to ash from that meteor shower."

He shook his head, eyes welling up. "She could see it up there from that ridge over the salt canyons—Sodom so small it could fit in her hand. She could have blown it off her palm with a kiss if she liked. *But she cared.*"

I looked at his sculpture. A woman, twisting from her hips, one arm reaching back, the other forward; chest ripped down the middle, heart exposed.

Roy's hands worked the mud, adding a dab of red glaze on her heart and expression to her face—wide eyes, raised eyebrows, mouth open, horrified.

"Half of her wanted to move up-trail with her husband, Righteous Lot; the other half of her turned back. See the power of spirit. All those muscles around her rib cage, the ones charged with shielding her heart, literally ripped top to bottom, like a curtain.

"She dropped like a rock. Couldn't move, not at all. Had to stay there and heal up. Lot left her and moved on with his daughters, seeking certainty and safety. She was left trailside, wailing salty tears. Other refugees trailing behind them found her. These people formed a village of salt miners. Both men and women used pickaxes on their stony hearts before using them to mine salt from those hills. They hewed out an interior life before they hollowed out the hills; learned to care for each other. Lot's wife suggested they call their village, Salt. She became a pillar of that community."

I looked at the label he'd inscribed beneath his figure, 'Splittina.'

El Roi said, "People called her Split. After a few years, maybe a decade or so, her wounds had turned to scars and no longer defined her. Everyone started calling her Tina."

Sarah was unimpressed. She said, "Can I change topics?"

Roy nodded.

Sarah said, "At least Split was safe. I'm not. Yesterday, on the street, I turned sideways, and my ex-husband was trailing by in a cart."

I said, "Did he see you?"

"No, not then. But I have this eerie feeling. He's about to rain down fire since he couldn't rain stones down on me. Crispus *loved* abusing me in every way imaginable. I lived in terror every day of that marriage. If he were any more wicked, he'd bust into flames."

I said, "Wait a sec. Crispus. Wandering eye, nose missing, and one leg?"

"He had that eye thing down, fooled a lot of folks into thinking he was crazy. All those fools are dead now. His evil eye has power in it."

I shivered, thought of how he'd escaped from the hospital by killing those guards, how he'd sawed off Gaius' head.

Shame intoned, she deserved what she got, just like you.

I tried to crowd her voice out by having a real conversation with real people.

I said, "No wonder you're stuck, Sarah."

Sarah passed her eyes from Roy to me to the sculpture. "We're pathetic. Slow and Stuck looking at Split. And yes, Crispus is a heap of contrariness—cuddly killer, sane lunatic, remorseful abuser, God-fearing Satanist. Talk about a divided self. He's it. Happened after his family was murdered. But I make excuses for him now and again; after all, how can you expect a crop of roses when all you plant are thorns?"

Inside, Fragile screamed, *let's run away with Escape, now! That man's way too scary.*

I said, *Breathe, Fragile!* We felt marginally better.

A hand, mine, reached up and yanked out an eyelash. *Cutter, how embarrassing! I've told you to do that only in private.*

She said, *at least I didn't cut you down the middle.*

Laz walked in with our squalling kid. He said, "My nipples don't work. Mike proved inarticulate, totally unwilling to discuss the maternal aspects of God's character with me, so I…"

"Shut up, Laz. Gimme the kid." We both grinned.

I said, "Guess who's in town?"

"I'm sure I don't know."

"Sarah's Ex. Crispus."

"Oops. Dangerous man."

Sarah looked at him. "Can you keep me safe?" Gave him her best, helpless smile.

Harlot said, *Oh brother. Watch out for that woman.*

Laz puffed up his chest a little. "Roy, let's talk to Mary and Martha's husbands. They're in town, visiting from Bethany. We can take care of this guy."

Harlot said, *Oh great! Maybe the big, brave menfolk could swagger over to hop-along and whittle him down to size. Get us all unstuck.*

I turned to wave goodbye to Laz just as Rahab's front gates popped open. Crispus limped through the door in front of a mule-drawn cart full of cronies and stuff hidden under wraps. He leaned on a pointy cane with a silver knob and shouted into the quiet of the courtyard, "Sarah, Lover Man's here! I know you're here—come on out. Give your Ex a big, sloppy kiss."

26

CLAUDIA

Julie, Pontii, and I walked single file, silent, back up the rocky trail to our hut on the hill. Julie looked confused—*what was going on here?*

Pontii's tone changed from almost human to officious. "Claudia, we'll speak of business matters later. I'm under imperial orders to secure you to the mainland while Vipsania Julilla Agrippina remains here. We leave immediately."

My cousin collapsed in front of our hut like she had been asked to fall on her sword. She held her head in her hands, started to rock back and forth, high keening lost in the wind. I knelt beside her, held her close. Tears on my cheeks surprised me—*my* tears, running down, getting lost in her chestnut braids.

I must be changing. These were real tears.

I murmured in her ear, "Julie, I'll *not* abandon you. I'll get Uncle Tibbie to release you back to Rome. At the least, I'll get him to send another so you won't be alone."

She wiped her eyes, double-fisted. Even so, her cheeks sheened tears, and the leavings trembled on her chin. "You made exile tolerable. Your liveliness, your laughter. Now, without you, loneliness will kill me."

Pontii motioned me along. I read his flashing eyes. *Stopper your bleeding heart. You lucked out. She lost out.*

I ignored him. "Julie, remember what I told you of Jesus? Their Jewish holy book has one main point, I think. *We are not alone.* God's arms around you are as close as a prayer. Jesus was with me today. I fell in the sea, and he drifted with me all the way back to our inlet. Both of you kept me alive—you taught me how to swim, and he didn't leave me alone."

I sat up and faced Julie, hands folded in my lap. I could see her struggle—wrapping arms around Jewish faith-vapor was tough work, even for a mystic like her. I said, "Take courage, cousin, the God-man has conquered even people like Pontii, empires like Rome."

She wouldn't meet my eyes. I took her hand, squeezed. "Julie, look at me! These words are not fog-wisp. Jesus is the real deal, God on wheels, come to save us from sharks." I looked at Pontii, my smile sweet as sugarcane.

Julie did not come to see us off. She sat on her black lava throne, limp as a sail with all the wind gone out of it. My words alone, without her faith, carried the weight of milkweed fluff.

Pontii and I managed to get his skiff past the break line without capsizing. Once out of the bay's mouth, we headed into a freshening mid-afternoon wind. An anvil-shaped cloud with rose-colored cheeks puffed up till its top turned black. Crackling thunder rumbled across the waters.

I held onto the center mast and looked behind me. Pontii had stripped off his armor and wore only his short leather tunic. He grimly tacked back and forth into this headwind. Not a bad-looking man, if you just went with appearances—a lean warrior type with a no-nonsense aura. Tall, dark, and handsome. Scratch under the surface? Out popped a conniver, eager as a schoolboy at a circus for advancement. The thought flashed across my mind. *He's not too different than father. He'll do well in Palestine—push his weight around, act like a sun god.*

I lifted my eyes from him back toward exile isle. Julie had gotten up from in front of our stone hut. I saw her in silhouette, sweeping; sweeping up her heart, and putting hope away. She soon dwindled from a real person to a stick figure. Stick figure shrank to black dot, and then the sky swallowed her and Trimerus itself.

I refused all my tears—lonely tears for her, survivor-guilt tears for me, fear-tears from being with this man, Pontii. I slammed the door on tears and looked ahead. We were maybe ten or fifteen miles off the coast. We weren't sailing directly into Vasto, the village where we'd launched to Trimerus.

I yelled over the wind, "where are we going?"

A clipped reply, "Aternum, military seaport, north, connected to Rome, Via Tiburtina."

I had no idea what he was talking about. I considered a startling option, raw honesty.

I yelled, "Jesus was the deal-breaker. He's laid claim to my heart. If you cipher that into our business deal, maybe I'll loan my body to yours, time to time."

The legionnaire glowered. *Insufferability was a valued commodity with militant extremists.* I counseled my wiser mind, *leave Pontii pilot behind, self. You don't need husband pot-luck even though your family's fallen on hard times.* The wishy-washy me wobbled, hung onto center mast, leaning left and right with the passing swells.

The further we sailed, the angrier the Adriatic Sea got. White chop slopped higher, now slapping over the gunnels.

I yelled over my shoulder, "Shouldn't we cut closer to shore? Those waters over there—they look calmer."

No answer. I turned to face him. Pontii had left the helm and was three steps away, sword stretched out in his right hand, black eyes hollowed and hardened by pride.

He shouted, "You'd give yourself to a Jew over *me*? Die in the storm, princess-bitch."

I backpedaled behind the mast, tripped, and fell. His sword flashed sideways, right where my neck at been. His sword stuck solid in the oaken mast. He wrestled with the stuck sword. Tugged with both arms, totally focused on getting control of his weapon—not his rage. Wind whipped the boom straight round and clocked him clean on the bean. Knocked him overboard.

He went under; then his head popped up on top of the next swell. Arms wind-milled, eyes wild. Well, no wonder, the man was in over his head—murderous ass. Leave him behind. I'd been saved by the Wind. Unfortunate for me, Jesus' Spirit-Buddy, blew a gentler thought into my mind. *Kill a killer, and the world is twice bad. His chance for grace is gone, and you sour your soul.*

Jesus had told me more than once, 'Love your enemies.' I sent back a very short prayer, minus the handshake. *Oh, crap.*

Before fear paralyzed me, I headed for the tiller. On the way by, my shoulder hit Pontii's sword handle, hard. Sword flew into the water. Sank. Didn't bob up, not even once.

When I grabbed the rudder, it was jammed hard right, spinning the boat in a circle. Wind had taken charge, working our boat like a wolf worried a bone. I added prayer's end piece, rapid-fire. *Help me do the right thing, forjesussakeamen.*

Pontii flapped in the wild, white water. His head bobbed up and then under, left of my circling boat. I pulled the rudder toward center, straightening out the spiral. A coil of rope, the same one I'd tripped over, slid through the slosh and around a bucket toward my feet. Skiff knifed by the terrified man.

I grabbed one end of the rope and threw the rest overboard. He grabbed hold of it. I pulled him toward the boat, hand over hand. As I pulled, the sail ripped top to bottom. The canvas luffed. A rogue wave bore down, covered the sky, swamped us. Mast snapped when wind bit where sword had hit. The bulk of the mast fell off to the right, grazing Pontii's bobbling head. A foot to the right, and it would have cracked his skull wide open.

I laughed in the face of all that was ludicrous. That included everything on offer at the moment. Pontii held onto the rope for dear life; pulled himself toward me. He timed the next swell and sloshed himself over the gunnels into the swamped skiff. *Jesus, please protect me again from a woman-eating shark. Uh, amen.*

That wave, like all waves, passed. But not before it brought the water level almost up to the slopping over point. We were the definition of wallowing-in-waves. I kicked him in the side, hard, and pushed the only bucket onboard his way.

"Captain Rage, start bailing out this frigging skiff, or we'll both drown."

27

SLOW

Laz and I walked over to Crispus and his cronies. Crispus stood on his one leg in front of his cart. He leaned heavily with both hands on his cane, showing off that crooked smile with all those broken teeth. His silver nose piece and crutch provided spice to the main attraction—that spring-loaded die of an eye, rolling around in the dice cup he kept for a head.

He motioned with a wave of one hand. One of his half-dozen gang members shut the door to the street and threw the bolt.

Laz said, "Hadn't seen you since that day up at Ben and Liza's general store, Crispus. Shiny nose you got now. Must have ditched Leah's leather one."

"And a nice pillbox on yer forehead, Jew-boy, 'long with them shiny curls down the sides a yer face."

"What brings you to our new home here at Rahab's?"

"Aww, my ol' heart was jus' a-breakin'. Missing my lovely bride from yesteryear, *don't ya know*?"

Laz replied, "She doesn't want to see you. Feel free to leave."

Crispus said, "Bein' a tad inhospitable, Mr. Dreadlock? Don't yer own holy book, in Deuteronomy 15, verses seven and eight, say to open yer hand wide to the disabled? Or is yur religion still hard-boiled an' left in the shell?" He scratched his stump.

Crispus' cronies spread out, a cast net being drawn tight. "Come closer, Jew, so I can see you better. Can't rightly sniff you so far off with my poor nose gone missin'." His cane moved under his hand, lifting slightly off the ground.

Vice tightened in my chest. Husband, not one step closer!

I looked at Laz, spoke with desperation. "Dear, we need to busy ourselves, readying our rooms for the centurion and all his soldiers. They're due anytime, aren't they, now?"

Crispus' wild eye steadied, looked me up and down, crotch to eyes, lingering on my breasts. "You bluff in cards as good as ya do with this soldier game, Honey-Lips?"

Dead level stare, eye to eye. I said, "Occupation isn't over, Crispus—only shattered into pieces. A string of crosses, outside the city gates, with you and your men on 'em, now that'll make for a Roman's centurion's wet dream. In memory of Tribune Gaius, *don't ya know*?"

Laz's hand was sweaty inside mine. Crispus' men froze in place. Crispus shuffled toward Laz, pointing with his cane, "Come here, young man, come closer so I can speak with ya private, away from that hen-pecking drudge."

My tight grip on husband's hand slipped some soul-soil under his feet. Laz's voice was resolute. "Crispus, if you want to wait, we'll come visit you at the foot of your cross."

God, save us from this evil man.

Sound of armor clanking in the street outside the door. Shouted orders rang through the air. Ground thumping, hoofbeats of heavy cavalry.

Crispus' eyes widened. His lieutenant approached. "Commander, let's leave, now!" They abandoned their cart. Two of his men picked him up under either armpit. They double-timed through the back gates, melting into the stream of passing travelers outside Jericho's walls.

Laz looked quizzically at me. We walked slowly to the front gate, threw it open wide, ready to receive Rome's best. We looked both ways, straining to see. No soldiers—only the regular market vendors, buyers, and neighbors. Business as usual, nine o'clock on a Thursday morning.

Laz took me in both of his arms. Long, slow breath of air. Shoulders dropped a few inches.

Thank you, Windy, for blowing the sound of safety all around us.

We returned to the workshop. Sarah greeted us. "Slow, I saw and heard the whole thing from a crack in the door. How'd you *do* that?"

I looked at her, shrugged. "Jesus' Spirit does amazing sound effects—angels, fire, thunder, smoke. Makes me downright worshipful."

"How best to worship this guy? Temple prostitution, like for Aphrodite, plus all my money? Whatever it takes."

Laz said, "Just do right, love mercy, walk humbly with God."[19]

Sarah and I went back into the workshop. The day was just beginning.

28

CLAUDIA

The sea taught us its day's dance, and we gained her certain rhythm. The closer we came toward the shore, the calmer she became. We followed the rocky coastline on our left, northbound. We swapped our one bailing bucket back and forth.

The outline of a city emerged from the grey morning mist. The city grew from a smudge to a slightly larger smear. Wood and stone buildings misted toward us, eerie, disembodied.

I ventured a few words into the air. "Your moods always *that* vicious, or sometimes worse?"

He hesitated, chanced a glance my way. "Couldn't be much worse. I suppose marriage is out of the question now." His face had all the expression of a peeled turnip.

"Might help if you talked. *You men*—one word for every hundred actions."

His face twitched. Probably regret pulling razor wire through mental knotholes.

He said, "Black rages break over me, time to time. Probably had something to do with that Jew."

"You're saying Jesus made you want to kill me?"

"No, not exactly. Maybe some devil made me do it."

"Pontii, get a grip. Grow up. Devils, Rome, the sea—anything but your evil self is responsible, huh?"

"Watch your mouth, Claudia. You can't unsay words, and I can't unhear them. Besides, ill words butter no potatoes."

"A real word chef, huh? Might consider switching your language recipe from murder to sorry-speak."

"Don't know that language."

"Souls speak lots of languages."

"I'm a soldier, not a soul."

"Some soldiers still have souls, even if they're scorched, for the most part. On the other hand, Jesus speaks pure soul food. He's all holied up."

"Wouldn't know soul food is if it hit me in the chops."

"Plainly. Here's my spin on souls. They're your balance beam of right and wrong. Like it was *right* to haul your sorry ass back in the boat, *right* to love Jesus, *right* to listen to my dreams, *wrong* to marry hastily for business and repent at leisure."

Pontii stared open-mouthed at me.

"Even you can learn new words, gestures, dream-speak, or touch, Pontii. They all speak. For example, *awkward* is screaming so loud right now I can barely hear myself think."

"That's a language? Huh. I thought a stray pack of dogs had been loosed in my head."

Ground fog swirled between us, providing cover. I worked the raw edge between us. "Soul-speak includes shy, sexy, or even rageful."

He chewed on his lip, face scrunched up, brows furrowed down. Spoke silence.

The storm scudded along, southbound behind us. A shy sun poked out of the cumulus and made nice with the earth. White steam ghosted up in tendrils off black rocks along the shore. We limped into the port, docked alongside the crisscrossed, creaking wooden pilings that supported a pier above us—remodeled sometime in the past century or two. A rusted iron ladder banged its bottom into pilings with each passing swell.

I examined the razor-sharp barnacles. *Hey there. We're alike. We suction into any post halfway stable, even if it's rotten.*

Pontii clambered half-way up the ladder, turned. He hung onto the ladder with his left hand and offered me his right. My cold-speak face sent him skittering.

I followed at a distance. He aimed us toward the 400-year-old Roman fortress that dominated Aternum's skyline. The main drag stretched along a river that veered west and north into mountain passes topped with storm clouds.

We trudged up the highway toward the fort, Pontii far in front of me. A circus of immigrants all vied for attention. Two painted jugglers stood at roadside, carelessly spinning cat-calls, jokes, and stilettos back and forth between them, a hat at their feet to collect coins. A brownish woman with a mottled face and hair in cornrows lugged wire cages behind her on a cart. Her cages were loaded with alarmed roosters crowing warnings. "Stay away. Nothing good's gonna come of this!"

A coterie of painted hags had stationed themselves just outside the fortress' walls, all young women sitting in a circle, faces painted with layers of rouge and contempt. A canvas shanty jiggled behind them, cries emerging, "yes, yes, yes!" The head harlot out front shook the tent post and yelled, "Time's up. Get gone."

Quiet moment or two. A man stumbled off, buttoning up his trousers. A teenager, maybe fourteen, sauntered from the shanty after her john, crumpling up the quarter-hour in her hands and dropping it behind her. She was a girl not yet grown, unhinged, spilling restlessness and contempt, trading perky breasts and unlined face for the coins she'd earned.

Her madame eyed me up and down. *This is our turf. Stay away.* I looked down at my body, became conscious. Threadbare, ragged singlet that was see-through in places. Bare, callused feet, muddy toes, scraggy hair plastered to my head. My royal actress self had gone missing. Only my scrabble-survivor remained, stripped to her studs, clutching freedom with both hands behind her back.

I entered the fortress' gates past a clutch of jeering guards. Pontii approached them. He waved them off, shut them down. I moved to a shady corner, sat on a ledge, and propped one stinky foot on the wall. Settled in to see what would happen.

A commotion of soldiers and officers swirled in front of me, taking on the rough shape of a square. The officer in charge shouted, "Legionnaires, the emperor and his five centuries of men arrive before sunset. This is probably Emperor Tiberius' only visit to Aternum, and it's a short one. Tiberius' fleet, arriving in two days, will take him to his war in Illyria. Dismissed."

My heart leapt to my throat. I would see my uncle for the first time since grandpa died. Would he do a loyalty check and then box me up, back to Trimerus?

Pontii chatted up a prissy-looking warthog of a man. He'd combed his thin, blond hair precisely, each hair arranged over his bald spot and curled around an enormous earring bored through his right ear.

Wartie-the-Combover waddled my way. Bowed with a fastidious flair. Cadenced voice, with the affected tone of the upward-striving. "M'lady, an *ornatrix* is at your command with food, drink, and a wardrobe of the latest fashionable attire."

I said, "You don't like my current gown, Herr…?"

He spluttered, "You knew I was from Gaul, Madame?"

"A faint accent that I hadn't heard since I lived in Rome. I was friends with a captured slave from Gaul."

"I see, Madame. My family was also brought back from Gaul as slaves." He raised his many-layered chin. "But now, I'm a free man. Your *ornatrix* will refresh you with delicacies, help you bathe, anoint yourself with oil and perfume, take care of *all* your needs."

I eyed him with amusement, picked my nose, examined my findings in detail, and then wiped my pickings in a smear on my ballroom gown. He stifled a gasp, turned on his heel. I followed him into the shadowy bowels of the fortress.

29
LEAH

Tiberius' expedition had traveled east out of Rome, traversing a high ridge's spine on Via Tiburtina. We were a group of five hundred or so, and camping overnight in a deep canyon, complete with a lovely waterfall. We were en route to Aternum on the Adriatic coast.

I roused slowly from my dreams after our first night there, contented by the sound of turtle doves' cooing. I crawled out our tent flap and admired how the grass had dressed in tiny beads of dew, night jewelry that glittered in stray sunbeams. Clouds had swallowed the ridgeline.

Gabe, our two-year-old, had slept peacefully between Rabbus and me but now had transformed into Mr. Grump. What *was* his problem? Nothing I did would comfort him. Then his father entered our tent, got on his knees, and played peek-a-boo with our son. Immediately, Gabe settled down, contented.

While playing with his son on hands and knees, Rabbus said, "I'm so happy Tiberius chose to rest here for a couple of days."

I focused on the sound of the waterfall outside our tent, its continual, thrumming sploosh. The morning grew soft around me. Rabbus said, "Sound of water soothes my spirit too, wife. Besides, I hear the weather in Aternum is extreme. You either get sapped with the humidity, or your prayer shawl gets blown back to Rome by a desert sandstorm. Down there, you can tell when the khamsin stops blowing. The cows fall over."

I laughed, "A new side of you is coming out, husband. I'm so glad for this road trip with you. I get to feel the dirt beneath my feet again instead of being a palace girl."

I looked around for our son. No Gabe. He'd disappeared. But where had he gone? I panicked and rushed outside the tent. Rabbus spotted him, thirty feet away, beyond the table where my bread dough was rising under a damp cheesecloth.

He'd gone to Jesus. After some time, Gabe wanted down. They walked hand in hand close to the waterfall and found a mud puddle. Both sat cross-legged in the middle of it. Each painted the other's face with mud.

Gabe first took a handful of mud, pulled Jesus' face low to his own, and carefully squashed the whole handful of mud on Jesus' chin. Gabe looked at Jesus, head atilt, to see if he was mad, like his mother would have been.

Jesus laughed. He put about the same amount of mud on Gabe's chin. Together they covered each other's whole face in a slow, careful way. Took time to admire their face-painting work. Middle Eastern Jews were now African Jews.

One of these newly brown-faced boys, the bigger one, pointed at a pair of hawks soaring in the thermals above the waterfall. They watched the hawks together for some time, even as we watched these two from our tent flap. Then the bigger Jew grabbed something in the grass and showed it to the smaller one. Rabbus and I held hands and walked over, listened in.

Jesus' white teeth flashed out of his brown-black face. "Gabe, this ladybug is playing dead because she's scared."

Jesus dropped flat in the grass, on his side. Gabe followed suit—two question marks facing each other on their elbows.

Jesus sat up, took Gabe in his lap. "But she's busy inside her bright orange shell. When she relaxes, her outer armor opens up. Her wet, inner wings dry, and then, she can fly."

"It's so wonderful how my Father made ladybugs, hawks, and you! What a Genius He is!" Gabe hugged Jesus and understood he was loved.

Jesus looked at us for permission, motioned to a quiet pool under the waterfall.

Rabbus said, "By all means."

Jesus' eyes crinkled with amusement, "We'll be awhile. Lots of mud here and Gabe needs his first swimming lesson."

We turned and walked back inside our tent while Jesus and Gabe went for their little wash 'n play. Rabbus laid me down on our bedroll, took off his outer armor and my underwings. We soared. I felt pretty. He gave all he had to me.

A stray thought wiggled across my besotted brain, 'now is a good time. Bless us with a child, Father, bless us on this Shabbat morning.' And then I drifted into a deep sleep.

When I awoke, I peeked through the tent flap. Rabbus and Jesus sat by our make-shift oven. Jesus had poured coffee into two mugs and stoked the fire under the oven. Gabe sat in the dirt close to his abba, playing with a tin pot and two sticks.

Jesus queried, "Have you resolved your anger about my prison rape?"

Rabbus said, "Nope. If Leah were to resurrect 'em, I'd kill 'em again."

"Feel the same way about those Jews who killed your parents?"

"They'd get the same treatment."

"Forgiveness ever come calling at your door?"

"Nah. If he poked his head in my tent flap, I'd kick him in the ass and send him packing. Tender guys like you need hard guys like me. This bread needs one knife to slice it up and another to spread the butter."

After a moment's pause, "Taking over Father's job is dangerous. Your sword may cut you off from Him and yourself."

"Don't be afraid for *me,* Jesus. I'll protect you from the rabble."

Long pause. Jesus looked as if he were listening to the wind. His eyes misted over. "Barabbas, it's me that will set *you* free from the rabble. [20] But this is not that day."

Another voice intruded, "Hey, you two."

Tiberius stood with another man behind the two seated men. Four guards faced outwards, covering the emperor's back. Rabbus leaped to his feet and saluted his boss. Surprised to see Julius, Jesus took two steps and hugged his old friend who stood beside the emperor.

The emperor nodded, "Relax, Rabbus. This is your time off from work. Julius and I were just out for a walk along the river. We were standing back of your tent, admiring your warrior in training. I might try copying his helmet design—seems to offer protection from stray thoughts."

I looked at our son. He'd put the pot over his head. The pot was so big it covered his eyes and ears and nestled around his chin. He beat on it with both sticks while he walked in circles round and round, singing, "I wuv's Jesus." [21]

Tiberius grinned at his new Imperial Guard. "As it was, we couldn't protect our noses from the smell of your fresh bread."

I slid from tent to oven. The bread was golden brown and popped up at the touch of my finger.

I said, "Sit, have some bread and a cup of coffee."

The men reclined, all four together in a circle around our small table. They watched me plant my bread knife in the top of the new loaf and slide it onto the table next to a bowl of butter and a butter knife.

Jesus said, "Hm. Look at this food for thought. Brings to mind how to resolve conflicts without a bunch of killing."

Tiberius looked at Jesus. "Say on, Seer."

Jesus looked solemnly at his emperor. "A few hours back, Leah prepared her meal for this moment. She took a tiny bit of dry yeast from her pouch, used Gabe's helmet to mix this yeast with milk, eggs, flour, and sugar—each ingredient different than the other. She covered the blob. While it sat undercover, we talked."

He looked at me, face quizzical. I nodded, giving him permission to share our secret chat.

"Leah and I talked about a conversation she had with your mother, Sire. They differed in their opinions on the divine. Your mother became quite furious. Flattened Leah with her strong feelings."

Tiberius leaned into the conversation, silent.

Jesus switched topics, motioned to bread. "It was magical, really, this bread.

Leah flattened all that had risen here—punched, kneaded, hammered it."

Jesus smiled at me. Earlier, he'd said, "Augusta can hurt you only when you're inflated with pride or fear."

Jesus continued, "Leah then put the dough back undercover. Too much light or warmth at the wrong time wrecks the whole process."

I remembered him asking about my friends here and in Samaria, the planting and harvesting of barley, the cleansed lepers. It had all seemed such a walkabout at the time.

Jesus continued, while looking at Tiberius, "Leah came back to the dough. Shaped it, slid it in the oven on its burial stone. It took some time to rise from its tomb."

Tiberius turned to me. "Did you ever rise after my mother flattened you, Leah?"

I sat silently, holding my now sleeping child. "Not yet. I rest undercover, in the dark."

Jesus said, "I suspect this journey will give us all we need to rise, be flattened, and rise again."

None of us knew how true his words would soon become. Evening fell. It sucked all light from this canyon where warm, moist air rose in columns, hawks and couples soared, and ladybugs stretched their drying wings in the dark.

30
SLOW

Crispus' cart and mules were gone by morning, but his memory lingered, and Sarah took to malingering. When I checked on her, she was curled up in bed, still as a held breath.

"The spinning wheel awaits, Sarah. Waits to shape you into your true self."

"Shut up, and Slow… down! I can't go there yet. Fear's twisted my guts into knots.

"You could move up the road. Get lost in the big city of Jerusalem."

"Na, I can get lost anywhere. Places aren't haunted—people are. Might as well stay here—that man's hate makes me a lost cause."

"Maybe you're not so much lost as never found. No fun hiding if no one's seeking—true for me most of my life. Then Jesus found a few keeper-me's inside my trickster whore."

"For such a practical woman, you sure get mystical as hell."

I winked. "*Don't ya know*? A lot depends on who you trust for what. For example, trust Jesus for safety. Trust your ex for danger."

The door popped open, and Crispus stood there grinning. He dressed like a rabbi in a black robe, phylacteries, sidelocks, and tallits. He held a box of sweets in one outstretched hand and his cane in the other. He bowed deep and twirled in a circle so we could admire him.

"Well, ain't I the picture! Ain't nuttin' got more grins than my circus, *don't ya know*! Both you beauties be souls of generosity, returning my chariot and steeds once the phantom troops had passed. I'm not even going to ask how you did that."

His words bounced like a wrecking ball among twigs barely rooted in dry ground, hitting here and there, scattering. I looked at Sarah and stood between her and Crispus, bridging the gap between her and her past.

I prayed to Jesus and talked to Crispus. "Take you and your candy elsewhere. You have no claim on her."

Crispus looked me over again, top to bottom. "Such a spitfire! An' squirting out of such beauty—I never smelled the stinkin' like of it. Unseemly, 'tis. Somewhere the Torah warns against uppity women, *now don't it*?"

He tipped his head to see past me to his ex. "Sarah, my love, why don't ya toddle over here to me, like a nice girl. Give your ol' rabbi-hubby a long smooch. Once you get a whiff of manliness, you be shiverin' all over again for my lovin'—ain't that so, darlin'?"

Sarah's voice quavered, "See this middle finger? Sit and twirl. Same tired old crap outta you. If you ever had an original idea, it would die of loneliness."

"Aw, sweetcakes, just as I remember. Such a winsome whiner. You tricked me once into a fruitless wander through your arid body. Purely the sheer milk of my human kindness. But you'll be delighted. Sympathy done been banished outta me." A leer twisted his mouth. He raised a thick eyebrow and dropped not only the deception but the candy. He lurched forward with his good leg and swung his peg leg in an arc behind him. His lurch loosened the string holding up his nosepiece. Two black booger holes now showed beneath his two black eye holes.

The distance between Sarah and Crispus snapped shut like a jackal's jaws. I stood behind him, off to one side. Grew teeth. He didn't see me take a thick wooden staff from the corner and swipe his good leg out from under him with both arms, swinging hard and low. "Take that, murderer!"

He fell flat. I came down hard on his head with the knobby end of the staff, once and then again and again, screaming oaths. Knocked him clean out, dented the side of his pea skull; beat his stump and side, crackity-clack! I threw his cane under Sarah's bed. It hit the bedpost. Something clicked. I shot a glance toward the sound. A thin, wicked-looking blade had popped out the cane's bottom. The tip of the blade was a couple of inches from Sarah's ankle.

I said, "Mind that cane. Probably poison-tipped." She picked up the top end of his cane and held the sharp end under Crispus' chin, ready to jab.

I said, "Hold on. God's better at judgment than we are. Let *your* conscience be clean." She settled for swiping the stiletto tip along the folds of his chin, leaving red ooze from ear to ear.

I called out through the window, "Laz, Roy! Come quick. Crispus needs deliverance straight to the Roman garrison."

I towered over the bag of bones under my feet, listened to shouts in the courtyard and the clatter of men running up the steps.

Cy had joined the two men I'd called. He said, "My eyes might be gone, but my hands still work. Let me at him, Slow."

Roy and Laz held the prisoner in place. Cy cinched knots tight. When they finished, Crispus' hands were both tied behind him to his one ankle. Laz stripped him of his rabbi disguise and covered him with burlap, carried him down the stairs, and dumped him in our horse-drawn cart in the courtyard. Sarah threw the cane in beside him, and the sharp blade nicked his ankle.

I said to Sarah, "Watch Michael for me. We've got a package to deliver. Back before dark, God willing."

She nodded. We melted into the main drag that was crowded with pilgrims. I sandwiched all my me's between my Laz and Roy. Crispus was under cover in the back. We headed for Herodium, some miles up the wadi, along the road called The Bloody Ascent. Crispus still had a reward on his head, payable in good Roman coin.

31
CLAUDIA

Kirkhardt-the-Warthog swished his fat hips up the spiraling stone staircase and pushed open a thick oak door on the second landing. Light poured out of the room into the dark hallway.

I followed Wartie into the room. A slip of a girl, perhaps mid-teens, stood in a streak of sun. Her long, chestnut-colored hair shone like copper. She stopped singing in mid-breath when she saw me and, in a moment, her smile wed sad and scared.

Wartie closed the door, leaving me alone with Chestnut and a tub of still steaming bathwater. The bed in the corner had several changes of clothing laid on it.

I queried, "Name?"

She replied in the ancient accent common to Gaul, "Kristel." She paused for a moment, "I'm a slave, m'lady. I was trained to care for all men's, women's essential needs. What might you need?"

"That bath and your song were both inviting. Go back to singing. I'll soak my grime away for a bit. Then we'll decide what comes next."

"Yes, m'lady." She volunteered, "Kirkhardt is my father's cousin."

I replied not a word but dropped my thin tunic on the floor and lowered myself into the hot water. Kristel gazed at my hard body, then resumed looking out the window, singing her song, but now softly.

Time passed. I snoozed. When I roused myself at a sudden sound, the sun's rays had stamped oblong squares of pale-yellow light across the floor. My *ornatrix* had folded herself into the window seat, head on her arms, fast asleep.

I stood, dripping, then stepped out of the tub. Kristel awoke. She moved toward me in a way that hardly moved the air. No small attributes, invisibility and forgettability, in such a young beauty.

She offered a towel. "Shall I oil your skin, m'lady?"

I gave her sharp glance. "No need. And, I can dry myself. For the past year, I was in exile, courtesy of Grandmother Augusta's command. No oils, no towels. Sun and wind dried me."

Kristel gasped a sharp intake of air. "You, a royal, in exile?"

Completely unformed thoughts popped out of my mouth, like a chick leaving its shell. "It's a favorite sport among royals. My mother was the result of an affair Augustus stumbled into. No one in my family, including me, will ever be included in any history books. Grandma's unspoken rule was, 'Never forget you're a mistake and you will *never* belong.'"

Kristel listened, enrapt.

I was amazed at my outburst. I'd never even *thought* that twaddle. How could I have known *all* my needs would include a slave with an open heart and tears? No one had told me exiled feelings come home to roost with other exiles.

I turned away from her, my eyes brimming with sadness. Voice hardened. "In this royal gladiator ring, one false step kills. Short sword of accusation, javelins of jest, trident and netting of rumors, daggers of eye-envy—all equal opportunity weapons for savaging fellow royals." I closed my eyes. My life galloped over me like a warhorse, images and memories tumbling together.

"M'lady, your life is harder than what I can imagine. At least I know where I belong."

I said, "The key to not belonging is not to love—anything or anyone. That way, no one can hurt you." I was silent, searching her eyes for understanding. She kept them locked on me.

"I failed at lovelessness with Grandpa, a man named Jesus, and my cousin, Julie. But Grandma still schools me in lovelessness. She's killed Grandpa, probably killed Jesus, and still has Julie in exile."

Kristel was silent, crying. Perhaps for me, perhaps for her. She watched me towel dry. "I'm lonely too. In that way, we are one."

Kristel stopped speaking with words and let her arms and hands speak service. She led me to a stool beside the tub, in front of a mirror. She took a few tucks in the waistline of my dinner dress and cinched up the shoulder straps. Once done with clothes, she combed and curled my hair and folded it up on top of my head with a torque of worked silver. She kohled my eyes, rouged my lips, and dabbed me with perfumed oils. Watching her work was exhausting, but the results were amazing.

Who was that person in the mirror? Make-up changed my face, but exile had changed my character.

Okay, so here I was, dolled up and ready to work for my dinner. What would be my earnings—a round trip back to Trimerus or a get-out-of-jail-free card? Note to self—*wheedle Uncle Tibbie into letting Julie come home.*

Kristel returned to the room after checking the evening schedule. Her face was a study in shades of shame. *Brilliant magenta mark, the shape of a hand, on her left cheek.*

She looked down. "Kirkhardt said the emperor asked for you, m'lady."

"Kristel, what happened?"

"Nothing to concern you. You have enough worry."

Her tide was at a low ebb, so I went digging in the little holes on her beach to see what snapped. "Go on, tell me, please."

"I'm worried about my uncle. I walk in on him in the kitchen. He supervises the cooks, you know, as well as housekeeping and such as me."

"A *very* important free man, by the sound of it."

She blurted, "He's always hated Tiberius, ever since the emperor chopped off his father's head."

I thought of my own father losing his head. All those headless torsos wandering about. I peered over the tub's edge from the stool where I sat. My headless body, reflected in the water, peered back at me.

She kept talking, adding to my collection of the headless. "His older brothers, also, chop-chop, offa their heads. Uncle brought back with child slaves. Uncle wants revenge."

I gulped. "Go on."

"I came into the kitchen when he was alone—preparing drinks on a tray. He didn't see me, but I saw him pour from a blue vial into crystal glasses on a silver platter. When he finished, he saw me standing in the corner, took two quick steps, and slapped me to the ground. He say, 'Stay quiet, Kristel!'"

"And then?"

She studied her feet. "I'm a show you to emperor suite, soon as you're ready, m'lady." *Fluttering in my chest—a trapped bird in there, seeking release.*

"You did well to trust me, Kristel. I'll not get you in trouble."

She led me through a maze of castle corridors, up two levels, and toward the castle front, overlooking the sea. We arrived at an alcove outside two oaken double doors, elaborately carved with the sign of Caesar's imprimatur, the sphinx.

Kirkhardt stood in the shadows. He nodded to me, handed a tray of drinks to Kristel.

Kristel knocked.

Throaty answer from within. "Enter."

We walked into a flood of roseate light, sheer curtains, light pink, billowing inwards like sails. Rabbus stood inside the entry door with another Imperial guard. Tiberius sat in an alcove, across from another man, someone facing away from me but familiar in form. He turned to face me.

Oh, *Jesus!*

I flew across the room. "Jesus! You came back to me!"

He opened his arms and held me, secure. My heart—and maybe his—pounded furiously. I touched his cheek and wiped a tear with my fingertip. Stuck it in my mouth. Yes, salty.

Uncle smiled. "Niece, so good to see you too. You remind of Vipsania, when we'd just married."

"Oh, Uncle Tibbie! I'm so sorry, uh, your highness. I'm re-arranging my heart to make room for *your* whole Emperor-ship thing."

"Quite all right, Niece. *I'm* re-arranging me too. We're all in a state of flux, with the possible exception of your unflappable friend here."

Jesus grinned at that, still wiping tears from his eyes. "I'm flappable, all right. But the closer I connect to Father, the less I flap, and the more I float inside Father's currents."

He turned and looked at me. In that moment, in the ocean of his eyes, I knew he knew. His spirit *had* been with me in the sea's currents, calming, comforting, helping me not to be terrified of sharks circling beneath me.

I looked over my shoulder at Kristel, who stood by the door. I said, "*Ornatrix*, please leave the tray there on the table. You're free to go."

She opened the door to leave. As she did, I saw the officer standing watch outside the door. Pontii. He looked over his shoulder and saw Jesus and me standing arm in arm. He flinched, disguising it as a good neck crack, left and right. Kristel closed the door.

I said, "I have a matter of concern about your security, Uncle. May I speak?"

Uncle Tibbie sat, motioned for Jesus and me to do the same. Rabbus drew near.

I relayed what Kristel had told me, word for word.

Rabbus said, "Perhaps I could appoint this steward as your official food and drink taster, sire?"

"Just, indeed," Uncle said. "Do it in the kitchen in front of his crew. A lesson for all."

Jesus reached into his backpack on the floor. He took out a piece of bread. He said, "These are some of Leah's leavings. Care for bread, Sire?"

My uncle was quiet for a while. Then he spoke up, "I suppose you'll say 'opposites are in that lump, like justice and mercy.'"

"Also, you might be missing the milk of human kindness."

Uncle said, "I'm a ruler, not a chef, or priest fond of pious eyewash."

Jesus nodded. "Ruling an empire and making bread are only things to do—no big difference between them. But Leah exposed herself to vulnerability, love itself. She let Father use her to raise you from the dead, out of courage and obedience, nothing more. Because of her obedience, her bread is superior to your rule."

Jesus' words felt like butterfly wings on my face, floating their wings up and down again and again. I didn't make meaning in his words. I let his presence fill me.

Uncle sat back, closed his eyes. Wind billowed through the sheers and filled the room. From out of this space, he spoke. "Change of plan. Bring the steward here."

Rabbus left to fetch Kirkhardt. I kept both my eyes on Jesus. His presence opened me like a ripe apricot falls apart of its own accord. The pit within me quickened with Jesus' kindness, gained in-sight, and became a third eye, watchful.

32
JESUS

The fat man in the brown toga swiped sweat off his head with one hand. He was a trembly mass, a mess of fluttering sighs and fidgety fingers.

Tiberius looked at the garrison commander who'd accompanied his freed slave. "I'm sure you understand, Silenus. The senior supervisor serves as taste-tester for me, wherever I go. Proceed with the drinks, taster."

Claudia and I had returned our chairs. Tiberius sat on a carpeted, elevated platform in a gilded chair. I whispered, *Father, show up and show off your glory.*

Kirkhardt's slippery hands shook. He carefully picked up the glass with *both* hands, but the crystal goblet slipped from his grasp anyway, shattering on the floor between his feet. A jagged piece of glass stuck in his ankle. Blood and wine mingled.

He jabbered, "Emperor, so sorry. I'll take away this mess. Bring you fresh drinks."

The emperor's eyes were cold. "Certainly, steward. Before you go, though, sample the remaining glass. If your hand isn't steady, my bodyguard will assist you."

Rabbus moved toward the tray, picked up the single glass, and held it to Kirkhardt's lips, nodding, encouraging, "Steward, drink."

The steward collapsed in a hopeless heap, knees crunching on jagged glass. He cried out, "Sire, when I was a boy of twelve, and you were a young general, you beheaded all the captured officers from Gaul, one by one. My father and two older brothers.... You laughed, sire! You laughed! You laughed as you brought down the ax on my father's neck. I vowed revenge."

Blood vessels in his temples pulsed, giving the impression of worms in there, frantic to escape. Kirkhardt ground out a few more words. "I poisoned your drink, and that drink has now poisoned me."

His right foot edged from purple to streaks of black. Black arrows fingered up from his ankle and down from his knees, joining in mid-calf. His breath grew ragged; eyes bugged out. Beads of red sweat rolled off his bald head onto the floor.

Claudia's eyes flicked toward me, then returned to the horror show before her. This intended homicide had soured into suicide. Rabbus stared, hand on sword, ready to bring it down on the steward's bent-over neck.

I walked to the steward. "Do you want your sins forgiven you?"

He looked up at me with the gaze of a man who knew he was utterly lost. "What's a sin, sire?"

My voice raised a notch, "Sin is like breaking that glass or what that represents—broken trust between people. Also, today, you broke God's law."

"What law and what God, Lord?" He raised his eyes to me.

"Love is the law, and I'm the God. Kirkhardt, your sins are forgiven, and your body healed. Live loyal to your emperor for as long as you may have."

I reached down, extending my hand to this fallen man. His faith rose to meet me. The streaks of red and black in his leg immediately reversed course. Purple-black foot pinked out, cuts healed, leaving only thin scars for remembrance sake. He stepped from his mess to me.

I said to Tiberius, "Emperor, your steward now awaits *your* disposition. If you mix mercy with your justice, he will be your most loyal servant in Aternum."

Tiberius sat cross-legged, arms folded over his chest, but he wore a softer mien on his skull and crossbones. He unfolded himself, stood. "All he said was true, and more. I was a vicious enemy, worse friend, and lethal family relation. No love to soften justice."

I replied, "Emperor, none is defined by their worst deeds. Love overrules Law. Happens every time Father forgives sin because of me. Millions of times every day."

My eyes, unbidden, bubbled up with something close to terror—like I was freezing in old grief, boiling in a vat of others' selfishness, from Eden to the end of time. Claudia grabbed my hand, not knowing what was paining me.

I glanced at her and said to Tiberius, "The future lies in the present, for those who can read it. My Father speaks it to my inner ear. I know another day, another way, someone will pay what is owed Justice for today's sins."

I shook with the certain knowledge of Love's cost. Neither Father nor I would let this cup pass from me. [22]

33
SLOW

Crispus moaned loudly from under his covering. Laz pulled our mules to a stop. He said to Roy, "We can't attract this kind of attention. Wait a minute till I gag him." We did, and he did. When I looked over my shoulder, I saw the whites of Crispus' eyes—bloodshot and wild with hatred. The burning in those eyes felt like a hot hand tightening around my throat.

In the distance, I could see the Dead Sea, a flat lake dimpled like hammered pewter. Sulfur stench blew uphill in a hot wind from the bottom of the world.

I turned my eyes up. Laddered silver-white cirrus stalled in their places. The sun broiled any exposed human skin cherry red by noon and black by sunset in this desert. Crags above and cracks beneath crawled with fiery snakes and scorpions. [23]

Another sight above us now, coming into view. Herodium towered over the desert floor. I looked for road signs, wanting to make sure we hadn't taken the turnoff to Hell.

Laz slapped the reins. Our mules increased their pace for a few steps, then slowed to their usual walking pace, just above a snooze. We'd pulled out ahead of an approaching caravan crowded with foreign travelers. These men were covered with the grime and dust of many days' journey.

Laz said to me, "Best to travel in the company of a caravan through these parts—safety in numbers. We may not think much or often about Satan. But you can be sure his demons call us by name and plot our destruction."

I said, "Aren't you a bit overdramatic, Laz? Aren't sword and arrow enough to worry about?"

Roy glanced at me out of the corner of his eye. "Satan is *millions* of times stronger than humans. The next time you confront him, how do you plan to battle? Stand there with your hand on your hip and say, "Satan, you're being naughty! Now just stop it!"

I wondered what I would do if called to confront this being. Roy must have seen into my mind. He said, "Our safety is not in numbers, but in Father and his Spirit, and His Word." He thumped the Torah scroll in the leather satchel beside him. I thought, *he keeps that thing as close as Rabbus keeps his sword.*

The lead camel driver poked his charge with a long prod. The camel picked up his pace. Ever so gradually, their caravan swallowed us right and left, fore and aft, passing us by.

My skin began to crawl. I felt my veil, fingering the edges to make sure it was all still in place, scooched closer to Laz on the buckboard seat. Cutter was terrified, as usual. She had a death grip on ma's paring knife in my robe's pocket.

The camel driver ahead of us shouted a command. Everyone stopped. The caravan's leader sat tall in his saddle, scrutinizing the road—no other travelers or soldiers in sight.

He threw off his ragged, moth-eaten cloak, revealing a fresh Bedouin warrior's outfit beneath. He swaggered back to our wagon. We were now firmly stuck in the bowels of his coil of camels, carts, and charlatans. [24]

He threw off our cart's covering. Crispus squawked urgent noises from behind his gag. Purpled face accented his distress.

Rough men surrounded our wagon, drawn swords inches from our throats. Other bandits unlashed and ungagged our prisoner. Several of them bundled him high up onto the lead camel's seat behind the bareback driver. The tyrant in his highchair cradled his swollen throat, spat out a scratchy command, "These idiots poisoned me! Kill 'em, take their mules, and push their wagon into the gully. Be quick about it."

I struggled to remember Jesus. Draw comfort and strength. But his memory had faded, growing more and more faint, year by year, like a cotton veil washed too many times and now threadbare. Hardly anything left in time of need. Only his faint voice, a whisper; no mouth or lips. What *had* he looked like when he was in the flesh beside me?

What I couldn't call to mind, Roy did. He shot to his feet, grabbing Laz's left hand with his right on his way up. Both men raised their hands together. Roy prayed in a loud voice, "Deliver us, Lord, from the snare of the chameleon and the viper's sting. Be quick, oh my God." They began to sing.

Their words of praise were still on their lips, along with my more timid humming, when the branches of the oaks quivered around us. The ground shook gently at first, then frantically. Trees reared and bucked. Sky curdled black with a fast-moving cloud swirling our way, barreling down-wadi directly toward us.

Men and beasts fell flat on the ground all around us. They were so terrified, so suddenly, that some cried out for the hills to cover them.[25] Those men's prayers were answered. Rocks fell from the towering cliffs above, covering many of them.

The fast-moving dust cloud joined nature's melee—cutting sand, thick as a wall, choked men and beasts. I looked to see if Moses and Pharaoh were nearby, engaging in a duel of plagues. Neither were present, but Windy certainly was out in force.

We, for our part, were not shaken by earthquake or choked with dust. We moved inside a second miracle, one of calm. All other humans and camels were having a bad day of it—all flayed by whipping sand or crushed by falling rocks.

Our wagon rolled on inside a bubble of protected space. Roy continued to sing one song of deliverance after another. Laz and most of my-me's joined in. Shame did not. Instead, she said, *you never could carry a tune in a bucket. Let those who know how, sing. You, shut up.* I stuck a gag in her mouth, turned up my volume. Wind whistled through my throat and the canyon's throat, all around. Our song became our weapon. [26]

Our spiral entry road snaked around the perimeter of a huge mound that Herod's father had built. The mound, thousands of meters tall, was shaped like a woman's breast. An acropolis had been constructed along this spiral highway—shanties, shops, feedlots, and a synagogue. Now many of these structures had been flattened. Sounds of wailing, calls for help.

At the very center-top of these breastworks was the tall nipple of a castle, erect, proud.

Harlot commented, *Herod the Great. Hmm. My kind of man. Obviously enjoyed pleasures of the flesh.*

In the midst of this general chaos, Roy spoke calmly, like this was an ordinary day, business as usual. "Herod the Great built these ninety-foot-tall outer and inner walls with an eight-foot trench between the walls.[27] Masada, south of here, is even more imposing."

Fragile noticed how many of Herodium's walls had crumbled; castle gates lay on the ground. The heads of her two eastern towers had been neatly clipped off. Red clouds of dust still swirled; sagging walls still groaned, along with the people under them. Men had all moved into the center of the castle courtyard. We waited there with them, wary for aftershocks, but few seeing God in the disaster.

Roy said, "God, open blind eyes. Let all see your hand at work." I remained veiled, half-seeing, half-not. Some of me believed in God's kindness when I looked through Roy's eyes of faith. Some of me sat still in Shame's shadow. I remembered Roy's sculpture, Splittina.

34
WINDY

Herod the Great's son, Antipas, hustled out of his father's palace and burial place, surrounded by guards. He shook his mane of stringy hair, white dust billowing off him in a cloud.

A man, pale as strained sand, trailed after the pudgy king. This emaciated man carried a set of ledgers and huffed along in the king's wake, hands white as goat's milk and eyes leeched of color. He had the surprised look of someone long dead, someone catapulted from a casket into a life of melancholy he could now enjoy.

A veiled woman in a purple, floor-length smock stood off to one side. She didn't even attempt to brush off all the plaster dust that covered her, head to toe.

All three heaved deep breaths, relishing their reprieve from being squashed into Herod the Great's necropolis, located directly beneath them. If I'd shaken the ground a bit harder, they'd have dropped right in.

Laz and Slow, joined by Roy, approached the other group. Laz kept his hands folded over his forearms, a sign of peace. Slow stayed a step behind him.

Laz called out to Herod Antipas, "A word, Sire?"

The king warily examined Laz and his companions, including the shapely woman hidden beneath her veil and hijab. Why were these strangers calm? What did they know that he didn't? He looked Slow up and down, eyes lingering here and there on her frame.

Laz said, "We are your humble servants from Jericho—I am Lazarus of Bethany, my wife, and El Roi, Rahab's proprietor. We were on our way to deliver the assassin of Tribunus Laticlavius Gaius, of Sepphoris, the late Caesar Augustus' son-in-law. The assassin's name is Crispus, a Samaritan commander of rebels, a man with a wild eye."

Herod straightened the olive leaf crown on his head with both hands and postured himself to his full height. Turned at an angle to better highlight his square chin.

He looked at the reed of a man standing behind him. "Chuza, how much of our tax revenues did that Roman fool extort from us on… what *was* the name of that doomed ship?"

Chuza, the albino accountant, seeped alarm. His habit was to hold chaos at bay by adding sums and subtracting out what didn't fit. On this disastrous day, life had not obeyed his rules—wipe feet with bleached towels, cut toast into exact triangles, and double-check accounts receivable.

Chuza looked at the veiled woman in the purple. "Joanna, dear, do you have a memory of those ledgers? I can't seem to rightly recall the exact amount, but I think it was considerable."

Slow remembered this woman from two years earlier when she was about to give birth to Michael. She remembered Joanna's voice, her timbre of casual competence. "Slightly more than two tons of gold bullion, husband—melted, refined, bricked, and stamped with Caesar Augustus's imprimatur. Soldiers carried that revenue out of the Jerusalem treasury two years, four months, and five days ago."

Chuza intoned, "There you have it, Sire. Just as I thought, two tons."

Herod heaved a sigh, fingers twirling his goatee. "What now of this half-wit assassin? And is there reward money to be gained if I ship him back to Rome?"

Joanna once again surprised Slow. "The reward for his capture is still available from Rome's treasury, in the amount of 50,000 sestertii."

Herod's mouth twisted, "Ah, yes. Now I remember Gaius, as well as my gold that he sunk in the sea, that incompetent dope. Where is this crazed, wild-eyed, pissant peasant so I can recoup a slice of my losses?"

Laz said, "Your highness, we were only a mile from here when his forces ambushed us in the Wadi Qelt. He had ordered our murder when El Roi prayed. Yahweh, blessed be his name, sent this dust storm and earthquake for our deliverance."

Herod turned his hand down and sideways, blew his nose on the pavement.

Laz said, "Perhaps, King Herod, you might still catch Crispus, if he lives."

Herod had a quiet word with his adjutant, who disappeared out the gate, barking orders.

Laz cast a look toward Slow. They stepped backward toward their cart. "With your leave-taking, Sire, we will return to Jericho. I'm sure your troops are more than competent to search out common criminals."

Herod commanded, "Your praying mentor can leave and take Yahweh's wretched earthquake with him. You and your wife will stay in our tower till this criminal is captured—or an aftershock takes the tower down. You will join my maintenance crew and repair my castle from your stinking Yahweh-quake. Your wife will attend to other matters I require."

The king turned away, saying over his shoulder, "As for me, I have little interest in that Samaritan wild-eye. Lunatics already surround me."

Slow spoke to her selves urgently. *Escape, don't leave! Fragile, stop screaming! And you, Cutter, take ma's blade away from my wrist! We'll get through this only if we stick together.*

Laz and Slow were "assisted" by two guards into the castle's gloomy interior. The guards led them by torchlight through darkened hallways. Elaborate paintings of Roman nymphs hid the hall's walls. A god copulated with each of these frisky maidens. The god's merry face, painted in flaming red colors, resembled Antipas' face. As the torches passed, paintings' bright colors bled to black.

Slow thought of what Laz had mentioned of Antipas' father, Herod the Great—how he had killed his wife for another woman and strangled several of his brothers in a fit of envy. One rabbi had said, "Your life will be longer as Herod's pig than as family member or friend."

They climbed four flights of spiral stairs. The ten steps in each flight led to a paved landing. On each landing, an oaken door. Some were bolted shut with a padlock; others had been shaken off their hinges. The guards unlocked the fourth-floor door.

An almost bare apartment lay beyond the door. Cracked walls exposed daylight beyond. As they stepped across the threshold, an aftershock swayed the tower. A window casing crashed onto the rocks below.

Laz hung onto Slow, his other arm raised in prayer. He spoke, voice trembling, "O God, though these towers dissolve into sand, stand with us."

Slow heard his voice as through water. She stared at the crumbly walls of their room and felt her inside supports crumbling. Her parts gained distance from her skin and each other. She felt disconnected, spacey.

She barely put these stray thoughts together, all in a row. *I'm married to a saint. Saint Lazarus. If he knew he'd be remembered as a good friend to Jesus, he'd be out of the running for sainthood, but he's clueless. And all my me's? We'll still have a presence, like the absence of light. But we'll not be seen—forgotten as quick as a dream in the early morning's light.*

35

CLAUDIA

Last night's banquet had been summarily canceled due to poisoning. Even so, tonight another banquet was being given in the emperor's honor.

Kristel, full of scuttlebutt, dolled me up. "I wish I was pretty like you. My face like mud wall. Hair straight like a poker." She held up the mirror for me to see her work. I stared so hard at who was in the glass that I scared myself. Kristel looked at me, envy in her eyes. If I could have, I'd have shucked beauty over my head like my worn-out tunic and handed it to her.

If it fits, take it. Never did me any good.

But who handled beauty artlessly without preening? I said his name to myself, lingering the name back of my teeth, rolling it over my tongue, polishing it like a stone in my mouth. I looked at my hair in the mirror, remembering Hippo using a few strands of it to stitch up Jesus' wounds. Was I still dissolved in his muscles? Didn't matter—Jesus left me feeling a part of him and him a part of me.

Kristel led me through back halls to the rear door of the banquet room. I looked through the crack in the door for the longest time. The place was packed. Uncle Tibbie sat at the head of a long banquet table at the far end of the ballroom. Anyone of even vague importance had been invited to this fête. Politicos, military brass, and those grasping for dignity. All shuffled toward the main entry door. Rome wanted a look at them. They wanted a look at Rome. All had plastered smiles on their faces while their elbows sliced upstream, hoping to get closer to the head of the table.

Every guest had prepared for this banquet. Who do *I* know that knows the gatekeeper at the door of the mayor's compound who knows the governor's best friend who knows the senator who plays cards with the consul? *Know-who* trumped *know-how* in Rome, as well as Aternum.

Uncle Tibbie spied me when I entered the hall. He whispered in the ear of his *maître de,* who seated me at his left side. Jesus reclined across from me, at Uncle's right hand. Julius reclined on the next cushion lower down the table than me.

And John? He wandered alone, below the foot of the table, gazing at wall tapestries—splendidly isolated. People he passed looked puzzled, noses sniffing the air, before they located the source of the smell and let him pass.

Kirkhardt stood to the side of his emperor, within his sight, and tasted every bit of food and drink brought to Uncle Tibbie. His new platinum blond toupee′ glistened in the torchlight as he waddled in and out of the kitchen. His jiggly frame groaned with pleasure at every morsel of food, every sip of wine. Uncle pointed this or that bit out to him, and, with a flourish of a separate knife, fork, or tasting cup, he sampled the emperor's wares. He practically kissed Jesus' feet as he went by, stepping spritely back and forth from the kitchen, singing a little tune, "I'm alive, alive, yes, indeed, I'm alive…!"

Rabbus stood with crossed arms behind Uncle Tibbie. He watched the whole proceeding with the practiced eye of the paranoid.

Tibbie turned to me, took a sip of pre-tasted wine, and said, "I'm pleased to have you next to me on one side and Jesus on the other. People who speak truth. Rare."

I was confused. *Was I being promoted to truth speaker?* "If you're interested in discussions of truth, Uncle, check with the guy on your other side. That's his specialty."

My uncle continued, "The truth is when I look at you, I see Vipsania. You remember, don't you, how Augustus made me divorce her for Julia. He and mother shed spouses like yesterday's fashions. Expected me to do the same. It's taken me years to recover."

Hallucination alert. I was a stand-in for his lost wife. 'Empress' did have a nice ring to it. And with Uncle, "love" could show up as a man *or* a woman, family relation or stranger. Whimsy won—if you lost favor, you'd become lion food, exiled, or poisoned. A Roman royalty play was never a loyalty play. One better titled, 'Slippery Options.'

My fantasy life was rudely interrupted by actual human conversation. Uncle Tibbie was talking to Jesus, "One of your Jewish kings had over a thousand wives, correct? He and Augustus both disavowed love matches."

Jesus eased that trademark, mystic smile onto his face and answered Uncle. "Solomon did use wives to seal political deals—but politics chipped away his heart from the outside in. Death of a thousand cuts."

Uncle said, "I didn't have Solomon's thousand marriages—only two. But they both fraught my heart with madness."

I leaned toward him. "And now?"

"My heart's maddened from absence more than presence. A mad potter spinning me around on his wheel. I feel his touch, but when I look, he's gone!"

Tiberius looked at Jesus. God-man looked back. Uncle blinked, Hope in his eyes. "Lately, I'm on another journey. Perhaps from nowhere to somewhere, perhaps a journey that might take me home."

Jesus said, "Father sculpted us all from nothing into something[28]—and what he made, he repairs—broken hearts, jaded hearts, hearts gone missing."

"You're hopeful, Jesus. But for a man in his 50's…?"

Jesus replied, "Solomon went from writing his hope-filled Proverbs, early in life, to a wise, but more cynical Ecclesiastes later in his life. He's one of Israel's heroes, but a hero who forgot how to be happy."

I said, "Forget Solomon, Jesus. How many Jewish, Roman, or Greek heroes ended up happy? *None*, that's how many. Zero. Why not aim for ordinary? You'd have a chance for happiness."

Uncle said, "What's ordinary, Claudia?"

"Exile life was ordinary. I learned to catch fish and gut them, plant seeds, weed our garden, swim in the ocean, laugh as storms swept over me, drool over fresh-caught fish cooking on a campfire. Little pleasures." I looked up, remembering. "Bigger pleasures became ordinary as well. I learned to love. I loved cousin Julie, loved Jesus' voice in my head, especially when a big fish yanked me off a cliff and set me adrift in the ocean."

Uncle said, "No complicated discussions of truth while in exile?"

"Nope. In my moments of falling—off a sinking ship or off a cliff—life wasn't complicated. It was deep."

Julius popped up, "Deep, huh? What's deep?"

"Simple, when you're in over your head, that's deep. Different from all these women who eye you, Julius. They're shallow and complicated."

He said, "Yep, caught that. Sorry, ladies, I'm already taken with a little Greek beauty, Sophia. We're to be wed after wargames in Illyria."

I didn't have the vaguest idea about wargames. I went back to my point about others' around us. "Uncle, all these people with ears like putty, jug ears stretching to hear a word from you. Creeps me out just sitting *next* to you. I can't imagine how it feels inside your skin."

"I'll never see any of them again."

I gestured at people lower down on the feeding trough. "I didn't have to worry about any of this on Trimerus." I stared at one painted, preening vixen against the wall. "That one over there? Puts me in mind of a female praying mantis. She eats her mate, all six legs and both wings, immediately after he does her. Very efficient. Mate and meal, less than a minute."

Julius smiled at me. "A bit more jaundiced than usual this evening, Claudia?"

I shook my head. "I'm rooted in what's real. My father's brains were eaten directly from his skull by a wild-eyed sadist. My brother was massacred by pirates, grandpa's ship sank, I almost drowned at sea, grandma exiled me. Even here, right now, if I say the wrong thing, I'll be back on Slammer Isle. My scalp is practically lifting off my skull."

I widened my eyes, offered an open-mouthed silent scream—a minor dramatic flair. I grabbed a glass of wine, sipped nonchalantly, and tried to calm myself.

Uncle asked, quite soberly, "So you were happier on Trimerus than you are here?"

"Not sure, Uncle, probably most of the time. But could you tell me if this Aternum junket is a loyalty once-over before I'm back in exile?"

Uncle Tibbie laughed. "Trimerus was mother's doing, not mine. She needed someone to blame so she could pop me to the top without suspicion cast on her. Everyone in the family realizes she is the Dowager of Assisted Suicide. It's only now I've enough courage to confront her, even if it is by gaining distance."

"So, I've officially served my time?"

He leaned over, mouth to my ear. "All royals worth their salt need seasoning. Your seasoning was spelled e-x-i-l-e. You're worth far more to the empire now than you were as the preening palace girl."

He looked at Jesus, "You too. Suffering's seasoned you. Sorry for you, jealous for me. What I'd like from you and Claudia includes your gain without your pain."

I pushed my luck. "Can you do two things for me, Uncle Tibbie? Let cousin Julie come home from Trimerus. And second, let me go with you on this journey. Perhaps I can be of service in your school of suffering."

"Of course, my dear. Done. But we're off to the empire's edges to get breathing space from mother. Another more pressing reason is your cousin Gemellus. He's gotten us into a bit of a war. Be warned. We might find ourselves covered with blood and guts, ours or others."

I decided in that heartbeat that it wasn't always best to know the worst. All I heard was that I could be close to Jesus, the god-man who radiated light from his sweet, combustible smile. That was enough.

36
SLOW

The next morning, two guards came for Laz. The taller, older man said, "Time to work. Rubble and rock need moving, bodies unearthing."

Laz got dressed and walked out the door behind the first guard, without breakfast. He'd not been gone from our room more than a few minutes when the door was once again unlocked. A flat-faced, tubby woman walked in, dressed in a burlap sack with armholes and a rope belt cinched around her waist. She had a broom in one hand and a pail of water with cleaning rags in the other hand.

She looked around at our shabby shell of a room and said, "Joanna sent me. Let's get to work. This place is a dump."

We talked as we worked. She was an Ammonite-Jewish woman married to an Edomite man. Both were conscripted laborers, unable to pay their taxes. She was on her hands and knees at the time, scrubbing the floor. I was washing down the furniture—two chairs and a table, bed in the corner.

She said, "This is how the king takes his women, pretty girl."

Scalp buzzed with fear. Why was she telling me this?

"I was pretty once, like you, long time passing. Last time he called for me, he told me I was sexy as a wet goat in a cave. Watch yourself, girl. Rumors are buzzing that he's got his eye on the new girl, the pretty one. That would be you. He gets what he wants. Some have overheard him bragging. Says he's going to do as other kings have done—take any bride he wants on her wedding night. The husband gets what's left."

I spoke a one-word prayer, *help*!

Joanna walked in the door. She was unveiled, dressed in a light green smock. She glided across the room to the table by the knocked-out window casing. She sat in one of our two newly cleaned chairs on either side of a simple wood table for two. She leaned back, closed her eyes, and let the breeze cool her. Her chestnut hair, shot through with shades of ash, blew back from her face.

Once situated, she smiled briefly at Ramona. "You can go now. Kitchen needs you."

I sat across from Joanna. Two glasses and a pitcher of water sat between us. Joanna reached into her bag and drew out a couple of egg salad sandwiches and two oranges. She started paring one orange.

Cutter eyed her curiously and commented to me, *looks like she's pared herself down. Look at her long fingers—small, quick, quiet. Her speech and movements cut to the quick.*

She pushed the pared orange at me and started in on the other one, glancing up at me now and again. While she pared, I wondered about the jagged, white scar that ran from just below her eye to mid-jaw.

She didn't believe in preambles. "Herod uses his vices to keep virtue from running wild."

I stacked her peelings neatly on a corner of the table. "So, what I've heard is true—he wants to bed me?"

She nodded. "Veils are handy. Covered women have their sanctuary overhead. But that doesn't stop a man like him. None of us keep what's ours, whether honor or virtue. Our lives, a brief borrowing of bones."

"Nothing to be done?"

"You can talk back and get your face slashed, like some women I know."

"Your husband didn't protect you?"

"He's a number's man. Didn't add up."

"How'd you get cut?"

Joanna looked to me like she was loosening screws from her floorboards. A memory popped out. "I was on my knees when I looked over my shoulder and made a comment."

"He must not have liked what you said."

Laughter unleashed from her throat, like a fox barking. "Nope, something about a tiny worm. About then, half my face suddenly hung off my skull."

She finished peeling her orange, daintily. "Here's my advice, shut up, keep your face intact *and* your husband alive."

There was a knock on the door. It swung open. A guard stepped in, walked to the corner, and threw a flimsy scarlet gown on the bed.

He said, “Ten minutes. The king’s summoned you.”

Joanna looked at the gown. “Same one he made me use. Let’s see if my bloodstains washed out.”

37
WINDY

A*ugustia,* a quinquereme warship, shot over the Adriatic Sea, smooth as liquid jasper, her sails full of what could not be seen. [29] Captain Sejanus commanded the twenty-ship armada. As one, this acropolis of wood and canvas moved toward war. The armada, powered both by wind and rowers was yare, closing with its target on the Illyrian peninsula's southern coast.

Rabbus sat next to Leah on their bedroll at the base of center mast. Leah held Gabe, Rabbus held her, the ship held them, and Father held the ship.

Rabbus said, "Interesting that Tiberius named this flagship after his mother. The carved figure on the prow is supposed to be Neptune. But the right half is an exact replica of Augusta, and the left half, an exact likeness of Tiberius. Her curls, the cleft in his chin, the arch of their necks. Mother and son, mushed together, take us to war."

Leah shivered. To calm herself, she turned to gaze at Son. He leaned on the portside gunnels near the prow, chatting with Claudia and John. She thought to herself, *I may forget many of his words, but I'll never forget how he makes me feel. Like I'm in the grip of all eternity.*

Jesus and Claudia turned from looking at the sea to watch the on-deck activities. A human target had been drawn on a canvas sheet, backed by bales of hay on the main deck. Archers and throwers lined up for target practice, knees bending for balance as the swells passed under the keel. Julius was next in line. His chest muscles sheened from jousting with his sparring partners. He faced away from his target, whirled around, and loosed his javelin all in one fluid movement. Dead center on the target's chest.

Claudia said to Son, "Ah, there's a man in love with his good looks. That was me before suffering drop-kicked me into womanhood. I still feel like both my feet are planted firmly in mid-air."

Son agreed, "*Kingdom* dreams blow *me* around, like these trade winds."

Julius distracted them, yelling loudly, "Ayrlo, hit the heart like I did, if you can!"

Ayrlo, thick-chested, panted heavily in spite of me blowing air into his asthmatic bronchioles. His spear landed closer to the target's lungs than its heart.

Julius play-acted, pretending his spear was a walking stick and he an old man. He approached Jesus and Claudia. "You lovebirds! Ya make me pine away for the good ol' days when I was yer age."

Son smiled at his friend's play-acting.

Julius changed from pretend *senex* to *puer* with a wink.[30] "Maybe *your* spear'll give life to our lady friend, Jesus."

Claudia clipped back a retort, "Violence to sex, in a heartbeat!"

Son looked over his shoulder at the flotilla of warships behind *Augustia*. I gave him two sudden images chock-a-block, shattering his equanimity.

Julius, screaming with pain.

John, hiding high in a tree.

Son asked me, *Windy, what's this?*

I said, *speak to them of violence. I'll supply your words. Inhale. Begin speaking.*

Son took a deep breath, held it, released. "I was thinking about pornography."

Claudia replied, quicksilver bright, "Taking your place with the rest of us mortals?"

Son said, "Violence porn came to mind."

Julius said, "Black leather, whips, bindings?"

"No. Porn's about power, and power's the ability to name what's real. I say Father's kingdom is more real than flesh. Porn says flesh trumps spirit—for sex and violence."

Claudia squinted at Jesus. "Say on."

"Invisible wars are much more deadly than visible ones. Those are the wars I fight for the sake of everything human."[31]

Julius smothered a snicker. "Saving us all, are you? You're something else, Jesus."

I whispered in Jesus' ear, *Get used to the mocking, Son. Friends, family, and foes will think you've lost your mind. Inhale. Ok, now you're full of my breath. Speak.*

"You're right, Julius. But one day, I *will* carry a sword of vengeance. Today is not that day." [32]

Claudia mumbled to Julius, "Never try to win a pissing contest with God-man. He shucks truth like fishermen do oysters."

Son said, "Julius, you spoke of wargames before you wed Sophia this fall?"

Julius stroked his spear tip. "In the trust 'n thrust department, its battle before bedroom."

Jesus shook his head. "Violence doesn't make the man—love does."

Julius' voice sliced off harsh disagreement. "Rome approves violence. Trained me in violence for the past four years in the military academy. Crowds pay to watch it. Even religious people leave houses of worship in the morning and line up for matinees to see people kill each other that afternoon. Guts, gore, and glory—*yeah, baby*!"

Claudia's outer vision fuzzed. I placed an image in her mind's eye. She saw her cousin, Postie, on his back, blood bubbling up from where she'd plunged a poisoned arrow in that pulsing hollow where his rib cage came together. She saw in sharp focus Postie lifting his face, holding his hand up to her for mercy.

She heard herself say, *Postie, will you hurry up and die! I have people coming for dinner tonight.* She'd felt only irritation. He was taking too long to die.

Her voice trembled. "I think of me stabbing Postie. I didn't feel that. But now my heart sticks sideways in my throat."

Son considered what Father would have him say. Father didn't want Son to say anything at all. Instead, Son's eyes bubbled with unbidden tears from my heart, his eyes, and Claudia's un-cried grief. Claudia slid along the redwood gunnel and slipped her arms around Jesus, whispered broken bits of comfort.

"Hey, you two, why so glum? You'd think someone had just been flayed alive." Julius made a cutting motion with his unsheathed sword like he was cutting into his chest. Fell in mock agony, writhing on the deck. He reminded Jesus of the six-year-old Julius, his playmate in Egypt when they were five years old, play-acting Anthony and Cleopatra's deaths.

Julius had grown older, but not grown up. How could he? Life's big questions hadn't yet hurt him. But this would be short-lived.

Claudia's head rested on Jesus' shoulder.

Ayrlo stood watching, half in shade, half in sunlight.

Son reached out to Julius and John. "Friends, come join Claudia and me." He looked at the man wheezing by the gunnels. "Ayrlo, you're also welcome."

Julius and John moved toward Jesus. Ayrlo moved away.

The four friends moved in a circle, three steps to the right, two back, rhythmically swaying to the music of my winds on a tilting deck. Their heads bent to circle center where I wove their hair, intentions, and thoughts together.[33] Son slowed the circle to a stop, looked at his friends carefully, one face to the next. "Today, we make deposits into Father's trust account."

Julius tipped his head to one side—*what are you talking about?*

Jesus continued, "Today we deposit our dance, prayer, and laughter in heaven's bank account. Tomorrow, we make withdrawals."

Jesus opened the circle of friends into a line that faced east. All of them saw what had been only a smudge. Fingers of red and yellow trees clawed up from the sea into the black mountain's scars. Row upon row of enemy soldiers lined the bouldered beaches below the forest. Chanting battle cries rose to the sound of drums. Banners snapped in the wind. Wooden barricades, X-shaped, twenty feet tall, stood between look-out towers that protected archers and slingers. Sharpened staves leaned seaward from the barricades.

This land was the next step toward home. Jesus would pass through this violent soil to get home to what? More violence. Violence to be dreamt by Claudia the night before Son's bloody execution. Violence allowed by her future husband, Pontii, soon to be Pilate over Judea. Violence thrust on Him by his own Jewish rulers. I moaned, whipping the air into a dirge for what was yet to come.

38
SLOW

The guard handed me off to a bent-over woman. Bright pink warts folded into the creases of her chins. Curly black hairs sprouted from the mole over her top lip. She led me through a tangle of hallways into the castle's basement.

Clatter-chatter, spinning wheels, shush-shush of harried maidens slippering along. Entryways lit by smoking torches shoved into wall sconces—female worker bees living hive-lives in service of King Bee.

My-me's did what they always do. Escape looked for a trapdoor that would drop her into anywhere but where she was. Fragile busied herself collapsing. Harlot put on her make-up. Shame wagged her finger, tut-tutting, "You made this bed being so sleazy. Now lie in it!"

Warty used the spiral handrail to heft herself up five stories, panting at each landing. She motioned toward the door on the sixth-floor landing. "He's in there. Best be spritely, sweet cakes."

A bored guard stood to door's right. His long spear, butt down, leaned outward. Waisted chain, heavy with iron skeleton keys, hung from his belt. He jerked his chin toward the door handle.

I opened the door.

The color purple slathered the room. Purple irises, roses, begonias. More smells and shades of purple than could possibly co-exist without a civil war breaking out. Door snapped shut behind me. Bolt slammed shut from the outside. I stood beneath a curtained window, a narrow bolt of sun slapping my face from the right.

Herod Antipas sat in a velvet chair made of silk fabric, magenta shading toward purple. A pile of used snot-rags lay at his feet. Absent-mindedly, he stropped a jeweled dagger with a flint.

He stared at me, a curious half-smile frozen on his chubby face. Arched eyebrows, painted purple.

A snake poked up between his legs.

He cried out, "Oh, my precious!" He reached into a basket for a hard-boiled egg, left it in his open hand. The egg-eater slithered across his thigh toward the egg, unhinged its jaws, and slid his body around the egg.

Once the egg had disappeared, so did the snake, uncoiling from the king's leg into another basket beside the king's chair. Herod rolled his eyes, now gazing out the window toward Bethlehem, the place where the innocents were murdered.[34] I looked up and noticed a jagged cord of pelicans, grey on brown, flapping south toward the Dead Sea.

Escape cried, *fly away. Let's go. He won't know.*

Herod shook himself back into the room just as I took a step backward toward the door. The way he fondled me with those frigid eyes, I felt like a naked beetle, speared on a stick pin.

Herod's pink tongue flicked over his lips. "I sent Joanna to you. She and that tacky dress are today's first object lesson. Drop it and turn around. Maybe the rest of you is as interesting as your face. At least I don't have to put a bag over your head, like the last two."

I summoned Harlot, my protector at the whorehouse in Sepphoris. *For such a time as this, please stay.* She promises nothing. Slid my right shoulder strap down.

Harlot fingered the bloody stain on the gown that wouldn't come out, the stain directly over my heart. She gave him a sultry reply, "You didn't mind using that blade of yours with Joanna, did you?"

The corner of his mouth pulls down like a fox snared by a hidden trap. His words snip off a comment, "Her disrespect needed a sharp lesson."

He chortles at his own wit. Irritation followed. "If you keep speaking, the lessons will continue."

Harlot said, "Not every student needs that school, my king."

A hand appears at the end of my arm. The other strap dropped. Dress fell to my waist, caught by the thin belt.

Herod's eyebrows arched higher. Tongue flicked out, then retreated into its wet cave.

Harlot's words spilled like clotted cream. "Would you care to help this dress *down*

while I raise *up* your standard?"

He chopped off his reply like a falcon snapping its prey's neck. "Drop it yourself, and be quick about it, Jew-whore."

She loosened the belt, released it.

My house caught fire. Each part of me was alone in a room, flames crawling up the walls. Fragile hid in the hall, peeking around a corner. She saw Cutter fumbling in the flames, on the floor, on hands and knees, looking for her lost knife.

Escape, dress trailing flames, floated out a window, joined by Harlot, also burning. The two were off, off and away to unknown destinations.

Shame cackled, lit more Lucifer matches, setting fires everywhere like a practiced arsonist. Smell of sulfur.

Herod's mouth moves silently. I catch up with his noise, "Couch, kneel, facing wall. Don't look back or talk back."

Fragile writhes.

Cracking sound of memory. Cynico. Sepphoris whorehouse. Room three. Ribs cracking, cheekbone breaking. I have no body. I'm made of memories, memories bright-lit by fire.

Attention arrows back into this room on a released bowstring. Man's big finger points. Points to naughty couch.

Where had that come from? Body floated to boxy, bad-boy cushions.

I now bent-over girl, head in hands. Very bad girl, me.

Big pig grunts. Bad me, bad, bad, bad.

Jesus? You here? Grinding tea leaves?

I'm here, child. Pay attention to me, not the bad man.

But Jesus, owie-pestle-banging-mortar. Chocka-chocka-chocka-clunk. Chocka-clunk! Up, down, chocka-clunk.

Jesus, please stay. Don't go.

His voice, *I'm with you, child. Listen to me. Hold my voice. Can you smell the broken tea leaves? Crushed leaves, now, all crushed. See me sprinkle tea leaves in pot. Pot's over fire. Fire's inside stove. Lovely sweet tea's brewing, child. Tea 'n me wrap you like a blanket. I'm here. I'm with you. We're together. Here, now.35*

Someone's crying now. Crying loud.

"All done now, please? Go now, go?"

Voice cuts air, "If I have to tell you again to get out of here, I'll cut you, whore."

Get dress off floor. Hold in front. Back, back, go back, baby-back steps. Head down. No look up. Hand feels face. No blood, no rips.

Goodgirlgoodgirlalivegirl

Big man yells. Door opens. Back out, shut door, soft-soft.

All done. Go bye-bye. Quiet now, quiet. No one sees, no one but Jesus.

39
JESUS

The storm broke over the sea and me in the night's darkest hour. Flagship *Augustia,* southernmost in the armada, was anchored along Illyria's coastline. Rain thrummed a staccato beat on the deck. I held the center mast with one hand and peered toward the fog-shrouded shore. The clouds parted for a brief moment, and the moon poked out, spider-veined with old scars. Down here, war awaited, ready to inflict new ones.

I began to sing, slow and steady, eyes toward heaven. Battle songs are so hard to sing alone. Then, out of nowhere, a voice joined mine. John had walked up behind me quietly and picked up my tune.

A moving image invaded my song and focused my inner eye in another direction. I saw an egg-eater snake gorging on a hard-boiled egg, swaying, spiraling upwards. Slow was on the floor, writhing on her hands and knees, flattened with terror.

Windy, what's happening with Slow?

He replied, *Satan's attacking her hope while her growth is still in egg form. Pray against him. Picture her parts slowly joining back together. She's been undone. But watch now. See her selves come together, pulled together by your prayer and my breath. Hold hope for Slow when she is not able.*

I sang-prayed these new words, *Spirit in me, Spirit in Slow, go Slow, grow Slow.* Breath sang in and out of my lungs. I led and John followed, singing descant. Windy blew my prayers, articulate in ways I could not fathom, through thin boundaries, from Italy to Israel.[36]

Light threw off night and cracked the dawn open. It crept on tippy-toes, afraid to show what the day would bring. John was not there to see dawn's whisper. He'd curled up in netting on the deck and had fallen asleep.

A creak from the captain's deck. I looked up. Tiberius stood, facing east. Bits of shadow moved between smudges there in the forest. Snatches of enemy war songs floated across the waves.

I climbed the ladder to Tiberius and stood with him on the bridge.

"Emperor, how do you see this day unfolding?"

He replied, "Seer, you tell me. That's why you're here."

I said, "What I see is this—dead bodies will cover this beach, these boulders, and that forest. Sea will turn red at the next tide. Two fingers pinch, squeezing what's in between into smoke."

His voice trembled with excitement. "Yes! Just so. Now *I'll* tell *you* what your vision means. Gemellus's army is closing a trap behind our enemies—four Roman legions are coming quietly up the other side of that mountain over there. The enemy is surrounded by land and sea. That's the pincher you saw. The gods smile on us, Seer."

Inside, Windy said, *Tiberius took your vision raw. He didn't inquire about meanings. He chips coal and thinks he's got diamonds. Happens when people confuse vision with interpretation.*

Should I tell him?

If you want to waste my breath in you on him. He must suffer more, longer, deeper before he's able to listen well.

"Sire, a question, if I may?"

Tiberius kept watching the dawn creeping up the shoreline. The four fingers on his right hand waggled, *ask on.*

"Why kill a bunch of people, yours and theirs, Sire, to get land you don't need?"

"You're asking me? *Your* Father's been into wholesale murder ever since Noah and the flood."

I continued to press my hope for peace outwards into the air. "Wouldn't a round table chat beat killing off the local taxpayers, Sire?"

"The problem isn't me. It's my grand-nephew, the consul here. Gemellus offended one of their two chiefs, Bato of Daesitiates. And, all right, another small thing. I *did* kill Bato's father. But that was long ago, on the same day I executed Kirkhardt's father. Bato was among the boy captives we brought home to Rome. Schooled in our best academies. Turns out we trained him to become a smarter terrorist. No fool like an educated fool."

"The law of unintended consequences?"

"Indeed. The other main leader in Illyria is Drusilla. Some say she's a demon. Others say she is the high priestess of the Druids. Both she and Bato are vicious in-fighters, but spies tell me neither have any hope of victory over one another or Rome. She and Bato agree only on one thing—you don't defeat your enemies only by killing their armies. You defeat them by killing their gods."

I said, reasonably enough, "gods can't be killed, correct?"

Tiberius shrugged. "Belief in them can die. Their gods take turns seeding doubt or blurring vision among the others. We've been peacekeepers between their warring tribes for generations. Many of these tribes are Celts from the north; a few are Druids from the south. When they don't have us to fight with, they're busy killing each other off. Darkness biting itself."

I said, "So there's no clear rule of law? And justice doesn't mix with kindness?"

"Correct. These gods are quick to get your left eye suspecting your right, your right arm stabbing your left."

"But today, Emperor, what do the Celt-Druids hope to achieve by warring with you?"

Tiberius worked to bend his face into a smile. Seemed like hard work. "Bottom line? They'd like to find working scales that balance hope, justice, and love.

"Picture this. Their guiding myth, on ancient cave walls, shows Hope as a child. This child leads a just Father, seen only in a vague outline. He's invisible almost and for sure blinded, his eyes covered with a rag. The visible Child guides the invisible Father among people. Father holds onto the Child's shoulder. This Hope Child, sometimes boy, sometimes girl, carries weighted scales. These scales, in these ancient drawings, balance love and justice."

I was silent, habitually in listening mode for Windy's voice. I also listened to Tiberius but adjusted my inner ear in Windy's favor.

She said, "And Son, never forget. You are that Hope Child."

Tiberius continued, "Another thing about this myth. The true Hope Child knows hope for love, absent rightness, isn't love. *That* sort of love is naïve, vacuous. *That* person's neighborhood hasn't yet been burned, its daughters raped, and its sons beheaded in front of their parents."

Claudia surprised me. She'd crept up the ladder and been listening. "Uncle, this man next to you carries spirit commodities, hope and such, like the nautilus shell carries spirals."

I said to her, "So, I'm your corner convenience store?"

Claudia replied, with a smile, "Princess of selfishness, remember?"

I hugged her. "Father's busy changing you, Claudia, and you've not yet caught up with the person he's destined you to be."

She squeezed my hand and looked at her uncle. "Jesus and you easily slide into such slippery talk. Destiny this and Hope that. Most of the time, it's all I can do to plan lunch."

Tiberius smiled. "Then get me breakfast. I smell it wafting up here from the galley below. Pork sausage from somewhere high on the hog."

He looked at me. "I thought our resident Jew would enjoy a change of diet. I need you at full strength, Jesus. Bato knows two things. You're our God of Hope, and you're on board this ship. My spies slipped that information to him. I used you as Bato bait to lure him into place."

I felt suddenly dizzy. Reached toward Claudia. "Hold me, please."

She wrapped her arms around me and muttered in my ear, "Uncle just put me in mind of the rat king who stayed in power by chewing his enemies' roots from below."

I didn't fully take in her meaning. My head was still spinning, and I felt vertiginous, one foot on the canting deck and the other poised over a void.

Father-Rock, steady both of us.

Tiberius queried, "Hear their war drums? Tempo's up-ticking. Bloodletting's about to begin."

Claudia said, "I can see their archers and slingers on the shore in front of the drummers. With the sun and clouds, they seem like chameleons in light and shadow."

The harsh cry of warriors, each one working into a frenzy, tingled the hairs on my neck.

Claudia kept whispering in my ear. "If we can see them, they can see us. And if you can be seen, you can be touched. If you can be touched, you can be killed. Uncle used you as bait, but let's slip his hook—slip away and leave Uncle to his little war."

I murmured back, "There *are* worse things in life than death. I wasn't made to run from conflicts Father has appointed for me to fight. He made me a candle on a hill, burning freely."

Claudia said, "But do you have to burn at both ends? I feel like Job, your patron saint. Or was that Satan who walked around the planet testing people? I forget. But that's not my point. Whoever's in charge of testing by fire, you'd think he'd have burned up by now."

Windy whispered, *time's not quite right to tell her your testing has hardly begun.*

40

SLOW

I lay on my bed, facing the wall. My scarlet dress rode up over my thighs. A man came through the door into this weird, round room with blown-out windows and trembly walls. I half-turned. Where was I? Who was this filthy man with torn work clothes and bleeding fingers?

Uninvited, he sat next to me on the bed. I flinched. He didn't seem to notice. Instead, he stroked my hair. I put space between me and my skin.

Scuttling noises in my head. Chunks of me running away.

He said, "Darling, what a day! We've uncovered a lot of bodies below. But you won't believe this. Do you remember the local rabbi I'd met from here at Herodium? His wife was going to stay with you while we men went to the Feast of Sheaves in Jerusalem. Well, we found a child beneath the toppled head of this turret, trapped between her parents' bodies. They'd sunk her in a crevice and then laid on top of her, forming a bridge with their bodies. That was the rabbi and his wife. Now their only child's an orphan."

I floated, detached. *Sacrificing their bodies for a kid counted more than barking from back of a Torah scroll, for sure.*

Haze of memories. Strong scent of purple irises, wrapping me in nose gauze.

The man said, "I thought we might show her kindness."

He liked little girls too. Probably dangerous. Very dangerous. I looked away. Eye to eye was way too close.

A little girl's voice, one outside my head? "My name is Yakhal."

She eye-checked with the man. Maybe she wanted to see if it was all right to speak?

Ack. Now I knew him. Maybe I was even married to him. The man called Laz said, "You remember that word, darling—one of the first ones I learned in Torah class? Yakhal means 'Hope.'"

I rolled off the bed and crawled over to the child. She was lithe as a willow sapling but looked a wreck. Like I felt. Her wild, raven hair stuck out at odd angles over almond eyes and sharp cheekbones and chin. White-powdered dust splotched her torn tunic. Bloody linen strips bound her right arm and wrapped 'round her head.

I squatted in front of her on my haunches and opened quivery arms, but only a bit. My hands, knuckles red and chapped, stretched out to her. She buried her head in my chest. Her whimpers grew to sobs.

I. Was. Lost. Shame said to the rest of us, *you're no older than her, broken in pieces. A dropped plate missing parts. This kid's unearthed. Way above you.*

Fragile and I cried with her anyway. Laz put his arms around both of us, weeping for no good reason. I felt better, also for no good reason.

Where were my-me's? Escape was probably zipping around the castle courtyard, shrieking like a scorched monkey. Cutter had gone, missing in action. Shame scowled in a corner, fresh out of Lucifer matches but content to lecture the rest of us. Bruise sat facing the corner, turning purple.

Strange, floaty images. Soft, joining comfort—a praying person, Jesus, puzzling over me, holding one part up to the other, seeing how we fit. He unbroke my pieces. His Spirit blew me around. Promised we'd stick together one day.

The girl-child patted my head, curious. Hope was present.

41

WINDY

Leah spooned with Rabbus on *Augustia's* pitching deck in the pre-dawn hours. I used Gabe to wake her. He had rolled out from under their tarpaulin, out into the rain. She grabbed her shrieking child, brought him back to her, pressed his mouth to her breast. Cries shushed to coos. I ghosted a silence around them, fog's sequestering—a mist so dense and low, its cushy butt sank into the sea.

Leah heard what others missed—quiet padding of careful feet slipping through the dense fog. The steps paused beside her sleeping husband, then moved along. Her preternatural hearing, Spirit school skills, caught the click of an opening lock, tiny rasp of squeaking hinge.

Leah whispered to Rabbus. "Husband, wake up. Quiet. Someone disappeared into the cargo hold over there, the one where all the ammunition is stored."

Husband checked his cloak for the cargo hold key. *Gone.*

Leah handed him a vial of oil from her bag. She always kept her lamp trimmed.[37]

"Hinge squeaks, husband. Careful."

He put finger to lips, gathered short sword and dagger from beneath his cloak. Slid over the wooden deck on bare feet. Silent cargo doors opened. Husband dropped in, disappeared from her view.

Leah, the warrior woman, dropped in as well, dropped into inner space. She pulled blankets over her and Gabe. Minded her heart.

Leah said, *Windy, please help.*

I swirled around her, whispering, *your sister needs you. She's dazed, divided. Ask Father to gather her parts together, gather her to Hope, and Hope to her.*

She began to pray but then hesitated, opened her mouth to request something else.

I squeezed her arm. *No need to ask. It's done.*

In the pitch dark of the hold below her, I came alongside her husband. I wafted a strong odor his way, a pungent musk of scalp, the sweat of a feral predator immediately behind him.

I said, *Rabbus, duck! Duck and stab. Now!*

Immediately, he dipped his head and thrust his dagger backhanded, angling up from his waist. A shadow grunted, folded in on itself. He pressed the blade home, harder, then turned and thrust the short sword out and up with his dominant left hand. Shadow went slack. Rabbus felt in the dark for the other's hands. Limp hands held a razor-wire garrote. Without instant obedience, Rabbus and not the assassin would have been releasing his bowels in death.

Rabbus pulled the corpse up the ladder one step at a time; poked into the pale and eerie fog. John slipped through the mist and helped Rabbus with the slippery, lean body. They laid the body out on the deck and bent low to look. Strange tattoos completely covered the man's face and neck.

Rabbus said, "He must have swum from shore, climbed the kedging anchor line. He knew where my key would be. John, there's an informer on this ship."

John flipped up the enemy's loincloth. Underneath, coiled around his waist, a sealed oilcloth pouch—flint, fuses, and powder.

Rabbus said, "If I'd come even a minute later, he'd have blown our ship sky-high."

John said, "If the enemy hit *this* ship, why not all the other ships?"

They ran to the forecastle, leapt up the ladder. Watchmen echoed the warning, ship to ship.

Their warning was too late. A cascade of ships detonated one after another, all synchronized to within a minute. Brilliant bursts of fire and thunder cannonaded through patchy fog in day's dawning. Patches of reflected fire goldened the flat, silver sea.

The famed Illyrian navy, rank upon rank of nimble galleys, appeared as if on command. Their galleys sailed quietly, from the north and west, pinching the Roman armada between Illyrian forces on land and sea.

Liburnian ships stroked at ram-speed toward Rome's heavy warships, their metal-tipped rostrums aimed at each of Rome's vessels, right below the waterline.

The enemy's chant broke the silence. Their cadenced cries rolled across the dawn's mist, "Death to Rome! Death to their god of Hope!"

From Tiberius' protected southernmost anchorage, all was eerie, invisible—'til I blew the fog apart for a moment so he could see. Once I cleaved the mist, Tiberius saw his battle plan had not survived contact with the enemy. The ash from this loss would drift far, settle slowly.

Commander Sejanus signaled his corpsman. The junior officer shot three flares from *Augustia*'s bridge, signaling the emperor's retreat. The other nineteen ships shielded his exit, took his beating.

The emperor ripped the top of his tunic. He paced the bridge, wailing, "Neptune, Zeus, Mars. Give me back my ships, my sailors! Restore to me the pride of Rome!"

Jesus stood behind him, silent.

42
LEAH

The fog blew in once again from the south and swallowed *Augustia* whole. We pulled up both anchors, slipping away in the pea soup, away into southern waters distant from the battle to our north.

Now it was twilight. We'd sheltered in a hidden cove, bobbing about at anchor. Our figurehead on the prow, a smushed together Augusta-Tiberius, proclaimed dominion over whatever lay beyond. The sun slid below the sea, winking out. I stood with John, Jesus, and Claudia, facing west. We silently took in this Artist's palate. Crisp gold lines etched themselves sideways into sky's pink and scarlet backdrop.

Tiberius had dispatched a scouting party before sunset. Their mission? Join us with Gemellus' troops. Captain Pontii led the chosen twelve warriors. The emperor had gone down their line before they'd left. Each man, from Pontii to the two least experienced, Julius and Arylo, had saluted him with a fist slam to his chest and a bowed head. He intoned a prayer over the group, invoking blessing from Mars before the scouts stroked their rowboat away into the night.

John interrupted the silence with a throaty aside to his cousin. "Jesus, this is a *really* good time for us to head home. We could swim to shore and set off by foot. This Gentile war does *not* concern us. You have bigger fish to fry. Destiny calls."

Jesus gazed out over the calm waters. The light of a rising moon reflected two forests and two skies kissing at the shoreline. "Bigger fish than obeying Father's call? My mission is clear for this chapter of my life—salt truth and light into Rome's decaying carcass."

John's head drooped, disconsolate. He examined his sandals.

Claudia said, "John, look at Jesus and listen to him. Salt hangs on him like seaweed on rocks. He packs Light and guides the lost—an all-purpose virtue generator. He opens his mouth and out flops love wrapped in truth. If I tried this, I'd sound like an empty sack slapping myself stupid in a stiff wind. I say this despite him just comparing me and my ilk to a decaying carcass—which I did *not* appreciate."

About then, Rabbus and the emperor walked over. Tiberius said, "And what of traitors, Seer?"

Sweat sheened on Jesus' brow. He said, "Just now, in my last breath or two, Windy advised me. The man you want is Arylo."

Jesus diverted the conversation, praying loudly, "Father, thank you for shaping your character into Julius' conduct over unknown ground, with betrayal all around him. And, Father, please protect John on his special assignment."

I looked around for John, wanting to ask about his assignment, but he'd ghosted our gathering.

Sound of a soft sploosh. Like a body dropping into water.

43
WINDY

Pontii's scouts thinned out across the ridgeline, single file. An old-growth deciduous forest, dressed in fall colors, lay below them to their right. Razor-cut light hit tree branches under a heliotrope sky. Blood reds and oranges competed for which tree could most dazzle the eye. The shadowed, misting forest to their left, evergreen with a few kapoks, slumped sharply down the mountain's side, jagging to the sea over lichened knobs of limestone and sharp-edged karst. Smell of rotting leaves, earth, and moss filled the air.

Pontii scanned the horizon and his footing, looking up and down, left and right, looking for Gemellus and his forces. The scouts' leader had no idea how little remained of the Roman fleet or how many legions the Illyrians had brought to the battle.

He knew so little of what he didn't know.

The scouts crept into a denser forest of huisache, oak, flame acers, maples, and lindens. Coarse, curlicued bark, like gnarled ears, absorbed low snuffling and growls that drifted in the air. Sharp-thorned branches cut quiet hands when men pulled them aside, peering over the next outcropping. A crop of late forget-me-nots hogged most of the light, providing cover for poisonous white oleander and purple hellebore.

Pontii held a hand to his lips, signaling quiet. His men, evenly divided into archers, slingers, and swordsmen, moved whisper-quiet. They didn't wake even the sleeping owl high in a branch of yellow-leafed linden.

Pontii's men crept deeper in these woods so filled with eerie disquiet and felt forces at work. This magic was *way* beyond what they could hope or imagine.[38] Julius was not finding this enchanted forest to his liking. His jokester-self was as quiet in absence as he'd been noisy in presence.

No one of these Romans knew Arylo was Bato's cousin, twice removed. He also was a child prisoner of war, brought up in Rome. He guarded his heart so well that his head rarely caught wind of his chest.

He'd kept in touch with Bato over the years through slippery meetings with shadowy intermediaries. Most recently, he'd passed coded messages to spies on the shore—a furtive candlelight sequence back of a cupped hand, short and long light-blinks. Arylo was a secret agent in a haunted wood, hunting for home.

Pontii had warned his men of Bato's tricks. During one break earlier in the day, Pontii said, "Tiberius may be a fox of many tricks. But Bato is a hedgehog with just one trick—disappearing in plain sight."

Ayrlo stifled a raucous laugh at his boss's cleverness. His laughter morphed into coughing that triggered an asthma attack. Arylo counseled himself between hacking fits. *Trust Cousin Bato. Hope in fiery Enji, the god of our youth. He will flame our enemies!*

Julius hissed, "Ayrlo, stop retching! You're going to blow our cover."

Julius' hearing verged on otherworldly. Even so, when Arylo quieted down, he heard nothing but the faint tapping of a woodpecker and wind listing through the treetops. He felt taut as a deer might feel, listening for the twang of a hunter's bow.

A harsh voice rang out, "Drop your weapons, now, or you be dead men."

Warriors had populated the woods. Moments before, these same warriors had appeared as trees. One Roman swordsman, Bentius, the fourth man in front of Ayrlo, drew his blade in a panic, head swiveling left to right. A hurling-ax, thrown from nowhere visible, appeared in a blur and buried itself in Bentius' chest. He fell facedown in a patch of oleander.

The voice rasped another command, "Drop to yer knees, hands behind heads."

Straightway, Julius dropped down. His two knees, however, had unhappy groundings—a two-inch thorn impaled his right knee, and a sliver of old, blue lava rock bit into his left knee. Julius stifled a scream.

Jesus' face flashed in Julius' mind's eye. He prayed, *God-man, hear me. You said you'd save everything human. Now, save me.*

Ayrlo puffed his way over to Bato. "Cousin, I've delivered my charges as promised. Indeed, I delivered the whole fleet."

He glanced up, eyes sparkling with the hope of glory.

Bato barked, "You were the loudest of all, you sniveling wheeze-bag. You and your kind shame all Illyria!"

Ayrlo collapsed, hung his head low, hands clutching his throat, trying to stretch open that traitorous tunnel. Sputum foamed his black, matted chest.

Bato was disgusted. He towered over his cousin, hands on hips. He offered Arylo a vicious kick—stop being such a spectacle!

Ayrlo's face purpled, even as Bato's face twisted with hatred for all-things-weak. Before he knew it, Bato's flashing sword removed Ayrlo's head. The severed head rolled face up after one full rotation on the forest's floor, caught by his hair in the roots of a tree. His surprised head set at a tilt with a clear view of his surroundings. He stared hard out of his draining skull, mouth open. Head saw body twitching next to him, gushing blood from his neck. His last look in this world was up and out at his cousin, Bato.

Bato didn't see that look; instead, he glared at his sword. "Darling, you did it again, without consulting me!" He sheathed her and shouted orders for the living Romans to bury the dead. Both bodies were laid side by side, dressed in nothing more than the survivors' memories.

Bato ordered his prisoners, "Take off everything that don't grow. Leave yer clothes and shoes in a pile. Take one step back; stand at attention!" They all stood there, stark naked. The victors gleefully divided the clothes and boots as spoils of war—shirts, leather tunics, shoes, and weapons all found new homes.

Bato watched from the shade of a whispering oak. He examined the survivors with his close eye. His far-sighted eye fixed on the anchored ship, down in the bay. He spoke no further word to any of them—including his old classmate, Pontii.

Everyone marched all day. The Romans' feet soon became swollen and pierced in many places, courtesy of thorny bracken hidden beneath red and yellow leafed mulch.

Julius was the last man in their ragged line. The joy of wargames was only a dying memory now. The proud stories of violence, battles fought and won, stories he'd thought to tell his bride at summer's end, were now telling him. He wanted healthy; I wanted holy. Together, he and I were busy composing a life for his good and Father's glory.

At day's end, they all arrived at the enemy camp—thousands of empty pup tents across a parade ground. A few sentries lashed the prisoners together inside a stockade. Julius felt as substantial as a laurel leaf clinging to a branch in a storm gale.

Imprisonment. Day one.

44
SLOW

I was one of two children in Laz's arms—the dazed, hopeless one. Gritty Hope was the other child. I laid my hand on the man's face, running it over his beard. Words trickled out of my mouth. "I know you. You're Laz. We're married, aren't we? I was gone for a while after that snake, Herod, knew me."

He flinched. I pushed back from him, held him at arm's length. His skin went from white to blood-red—from neck to tip-top of head. His fingers twitched.

His anger surfaced my own. A seething fire ripped through me like wind through wheat, stoked by rage. Flash fantasy, *Herod, impaled on a stake.*

Cutter dreams, the me most burnt by rage. I mostly gave Cutter no voice, but she had her imagination. It was all I could do to keep a grip on her knife. She intoned, *I dribble your rage outta you, one eyelash at a time, one red line on your arm after another. Without me, you'd explode. You'd think you're a bright-haired, basement woman— kind, lovely, and helpless. Then, one fine day, boom!*

Laz said, "Fine protector I was. I was tricked into sorting rubble in front of me while a plague swept through the backdoor."

Hope looked at both of us, frantic eyes swiveling back and forth. She burst into tears, sniffled, hiccupped, "Which one was I? Rubble or plague?"

She turned to leave.

I pulled her back to me. Looked at her eye to eye. "What you see are good people at their worst. We clean up good. Our son, Mike, needs a big sister."

Hope stared at me as I spoke. She gulped my words like whirlpools suction seawater.

Joanna peeked around our half-open door. I was a half-baked pot in an oven, peeking out at a potter peeking in, dribbling glazes of fear-orange, black-dread, and red-shame.

Joanna said, "All done, Slow. Safe for now."

She barked out another of her guttural laughs. "I walked through the women's warren—all those jangling bracelets in the basement. Word was, 'King reaped a small field and was *not* impressed.'"

Joanna kept talking. "And during this morning's business meeting, Herod told Chuzo he didn't like yesterday's adventures in romper room. He said to get rid of the baby pretending to be a grownup. Send her packing back to Jericho."

Harlot's face burned. She hadn't been good enough. The rest of us felt glad. Fragile had her place. She'd rescued us from more abuse.

I turned to the child in my lap. At that moment, a ray of sun filtered over Hope, lighting her up, like gold dust had fallen from heaven, and given her a good once-over.

She said, "My abba said dogs lick you when you feed them, but devils bite you." I didn't care if I were dog or devil. Either one could help Cutter work on Herod.

Hope ruined my sweet revenge. "Then Abba said, 'Angels give back good when given bad.'"

She pulled a crumpled violet from her pocket and held it up to me. The crushed flower gave off a sweet fragrance. She said, "This was under that big stone with me, the stone that killed Abba and Ma. Let's leave it when we go. Mr. King might find it."

45
WINDY

It was an easy swim. Mostly John side-stroked toward shore and then crawled over weedy rocks onto the beach. He had belted supplies around his waist under his camel skin tunic. He wanted to be on a different track than those scouts, a path that took him home to Israel. He headed south and east. Walked about a half-mile. But then, against his will, I stopped his feet from moving. He stared at them, wondering. I headed him back the other way, and he followed my lead. The scouting party was ahead of him, barely in sight. If he'd waited much longer, he would have lost them.

Once the scouts settled down to rest that night, he whispered up a giant fig tree with bright, glossy leaves that gleamed in the moonlight. He found a notch in the branches and prayed, *Spirit, fill me, like Jesus.*

I blew his way, cooled his brow. He heard my voice but didn't know what to make of my words when I said, *who do you think moved your feet? The One who breathes you every minute of your life.*

He tucked himself inside his bedroll and slept.

When the sun rose, the legionnaires started north once again. John waited and watched. Shadows rose from the ground. He couldn't discern if they were spirits or men. These beings materialized out of thin air and followed the scouts, before, behind, and around them on all sides. Silent, invisible.

These shadow-warriors sprung their surprise in late morning. Bentius went down, ax in his chest. Bato chopped Arylo's head off.

John muttered to himself, *who is that man? He seems more demon than person.*

I answered, matter of fact, *that's Bato, inhabited by Enji and his brood of demons.*

He said, *Windy? You're speaking directly to me now?*

I replied, *you asked me to fill you.*

He said, kind of surprised, *huh. You listen and respond to me? We travel together now, like you do with Jesus?*

I threw down this body memory, one he'd long forgotten, *you don't remember leaping for joy in your mother's womb when Mary, newly pregnant with Jesus, walked into the room. Even then, I quickened you to recognize Jesus.39 I'm still with you.*

He replied, *I know me. I'll forget you're in me or confuse you with my thoughts. My ancestors did that all the time. Promised not to forget, and then ignored You. I'm an ordinary person, Windy, forgetful.*

His attention re-focused on what was happening below him, and he promptly forgot me. The Illyrians had stripped the Romans and all the men, captured and captors, set out along the ridge. They aimed themselves toward a yet higher ridge that reminded John very much of a sleeping dragon's head.

I whispered in John's ear, *follow. I'll shield you from their ears and eyes.*

He slipped from one tree to another, picking his way through the decaying leaves of yellow and orange as well as vermillion, the purplish color of fresh liver. I fingered the musk of something stinky through his nose.

John, see these demon spirits? They've shaped themselves to look like bear, leopard, and lion. They pad all around you, voracious.

I did smell something, Windy, but I thought it was me. I'm pretty rank.

I brought him up short. *When you don't know what's going on—inquire! It's only been a few minutes since I reminded you to constantly check with me.*

Sorry.

We kept moving. Captors and captured, John and me, demon beasts at a distance, traveling apart and yet together, quietly. We arrived late in the day. A sea of empty tents on an open plain surrounded a central stockade. The chained prisoners were shoved inside the stockade.

Half-dozen ant mounds set on raised platforms, in a half-circle. These mounds of ants, like tiny priests on altars, swarmed in front of the stockade's entrance. An eternal flame of sorts burned in the center of this half-circle.

John perched high in a flame tree along the side of Sleeping Dragon Woods. He could see the bay east of here where the Illyrian navy had finished their work. Rome's proud armada cindered toward the waterline. The ships that remained were few—charred, black slippers, half-masts, weak chimneys, altars to defeat.

John listed in the breeze and listened to me. I rocked him in the treetop and didn't waste my words. I caused a deep sleep to fall on my servant. He'd need the rest.

After some days, I woke him. His outer world narrowed to the fragrance of the tree leaves, the ambit of his eyes, the touch of his fingertips on rough bark. Sun inched across the sky, time and again. His stomach shrank, and his spirit was enlarged.

Even so, he was overcome by a fit of righteous indignation. *Windy, I can't bear to watch that vile Roman whore seduce Jesus. Does he really think this is how Messiah should act?*

Jesus is in my care, not yours. He's like you, busy learning from me who he is and who he isn't. And John, remember that your violent thoughts toward my child, Claudia, are the same as murderous deeds.[40]

But you can't approve of what's going on between him and that hideous woman, can you?

My laughter rang in the wind.

Are you laughing at me, Windy?

Remember Jesus' words not so long ago. Father creates and judges. I comfort and convict. Jesus loves. Are you greater than your cousin?

Well, that shut him up. He cut a few branches with his hatchet, shaped them with his knife. Let the crumbled shavings of violence become his new bedding. He slept again on the bed he and I had made.

46
JOHN

It was the sixth day.[41] The parade ground gradually filled with soldiers who massed into formation before Bato. He paced before them, showering sparks off his dagger, the one he called Precious. He twirled it horizontally, with one hand, shoulder high. He shushed his furiously rattling sword, a sheathed *sica*. "Darling, quiet. Your time will come."

A leashed bear waddled behind him.

Bato addressed his army, poured smiling-laughter-syrup all over them. The army reveled in his praise. They returned the praise when he was done—names of god and leader twined together, resounding, thumping, stomping, a repetitive crescendo, "Enji-Bato! Bato-Enji!"

Bato dismissed them to their tents after he'd eaten his fill of adoration. He rested in the shade of a red kapok. His chef whetted his appetite with meat morsels off a sizzling spit, meat he washed down with blood-red wine from a silver chalice.

An hour passed. Napping Bato awakened with a start and looked at what his back-kitchen chef had cooked up for him—four lines of white powder, laid out on a smooth, polished stump in front of him. Bato got on his knees and bowed his head, as if in prayer. He then walked his nose through one line after the other, like a hog snuffling down slop.

Once refreshed from whatever *that* was, Bato put on his armor. A bronze helmet with a crested purple plume swooped down to his chin, covering both sides of his impossibly long face. His flashing smile and jutting jaw set off his metal teeth. A bronze torque of snakes writhed around his neck on both sides of his throat. Their mouths were open, fangs exposed. Leather straps and metal buckles fastened bronze breastplate and greaves. Bear teeth and claws etched his armor.

Bato pranced around the parade ground, still conversing with both *sica* and dagger. Darling rattled for release from her scabbard. Precious flashed in the sun.

His voice was crisp. "Precious, let's see what food you can fetch today for daddy."

Bato's underlings had staked out Pontii. They'd conversed, Bato and Pontii, but in low tones I couldn't hear. Abruptly, Bato bent over the captain, hands quick, slicing skin off Pontii's front, shoving strips of flesh in his mouth. He flipped tidbits to his bear. The bear slathered wildly, turned in circles, standing and dancing for his next hand-out. After some time and more than a few Pontii scraps, Bato said, "No more for now, Sperm. Rome must feed my followers." [42]

Bato staked out Julius next, dangling strips of Pontii's flank before him. "Nothing to eat for six days and nights, soldier? A bit peckish, are you? Case of the rumbly tums?"

Julius was silent.

Bato continued, "And Julius, son of Egypt's past Prefect, you do know that you and my old classmate are merely appetizers? The main course, of course, is Jesus. That's the name he uses here in this world—or so say my spirit guides. Other worlds, other names. My guides are rarely wrong. They've heard him say, both here and in other worlds, 'Eat my body and drink my blood or I'll have nothing to do with you."

He put a pious look on his face. "And who are we to disobey such a god?" [43]

Julius turned his head and vomited.

Bato said, "*My, my.* Julius' puke on big, bad Bato's boots? Bad form, I'd say. Have a little lick, Spittle. Use your own tongue, or I'll cut it out and have another wipe my boots with it."

Julius licked up his vomit. Pled for mercy, promised cooperation.

Bato brayed, "Violence *is* more than ideas in a classroom, cadet. Think you can fool me into eating your empty words and think they will strengthen me? Let's not fool ourselves. Your big ideas are not yet digested."

He laughed. "You're no different than the rest of his followers. Jesus is far more food for thought than what you can stomach. But no matter.

Speak, Meat. Tell me what Jesus fears. Where are the tiny cracks in his surety? Feed me knowledge or feed me flesh. Your choice."

Julius kept his mouth ratcheted shut. As a reward, Bato flayed his chest, thighs, and arms—like he'd done to Pontii. He hand-fed Julius to his captains. Julius howled and barked obscenities, point and counterpoint, under the baking sun.

Bato glanced over his shoulder at him. "So annoying when food talks back to you."

He stuffed a rag in Julius's mouth and as he walked away, he said, "I forgot. Don't want to be inhospitable. Segorias, bring a wee bucket of our priests over here. They mustn't miss their chance to visit with Rome. One bitty bucket for each man."

The officer put on protective leather vestments, head to toe. He climbed one of the six altars and scooped up two buckets of army ants, one in either hand. He climbed down, careful not to spill on his fellow captains who lined the pathway. He walked to the two flayed men, dumped one pail on each man's chest. Black-jawed saw blades ground meat to meal.

I said, *Windy, I've admitted my violent thought and asked forgiveness. But, even so, could I turn into Bato?*

Windy replied, *all humans are murderers, guilty and proud like Bato of angry thoughts. But you, John, you're on a course of repentance and renewal—not sliding down, and down again, from man to beast, like Bato.*

Windy, will violence eat us all alive?

He said, *Choose the meaning you put on meanness, John. But this is what I'd suggest. If you choose violence today, violence will choose you tomorrow.*

47

WINDY

A curious swarm of creatures marched from within high, iron gates built into the bowels of Dragon Ridge. These armored soldiers and their beasts marched in cadence—full step forward, half-step back, a little shoulder shimmy, then another full step forward. Tambourines and drums called cadence. Rumblings and icy blue steam trailed after them from within those dark gates.

Their chieftain, Drusilla, was a button of a woman, with blue-white hair and almost see-through, glossy skin. This elfin queen was dressed in an ice-blue gown and rested on a pelt of blue fox. She was possessed of a regal haughtiness that dimmed any who merely preened, like a rare blue moon might dim a common constellation.

A pointed horn, the color of sapphires, grew out the back of her head. This horn of power arched up and over her head, its exposed point glistening. Her coiled hair was coiffed neat as a hummingbird's nest—all tucked in, not a hair out of place. Contrary winds switched the tail of her dress back and forth.

John asked me, *Windy, is this living thing human or demon?*

Watch and learn, John. Drusilla is a hollowed human, so long inhabited by Satan that each is unbounded. One flows into the other. Human and demon parts take turns streaming each another. See how she perches on her custom throne carved so precisely; how she leans forward, knees together, feet paired and touching, slippers resting on her ice-carved dais.

Drusilla's throne was a mosaic of blue jewels hewn from within her ice-mountain—deep azure sapphires, meridian blue topaz, light blue diamonds, and sky-blue aquamarine. These shimmering blues blended in dazzling reflections of light. Beams of crystalized blue light emerged from within these jewels.

John, don't look at those beams for long. They'll scorch the back of your eyes.

Ack! Looked too long. Eyes hurt now.

Look and listen to Me, not her. Mind my heart or list her way and adopt her world view, bit by bit.

Drusilla's mobile dais, a seven-sided ice carving, stretched ten feet across and four feet thick. Bleached skulls, each wearing a diamond diadem, set on spikes anchored midway along each of the seven sides. Blue flames of icy fire trailed from the skulls' eye sockets. Steam drifted out their mouths and trickled down the spikes.

Six single-horned beasts, eight-foot-tall blue quadrupeds, each a ton or more in weight and yoked together in two rows, supported the queen's dais and throne. One single, larger beast led the other six and had three longer horns. These seven beasts carried the witchy queen's dais on rods between their rows—not unlike how the Ark of God had been carried on rods long ago. The beasts' horns were like curved spears of sheer ivory, iridescent silver-blue. The beasts' open jaws were crowded with grinding teeth that dripped a steady drizzle of royal blue blood.[44]

John said, *they all show signs of a true-blue mood. Their eyes, huge but hollow.*

Excellent intuition, John. Your feeling self is warming up, even in such a cold climate.

Pale blue mist swirled in tendrils around Drusilla's body, like smoke coming off an unholy altar. She settled herself outside the mountain's gates. Claimed eminent domain by sheer force of presence.

Bato cut a swath through her surrounding guards, holding his head high.

Drusilla cried out in a voice that belied her diminutive self, "Hail, Bato! United, we conquer!"

Bato bowed stiffly. "Dru, you're putting on quite a show today with your new incarnation. Quite a get-up. Always a pleasant friction when we're together, *neh*?"

Her icy look enveloped him. A blast of arctic air. "What information do you bring of this new god's weak underbelly, Bato-boy?"

Bato harrumphed. "Fine talk from one who's not fought a fair fight in all her days."

"If I'm in a fair fight, obviously I've failed to plan. But that's never happened. Besides, what do *you* know of blue-blood matters? I care not for their emperor or the disgusting red ooze of your raw-meat legions. This novel god from eastern shores is far too shiny. One who speaks with his authority could convert millions!"

Bato laughed. "That rack of lamb will hardly feed me, much less my captains."

"Bato, mark my words. This one is dangerous. A serious competitor. We must chain him for a thousand years."

Drusilla dabbed at her pixie nose with a blue lace hanky. She commanded, "All eyes on this Jesus, flesh-eater. Set your demons loose. Excavate, expose, exploit any found weaknesses. Other gods like yours from the south are laughable—like being chained behind a farting camel on a caravan to nowhere."

She covered her mouth, yawned.

Bato strode over to her dais, roughly shoving past the lead horned creature. The blue beast bent to examine him. Like he was a piece of straw. She tossed her head and stuck one of her three horns in his butt as he passed. He whipped Darling out of his scabbard and slashed upwards toward the beast's neck. The mastodon, with a flick of her horn, sent Darling flying into the dirt where she flopped around, lively as a rooster with a fresh wrung neck.

Blue beast and Bato faced each other. He eyed her chunky knees. She looked down at Precious in his other hand, inquiring with a look if he wished to be totally un-manned.

Bato refused to look up. Instead, he sheathed Precious and muttered to the blue beast, "You're for the stewpot, carcass."

Beast chewed her cud, burped up a choice wad of disgust, half-digested. Squirted a direct hit on Bato's head.

He's a spark away from combusting, Windy.

Indeed. Short-fused and proud. But wait. See what happens in this house divided.

Bato's southern warriors, over two thousand, had fanned out around Drusilla's hundred palace guards and seven horned beasts. Her blue Druid flags were lost in Bato's brilliant reds and oranges. Bato's warriors stomped out a victory song, shaking the very ground beneath them.

Drusilla surveyed the swarm from her elevated ice platform.

Bato mounted a mass of his soldiers. They knelt on hands and knees and hoisted him on their shoulders. Together, they formed a platform of swaying flesh that matched the height of Drusilla's dais. He positioned himself directly across from her for a face-to-face summit talk. Signaled for quiet.

John, watch their noses tipping this way and that, sniffing out hidden intention.

Bato barked, "Dru, what of Gemellus' four legions? Your job was to contain and crush them."

Drusilla answered tangentially, "*Me* contain them, for *you*, Enji spawn? Why corral such drivel for a vomitous voluptuary gone bad?"

Bato blew out chunks of uncontainable fury, a blow torch of impotence jacked up by his white power powder. "I crush the weak, Witch."

Drusilla said, "Anthropophagus, you prove my point. Murder's in your mind, and it's hardly original. Cain beat you to it."

Bato spat, "Strength trumps fancy words." Bits of Julius-puke still adorned both his boots, but he refused to see what was beneath him.

Bato brayed, "We searched and stripped each Roman ship before we fed their sailors to our priests. Your high-sounding voice cabbage—not worth a fart. No food of merit in the Roman scouts either. All gristle and gluey, undone fillings in my cooks' pot pies."

Drusilla said, "Bloody to the core."

Bato squared his shoulders, as confident as thousands surrounding hundreds could be.

Drusilla's smile was faint, vague. Her nostrils flared slightly. "I sniff the stench of your effluent. Such stench usually flows from sewers, but perhaps your snout can't sniff out what's going on here? Ah, but back to business. You may now bow, Bato—like you do for your nose-feed. Humble yourself, and I might drop a pearl of wisdom in your open mouth."

Bato remained stony, erect, immobile. The crack in their alliance fissured further. Hell peeked out of it.

The ice queen smirked. She moved her feet apart a tiny twitch, leaned forward, elbows resting on her knees.

"No obeisance? Well then, you're choosing another course."

Bato yelled, "Men, take her down! Drag her and the Blue Bells to Enji's altars."

Drusilla used her scepter to slip the top of an incense pot to one side. Pressured fragrance of blended simples poured forth. She pronounced an incantation.

Bato morphed into a hedgehog. First, he lost his balance and fell on all fours, crashing between the men who'd been his pillars. His followers moved back, allowing him space, faces aghast. He needed every bit of the space, for as soon as he hit ground, he expanded sideways, bursting his armor. His skin grew bristles, and he began to bray. The deeper donkey bray gradually transformed into a higher-pitched hog squeal.

While still in the act of squealing, his hands and feet turned cloven. His helmet popped off; nose flattened into a snout. Gimlet eyes grew pink, crazed.

He stared at Dru, frantic. But how to stop a meat-ax in mid-air? The words had already left her lips. He spun in tight circles; became his own horror show. Sounds tumbled out of his snout, igniting as they went, setting his tail on fire. Bato augured into a shallow pit of his own making.

Bato's mighty men followed their leader's path in death as well as life. His soldiers, from captains to privates, morphed into hedgehogs. Each, uncontainable, popped out of old armor and swirled on brand new split-trotters. Many held their new hoofs in front of gimlet eyes, staring at what had become of their bodies.

In the normal way of life and death, one's final scream or whimper includes all the nights and days that led to it. Each nip and bite of sarcasm or shame, each mindless day of grazing on family with excess or absence. And then, in a moment, murmurs crescendo into heart attack. Shell of isolation bursts into stroke. Living bodies become dead meat.

Thus began a chorus of wailing screams one hears only in a slaughter yard. Beards of newborn hedgehogs bapped up and down beneath snouts. Shock spilled through razor-sharp teeth. The terrible song of demons rang across the mountains and valleys.

Drusilla cackled loudly and vaguely pointed toward the cliff with her regent's staff. Bato and the Hogs began an unthinking, impulse-riddled, death-dash-dance toward cliff's edge. The ground thundered as they plowed through the ant mounds, trampling Sperm-the-Bear and all the tents. They scattered and crushed, galloping unbridled to their peculiar ending.

In less than a minute, thousands of hogs had pitched 500 feet down into the sea, tumbling snout over hoof. The old saying had been true, after all—hedgehogs have one main trick, they disappear in plain sight.

After Bato and the Hogs had danced to their death, flattened tents and hoof prints were all that remained. The lead quadruped, Mildew, turned her sad, blue eyes to Drusilla. *What next?*

Drusilla motioned for Mildew to lead the others beneath the towering kapok tree. She rested on her throne in the center of that shade before daintily stepping down from her dais.

The tiny blue queen looked up through the dense foliage. She said, "You can come down now, John."

48

JESUS

A*ugustia* bobbed between her two anchor lines in our hidden bay. Tiberius, Sejanus, Claudia, and I quietly watched dusk thicken from pale to burnt orange. After the sun disappeared in a low-hanging cloud bank, we entered the emperor's cabin. We all collapsed in rickety chairs around a table splotched red and white with candle wax. A single, unmade bed in the corner was laden with layers of dirty wash. A fine, adolescent cabin desperately trying to look adult.

A maître d' served us our evening meal. We washed down a dinner of ox tongue and aged cheese with red wine and wandering conversation, all the while skating carefully on the thin ice of good manners. Tiberius cut his tongue to slivers with a jeweled dagger. He wore his face seriously, eyebrows glowering over recessed, button-black eyes. Cracked fingernails were mooned black with dirt.

After supper, Claudia handed me a glass of port from the emperor's imperial cask. I pulled my chair to the porthole and gazed across the riffling waves. A smoky, full flavor hit all the spots on my tongue—sweet, bitter, tangy. Being human had its moments.

Windy said, *best not to settle into the appetites of royalty.*

I answered, *it is nice to sit back, put my feet up.*

The emperor broke into my interior chat. "Haven't seen your weird friend lately. What's his name? You know, that fragrant fellow."

I said, "Father's Spirit appointed John as night watchman for your lost sortie."[45]

Tiberius queried Sejanus, "Millions of sestertii sunk along this stinking coastline. Why waste good money pursuing bad people? I'm of a mind to sail for Capri."

Windy, he's like Herod. Counts his money and ignores people.

Windy blew a deep breath into my chest, calming my frets.

Claudia segued into the conversation. "Uncle, why betray Gemellus? He's your successor."

Tiberius answered, "Ah, he'll be okay. He'll regroup his forces inside Scodra's city walls."

Windy poked me right under my ribs. *The emperor must find his scouts and John. They need you.*

I said, "Emperor, pardon me. Father advises a different course. We're to save you, your scouts, and John from the folly of a fatal independence."

Claudia eyed me. "John wanted you to rescue him. That's why he left."

I repeated some of her words back to her, "Yes, I *am* on a rescue mission."

I was like Abba when he was daydreaming. He could repeat Ma's words exactly, but his head was elsewhere. Sometimes I couldn't listen to Windy and deal with people. This was one of those times.

Windy's voice boomed in my inner ear. *Tell Tiberius to turn this tub around. Go back to where he was hurt. He will only find himself, his true self, at the point of his pain.*

I repeated Father's words, given through Windy.

He sipped his drink. "Why should I listen to '*Father's* words?"

"Sire, you trained your few legions not to question why—only do and die. Should the Emperor of the Universe have lesser rules than you?"

Tiberius' face scrunched up. He looked mad. Spewed a few words. I didn't hear them. I was listening to Windy.

The bay is a graveyard—sailors, ants, and hogs are there. Begin there and climb out of that grave. The Blue Queen awaits. She has John. Go.

I mused aloud to Windy. "The path begins with an underwater cemetery? And who's the Blue Queen?"

The emperor said, "Jesus, what *are* you raving about?"

Huh, gas came from Tiberius' mouth. I think it was attached to words.

Windy said, *you need practice in cheating the grave. And don't forget. That egg-eating snake wants to swallow you whole before your true ministry begins.*

I muttered aloud, "I'll do what you say. But on my way, could you tell me what to do about this snake who thinks I'm still an egg?"

I glanced up. Claudia looked puzzled. Sejanus placed his hands on the table and levered himself up, like an obelisk being pulleyed into the air. He left the cabin, scratching his head.

Windy kept warning me. I relayed her words to Tiberius. "We have to go back to the Bay of Defeat. These waters are now full of dead hogs, army ants, and sunken ships with the bodies of your Roman sailors still on board."

Tiberius stared my way. "It's your *mind*, Seer, where bones are scattered and snakes lurk. Besides, I like my graveyards tidy. I want each soul labeled in a box with a marble crypt around it. I hate it when the dead wander in open water."

I said, "Emperor, perhaps it's time to switch."

He lifted his eyebrows, querying.

"Switch from *futile* power over the dead to actual power in life—honor the dead, but love the living."

He scratched his chin. "Perhaps a few angels are on the loose and can't be penned in."

Claudia nodded, "Yes, Uncle, the angels. Don't forget the angels."

All this outer conversation subsided into brain fuzz. Windy kept talking. *I'll not tell*

you now about how to handle the ol' serpent. Not yet—that hour is still coming. Father will always be clear. His mouth to your ear through my breath.

I replied aloud once again to Windy. "I'll not say no to Him. He's my goal and purpose."

Tiberius looked at Claudia and said, "See, he admits it. He conspires with John."

I half-heard Tiberius. "What are you saying? We are One."

Claudia rolled her eyes, "Excuse me, Uncle, while I relocate him. Jesus, earth is calling."

She looked at Tiberius. "Uncle, the boundary between this world and the next is very thin for Jesus. You and I define reality in much the same way—then we congratulate ourselves on being sane. Jesus has never quite agreed. He's into air travel; gets lost in cracks between worlds."

She turned to me. "God-man, come to me!" She took my face in her hands, blue eyes clear and lucid, two inches from mine. "I'll follow you anywhere, Jesus, but you take these zingy trips all the time. Next time you leave, I want to go with you."

I muttered aloud to Windy, "Okay if she goes? This could be a death trip."

Windy said, *no problem. Train her further. I'll protect you.*

Claudia said, "Death doesn't attract me. But if death does come, can we die together?"

I looked at Claudia, "The die *has* been cast. My path is dangerous, steep, and narrow. Are you all right with that?"

She smiled at me, palms up and open, head nodding.

Tiberius looked sternly at Claudia. "There's a thin line between thinking you're a god and actually being one. And you know the odds on that score."

I humbled myself before Tiberius; took a knee. "Return to the place where you were wounded, Sire. The path to maturity always takes you through the Thresher."

Tiberius stared out the porthole. His eyebrows seemed to wander, aiming toward each other but missing in the middle.

"Sire, ignore my words at your own peril. This ship will sink, just like your armada, if you ignore me."

Claudia said, "Uncle, he does this all the time. Slips out a prophecy or two in a serving dish. Wants to see if you'll sample his wares."

"Generous to a fault, Claudia, but doubtful. Feast on army ants in a Bay of Pigs? You're a girl crammed full of hormones and will believe anything he says—stupid stuff, crazed ramblings."

The emperor appeared to make up his mind. He turned to me. "Jesus, lay down. It wouldn't be right to leave you here with the enemy—a man like you with a fevered mind. I'm more righteous than that. We'll take you home for modern medical care. They can put leeches on you; bleed black humors from your mind. Meanwhile, Hippo will give you calming herbs."

Claudia said, "Uncle, a memory came to mind. I fell into the sea off a cliff while on Trimerus. I swam the way I thought best, straight for shore and safety. Ocean's currents were way bigger than me. They took me another way."

Tiberius replied, "Interesting daydream. What does this have to do with me?"

He stomped out the cabin's door and yelled in his emperor voice, "Sejanus, anchors aweigh! We sail for Capri!"

49
SLOW

The pockmarked moon was halved. Cloud wisp whittled that half down to a silver sliver. "Hey," I said, looking at God's sky jewelry, "I know how you feel. Heat's gone elsewhere, and look at what's left of us." The moon said not a word.

Laz and Hope and I rattled toward Jericho, a few miles northeast from Herod's palace, and mostly downhill. A skip 'n slide full of shadows in this part of our journey. Laz left his whip in its stand beside his left knee and settled for clucking and churring instead of slapping leather on Goodness's back.

Our placid mule whinnied contentedly. She had no need to speak about what wasn't on her mind. She wasn't worried about Crispus lurking in wait. Wasn't replaying the past. Wasn't rehearsing the future. Instead, she ate from her feed bag, breathed the same air as me, and walked the same earth, grounded and grateful. I felt jealous of this mule, envied her contentment while I held onto the buckboard, trying to slow my sense of free fall.

Escape fell off the wagon and lay in a curl by the roadside. I watched her in my mind's eye and felt littler with her loss. Missing people was a full-time job. Mother, Father, Leah, Jesus, most of my-me's. Moody mourning was like breaking rocks with a hammer. But if I worked at it hard enough, maybe a memory would come into focus. Maybe I'd feel more substantial than moonlight over mist.

Inside, I cast a long eye toward Escape, back to where she'd ditched the rest of us. I gentled her back into my arms, the same arms that steadied our miracle child, Hope, born from the rubble. I'd put her in my long nightie for our night journey. She napped, snugged between her new parents, legs hidden in a twist of white cotton fishtail.

A jounce from the rutted road awoke her. She jumped up and down, pointing out the lights of Herodium behind us and Jericho in front of us; bounced about, shivering with excitement, a living Hope.

I sucked some liveliness from her and felt only a little guilty, stealing her joy. She seemed to have extra. I took a piece of pleasure from her light green eyes, eyes the color of celery in springtime. Her hugs also soothed me, though for the most part, I was haggard as a beggar, with a sack of pulp for a brain.

Inside, Cutter mused on how to get back at Herod. She made me the point of her anger since Herod wasn't available.

I advised, *foolish thoughts, Cutter. Collect calm instead.*

Cutter ignored me, her will strong and sharp as a bone saw. *If I can't get to Herod, I'll*

take whoever's available. Like you. She surfaced, floated a hand up, and picked me like a lock. An eyelash floated down in front of me. She said, "Don't mess with me, Slow. I've got pluck."

Harlot said, *even professionals like me get brittle if beaten too hard, too long. Pay attention to Bruise. She's gathering herself in patches on your backside.*

I replied, *No thanks to you, Harlot. You floated away, out a window, when I'd asked you to handle the king.*

Harlot was quiet, silent as the stars. Then she said, *I couldn't stay, not for that hateful man. Besides, Escape needed adult supervision.*

So, only Fragile and Bruise had the guts to stay for the rape?

Shame filled in for Harlot. She replied, *and where were you, High 'n Mighty?*

A warm wash came over me, and I hid my face from me.

A sudden image of Jesus. Little spikes of light came out of his body, as if white-hot fire, or bits of starlight, were shooting out of him all over.

Windy's voice, *we didn't leave you alone. Jesus came for us. He suffered with you.*

I whispered words into the air, words I didn't know I knew, "God, keep Jesus sane, even when others cram doubt and hate into him."

Laz overheard me. "His own brothers think Jesus is nuts most of the time, especially James. Is that what you had in mind just now, Slow?"

"I don't know why I'm praying this, God. Maybe faith mixes with my garbage. Dunno. But I'm telling you, God, so you'll remember, Jesus is the best person you *ever* made. Keep him on track, doing your stuff for you."

Our new daughter looked up at Laz and then at me. Her face shone bright with belief, even in the dark, even though she knew not the man I spoke of.

Her touch, her word, comforted my-me's, particularly my little ones—Bruise, Escape, and Fragile. All of them, about Hope's size. Cutter was more muscly, older. And Shame refused comfort; instead, she sat alone, disconnected from the rest of us.

My many-me's, dark and light, full of certainty mixed with doubt, rolled down the hill with Laz and Hope. Moonlight poured to earth, lighting our path and coating us in silver.

50

JOHN

I heard her voice but didn't take it in. That tiny, blue-haired woman, colder than a month of Januarys, had spoken to me. I was above her. Invisible, right? I was *good* at disappearing.

While I was thinking these thoughts, she spoke to my tree. Something bright and streaky fell from her mouth and knocked my fig tree over. I got a glimpse of her on my way down, standing there with her finger out, pointing the tree away from her throne. A quirky smile stitched her face.

I used both hands to hang from my branch. I felt dazed and dopey, maybe eight feet off the ground over an earthen hollow. My tree's roots sizzled.

The blue witch walked around my hanging tree. She said, "There you are, hiding back of fig leaves! You sons of men! All wizened, burnt roots. But no matter, I'll send Mildew over. She *loves* men, but not as much as she used to."

The leading blue beast, the one who had horned Bato, slipped her traces without any human help. I realized in a lightning stroke—I was like her, unhooked, unattached.

Mildew positioned herself beneath me. Woefully looked me up and down with her huge brown eyes. Reminded me of a human in extended mourning. *Hmm. Windy, is there a human locked inside her, unable to speak or escape?*

Drusilla must have read my mind. "Milly was once a gabby princess possessed of too many words. Saturated in desire."

"What happened to her?"

Blue said, "I love beasts. Well, that's a bit excessive since my affection is without cloying kindness." She sighed, disabusing herself of anything remotely warm. "But beasts *do* take an edge off my contempt. People *are* problematic. They can speak. That's an immediate problem. For example, you. You have quite a mouth on you."

"You didn't tell me what happened to her. And I say what I'm supposed to say. No more, no less."

"Let's make that less. But about Milly? Cat got her tongue."

What?

Another sly smile. "*Meow.*"

"You do know who rules this small ball, Planet Blue, don't you, John? From way out there in the cool night sky, this speck of blue is quite beautiful—and oh so silent."

I set my feet on the beast's shoulders and lowered myself on her neck, complete with a horn to hold.

"You and your flapping tongue would be quite fetching in a camel cage. You wouldn't be nearly so bothersome as a camel."

"Got clothes, Blue?"

She rolled her eyes. "You do look silly, sitting there naked on Milly. Get down. Speak with me, but sparingly."

I jumped down, saw a loincloth with camel hair fringe at my feet. I put it on and stood my ground. Lifted my chin.

Acting confident isn't the key. Try dependence on Me.

Uh, forgot again, Windy. Sorry. My mind wanders in my wilderness, like Moses' crowd, post-Egypt.

Blue sat still on her throne in front of me, head tipped sideways, amused. She left shadows splashing all around, even at high noon.

Something's majorly out of whack. What's up, Windy?

She doesn't cast a shadow. She is a shadow, wrapped in illusion.

Drusilla handed me a platter of roasted locusts, smeared with honey, "Eat hearty, John—I know your dietary preferences and believe me, you need more roughage in your diet. For example, these blue-bell popsicles. They're more popular in the Mediterranean diet." She sucked on an icy blue stick with a flower sticking out the side.

"Keep smacking down all these fried locusts, and you'll start to swarm. No matter. We Druids believe in feeding our guests before we inquire of them."

"We Jews believe in compassion before inquisitions. Any soldier's woundwort, Gideon's balm, or pain powders in your bag of tricks? I know two men in desperate need of care. Once I take care of my friends, I'll speak with you."

"Brave words, beggar-cum-chooser. Dictating terms of engagement after what you've seen? What I did to those other men I could very well do to you."

I turned on my heel from her frigid air. She said nothing, did nothing.

I unlatched the gate and threw it wide open, examined the prisoners. Pontii and Julius were still alive, along with the rest of them.

I stood, wondering what to do, when a canvas shelter appeared over the men. Other items also appeared, loaded with flat-out spookiness—jars of cool water, platters of fresh fruit and meats, pots of ointment, and strips of bandages. Manacles fell off the prisoners' feet, invisibly. Real swirled inside the unreal, blurring the edges of both.

The conscious men began to gorge on cheeses and meats, fish and fruit, bowls of wine. They were wild-eyed, shoveling food in their faces with both hands, spilling wine down their naked chests.

I said, "Romans, make pigs of yourself, and Blue will too. Be men, not animals, or you'll soon be split-trotting over the cliff."

I looked over my shoulder, out past the stockade gate. Drusilla daintily filed her nails with a turquoise icicle rasp. Her image shimmered in ice-shade. One of her creatures fanned her with a long-handled leafy vane made of royal blue peacock feathers.

Another attendant, decked out like a Pharisee in dreadlocks, tallits, phylacteries, and an indigo-blue robe, handed her a jasmine mint julip, ultramarine liquid sloshing amongst sky-blue ice cubes.

John, notice that he retreats facing her, bowing low, smiling with practiced sincerity. He's terrified she might turn him into a goy.

Windy, did she give me this stuff, or did you?

John, she did. Use the stuff she provided. I'll weave good out of bad.

I took the supplies, sat under Blue's canvas shade on my haunches between Julius and Pontii. The two men shallowed air in-and-out, maybe five or six air-sips a minute, heads lolling off to one side, lips cracked, wide open. I felt for a pulse in their necks—*fluttery.*

Pontii's raw guts still crawled with a few army ants. I washed all the ants away and applied balms. Put pain powders on their tongues, squeezed water from a wet cloth into their mouths. Julius started choking.

John, turn him on his side, gentle-like, and help him cough the water up and out. Yes, like that, good.

I bound their chest and stomach wounds with swaddling strips loaded with ointments, under Windy's directions. I worked my way down to their thighs, looked away from the bloody holes where their genitals had once been located.

Balius, one of the archers, stopped his feasting and came over to me. "Let me do that. The weird lady out there is motioning for you."

I approached, shoulders back. She said, "Admirable compassion, even if you are importing the Ghost. But don't depend on fickle Windy. Blows where it wants. It can't make up its mind—male or female. How do you expect help from addled Gender Dysmorphia?"

Blue spoke as nobles might, words rolling rounded out of her mouth, sliding from one tonal register to another. A living legend in elocution.

I tested a locust on the platter before me. Nice crunch. Ate another. A blue fizzy ice drink appeared at my right hand. I sipped, looked up at my hostess.

Drusilla had sharpened her gaze into a honed blade. Introductions were done. Time for business. She said, "Whilst you were tending those imbeciles, I've been reeling in your cousin, the lunatic Hope-God. Tell me more of his bouts of confusion, needs for specialness. This is more than Transient Global Amnesia. He's a caravan wreck. Psychotic dementias, character disorders, mood disorders—all wrapped up in an anorexic, confused, mudder messiah."

She held up her little fist to the southern horizon, sighted over it. "A spritely breeze will shortly re-direct them."

I said, "Men and beasts, even nature, bows to you, Witch of Planet Blue?"

Her sapphire eyes glittered. "Without my order, rulers rob and rape. Caesar makes off with the silverware. Refugees bang on border fences. Starved elders, diseased children. Things get out of control."

Two violinists appeared, tuned up. Drusilla stood and sang an ordered, lyrical aria. She sang as if she was saving everyone within the sound of her soprano. Her voice was so pure, so light, that it brought down a sweep of angels' wings, leaving me vulnerable to the hold of her voice.

Drusilla roused from showering us all with her glory. She even noticed I was still present. "Didn't you just love how I made you suddenly hopeful? And John, don't ever confuse the Mistress of Hallucination with me. You only *think* you hear God's voice. Continue that, and soon you'll be acting like a common nutter wandering barren backroads, turning into your cousin. Bah. Look at me, young man! I'm what you seek, in the flesh."

The ground began to shimmer beneath my bare feet, like a new earth forming even as I stood there—forming under me, forming me.

Blue's voice sounded so lyrical, so sweet. Her words sounded like they'd passed through honeycomb. "Cousin-dear confuses hope with naïve optimism. False messiahs like him turn true truth-seekers away from the blue globe's real Ruler." She pointed both forefingers to her own perky self.

Her eyes bored down on me. "Consider this, John. Even his *brothers* realize Jesus is off-his-rocker-coo-coo. Divino-Demento. Just ask James, Jude, or Justus."

Drusilla grinned. "Think of it. He claims lowliness of heart. Humility? My ass. It's a power grab, John. Unfortunately, dear boy, your discernment is dismal, so I'll boil it down for you. Jesus has configured himself as a mild 'n meek manger boy, not what he really is— a usurper of true authority. And you, brooding loner, you've bought it. Every time he farts, you stand up and clap like a trained monkey—now *that's* pathetic. Get a life, locust-eater."

I felt shaken. Had I really been wish-fulfilling? I sank deeper in quicksand. Maybe Queen Blue *could* shore up my sinking faith.

Blue said, "Just the other day, outside Herod's palace? You shared your dream with Jesus—ah, you know, that ever so vulnerable self-disclosure? Dreamt of you being pregnant with *still-born faith?* Brought a tear to my eye."

I forgot my sinking in quicksand. I got mad. "Not fair, eavesdropping like that!"

"Oh goodness me! Quick, let's call the authorities! Well, golly. I forgot. I am the Authority. Only I have the power to raise you up, little man. Look down and see what I mean."

I was horrified. *How did that happen?* I looked up at Blue, and she'd grown younger, strikingly beautiful. Her hair was blue blond, her form flowing, features runic with a sharp definition of jaw and cheekbones, eyes cobalt blue. Her breasts had grown voluptuous, her gown almost transparent. She removed her throne from beneath her, vanished all other eyes around us, and stroked my chest and stomach with her light touch.

I covered my embarrassment.

She twinkled a smile my way. Blue and I lay together on a bed of light blue clouds, soft, inviting. A breath of fragrant myrrh, my favorite, wafted our way. A copy of the scriptures lay open to the Song of Solomon.

Blue purred, "Come join me for a Bible study, young man. Recite some verses of holy writ in your lovely baritone voice while you rest your head between my breasts. I'll minister to all your needs." [46]

John! What are you doing? I've been talking, trying to get your attention, but you've tuned me out. Stand up and shout one word, 'No!' Do it now.

"NO!" I thought I'd shouted my refusal, but when I opened my ears, I'd only whispered it.

Work, John, exercise your faith!

OK, Windy. I'm on it.

Blue's voice cut through my conversation with Windy. "Blow-hard trying to seduce you away, Johnny-boy?"

Blue sat back on her throne. Looked like she had in the beginning, a button of a figure. "Perhaps I'll wish-fulfill you. Change your ruff-tuff male body into a hairless pregnant virgin, eight months along with a stillborn fetus. Now, *that* would be a real hoot." She poked Millie in the flank, winked at her.

I said, "Greater is He that is within me than who *you* are within the earth, Blue."

"Means nothing. Jesus' glory train will also come to exactly that—nothing."

"Father won't allow you to swallow the Kingdom. *Everyone* has moments of doubt. Jesus' words and deeds are real. True love, his seal. Cold hate's *your* deal."

She replied, icily. "And you're a bleating camel in the wilderness. Change camels in mid-stream, Crying Voice. Use your rhetoric for a true powerhouse such as Me. You've only seen only a tiny bit from my bag of tricks."

"Your tricks, Blue, smoke and mirrors."

"Ah, camel boy, you wear your destiny like a hangman's noose. Ha! You're no more than a short arrow shot from a flaccid bow. Glory Hound cousin wants a different destiny. He *hopes* to get Tiberius into service of the Greater Emperor. Meaning himself, of course. And what else? Ah yes, he *hopes* to bed Nympho Claudia. But your weak-weenie cousin?"

She shook her head, eyes dripping merry sadness. "Erectile dysfunction, so common among the children of men. But for a *coming* messiah? Such a sad, *sad* situation."

"Seducer, you confuse his gentleness with weakness."

"Fine talk from a half-baked worm living inside a see-through fig leaf."

"Repent, Blue. You're always changing *appearances*—try changing your *character*. Outside, a frozen cross-dresser. Inside, you're the northern bombast Daniel prophesied—squawking for adoration to anyone in hailing distance." [47]

"My weaponry packs *way* more punch than your limp Branch of David. I'll overthrow Rome, put a chicken in every pot, and bring *Pax Drusillax* from sea to shining sea. Wise up, join me. You might graduate from sewer sweep to much, much more."

I started to reply. Didn't get a chance. The ground rose to meet me. When I came to, I'd been staked out on my back next to an anthill, the only one that survived the stampede. A mound of army ants seethed a few feet away.

How did this happen? I'd been standing in the cool shade, loincloth in place, looking at Drusilla a moment ago—a civilized conversation, even if desecrating. Now here I was fifty yards away in the sun's torrid blaze. One army ant, an advance scout, found the big toe on my right foot and sank its teeth into me.

51
CLAUDIA

We left on the next high tide. No wind, sails empty. Rowers stroked *Augustia* southwest into the sunset and a dead calm. A sky on fire reflected blood-red light over glassy waters.

Uncle, I suspected, wouldn't be averse to kicking back in Capri, diddling a few younger, nubile partners of both genders. Cousin Caligula had preened, proud to be a rising star in Uncle's harem there at Villa Jovis.

Jesus sat on a waist-high cargo hatch in the stern, head shuckling up and down, lips moving. Occasionally he'd pop his head up, look at the northern Illyrian coastline disappearing behind him, then turn his head back and glance at the southern skies.

I came up behind him and rested my hands on his shoulders, my fingers talking to his knotted neck. I cooed and clucked over him, a nest of unsaid words in my throat. Jesus relaxed backward into my wings, onto my breast. His chestnut hair blew back, and a few strands stuck on my open lips. He crossed forearms over his heart and held my hands, his right on my left, his left on my right. Cross *my* heart and hope to live, I desperately wanted us together—twinning, twining, indistinguishable —coming from and returning to his Father.

He said, "Windy says we'll arrive in her time, but I don't see how. Where I want to go is vanishing behind us."

I said, "I get to where I'm going by moving from where I've been."

"Does direction have something to do with it?"

"Nope. If what you've told me is true, Windy is the one blowing the times of our lives. Didn't you tell me that he sometimes gets us up by heading down? Nothing is wasted."

He looked over his shoulder at me and grinned, "Wow. That's true stuff I should be spouting. But I needed your reminder. Thanks."

"I haven't been in truth school with you for nothing. My ears work, and my brain ticks along, even if my heart is slow to catch up."

He kept me in his sight, steady like. "You move like a flower in the wind, like daffodils in spring, like kindness."

My heart raced. *This man loves me.*

We moved out of our hidden bay into open waters. Wind picked up out there, helping the rowers along. The open water's long swells took hold of her, deck smoothly tipping and falling, ship steadying into its sway and buck.

"While I was massaging your tight neck, I remembered your voice in the ocean currents along Trimerus' coastline. When I focused on you, I wasn't afraid."

He said, "Windy messages Father's voice to me. I do the same for you. Tune to His voice and learn our lines. She's a million times deeper than the blue sea, higher than blue sky, or anyone claiming to be true blue."

Why was he talking about blue this, blue that? We looked over the shifting colors of the sky and sea. *At least five colors of blue. Oh, dense me.*

Uncle arrived on cat's feet, like a panther. "Been able to cool down Jesus' fevered brain with a neck massage, Niece?"

I said, "Passing the time together."

"You remind me of the proverb, 'Love makes time pass. Time makes love pass.'"

"Well, that's hopeful, Uncle. I guess all things *do* come to pass, but some pass like a kidney stone."

Jesus switched gears, "I get visions of an army of ants eating John. I need to be with him, not sailing into a sunset, Sire."

Uncle said, "Beautiful sunsets—much more attractive than cannibal armies."

"Sire, you're in charge of your empire and this boat. Father's given me a far greater command.[48] John's spirit and mine, join. Father uses our faith to protect John, even when you don't."

He motioned over his shoulder and mine, "We'll be back there by tomorrow."

Uncle Tibbie said, "If your Spirit is so potent, stop worry from eating me. An army of ants is chewing sorrow into *my* body, ruing the deaths of those sailors who died to protect me."

"Winnow worry with obedience, Sire. When I obey the little that Father gives me to do, he's in charge of consequences. Disobey, *like you're doing now*, and the consequences are on you."

"Seer, I don't have your hotline to heaven, and there is no higher power on earth than me. I do what's best in my own eyes."

Jesus said, "Before Claudia came, I'd been praying and watching the sky in front of us. Nothing but clear skies each of the six times I'd checked. Now, since you arrived, I checked again. Do you see that tiny cloud in the dusk, that one the size of my hand? Windy swirls behind that cloud, gathering energy. She will blow us back to where we need to be—regardless of your orders, Sire."

Uncle was dismissive. "Rave on, Seer. I was dreaming of sunny Capri, my idyll away from mother. Peace and quiet on Capri. Distraction is what I need, and that's what I'll get."

I thought, but didn't say, *denial's a fluffy four-poster bed, Uncle, complete with canopy and two steps for mounting. You can lie there, cuddle with partners, and look down at who's eating you.*

Uncle stood, arms crossed, feet solidly planted on the lilting deck, a picture of power. He looked honorable, determined, prejudiced, and pig-headed—in other words, a man. A man with a jeweled scepter, but a man, nonetheless.

Wind picked up, slapping waves on our bow, sending spray across my face. *A vision. Storm on spinning chariot wheels, inexorable, unyielding, morphing into a monster, lunging present into future.*

Jesus whispered to me, "This storm will pitch down sideways with heavy winds and waves very soon." [49]

Jesus turned to face Uncle Tibbie. "Ready *Augustia* for a storm that will soon arrive and blow us back to Disaster Bay. There, above that bay, in the mouth of a cave, a wall will thresh you. Winnow you through to the other side."

I took Uncle Tibbie's arm and whispered in his ear, "Whatever he says to you, do it. The wind and seas obey him."

Uncle's eyes flicked from me to the calm all around us. Doubt and belief stormed across his face, each in turn.

He climbed to the bridge and clipped out a command. "Sejanus, prepare the ship for a storm."

"But, Emperor, our sails are full for the first time. Smooth sailing for our night passage."

Uncle silenced him with the wave of his hand.

52

WINDY

The next morning, Slow woke up at home in Jericho to the life I designed her to live. The sleeping pallet they'd made up for Yakhal was empty. Slow crept to their bedroom door and cracked it open.

Yakhal and Michael had found each other. They were now deep in play—enacting the old story of Joshua fighting the battle of Jericho. Michael marched himself on his knees, pushing toy soldiers around a wall of wooden blocks.

Yakhal sat inside the walled city with two dolls leftover from Slow's childhood—the ones their mother had given Leah and her. These were two of the few things that remained from their mother. The prettier of the two dolls had a scarlet thread in her hands the color of pomegranate flowers. Yakhal stood this pretty doll on the other's head. She kept turning her body in a slow circle to keep an eye on Mike and his army.

I glimmered awareness into Slow—her standing on Leah's shoulders, seeing tomorrow through her sister's love.

The seventh time 'round his Jericho wall, Mike yelled, "Down! All fall down!" He used his bossy voice and flattened the wall with both hands. Danced a victory jig.

He jigged his hips left, then right. He jumped up and down, a celebration storm in a small package. Yakhal danced with him for a bit, but then she stopped and busted into tears.

"What wrong, lil' gurl?"

He didn't even know her name yet. She was just a new playmate who'd shown up.

Girl cried, "My ma and pa fell under big blocks. All gone, all dead."

Slow's boy-child sat, put his arms 'round her, and cried too—not knowing anything but feeling deep and true, as little children do.

Laz had snuck up behind Slow, watching. They joined their children, one arm 'round each. Yakhal slipped her arm around Slow's leg and hugged her with artless affection. Slow gazed back at her, beleaguered kindness in her eyes.

They sat in a circle, children inside, and parents forming a Jericho wall of protection around the children. The war wasn't over, Father's kingdom not yet visible. But for now, their fragile circle of safety was in place.

Laz said, "Michael, meet your new sister, Yakhal. Yakhal, meet your little brother, Michael."

Their new child looked at them, "Can you call me Hope, not Yakhal? I feel better when you call me by that name."

This new family began their life as a foursome—Slow, not Go; Hope, not Yakhal; Laz, not yet resurrected a second time—and Michael, a boy, and not an archangel.

53
JOHN

I was still staked out. When the one army ant bit me, it hurt like someone had stuck a lit match in me. The black ant zoomed back to get his pals. Word spread like wildfire. The black, seething mound reshaped in tidy columns and headed my way. *Yum, fresh meat.*

When only a few inches away, they hit an invisible wall. The columns split, half toward my head, half toward to my feet, encircling, looking for access. I thought I could hear their fury, their snapping teeth. They stacked up a couple of inches from my body, behind my wall of protection—fifty, hundred, thousand-deep, clawing toward dinner.

Blue sat shaded, at a distance. She finally became curious enough to pick her way in my direction. She looked at my wall. The Pharisee slid a pedestal under her.

I said, "Blue, God is at work, providing protection through prayer—Jesus' invisible prayer has built this invisible wall."

She had nothing to say.

Windy said, *you're right. Jesus did pray for you. I improvised. Take a look, John; look up if you want to catch a glimpse of Me.*

A blue swirl, shaped like a tornado, filled the sky over me. The cloud was topped with a thunderhead with long lips and puffy cheeks.

A real blow began. Rain began to fall, first in light, misty drops. Then, a downpour. I looked around. Blue was implacable, on her pint-sized throne, looking down at me.

She said, "All right. I've had enough. Your wall's about to fall."

I said, "Wall or no wall, Ghost's liveliness trumps your deadliness, Blue. Fire or ice, Bato or you—doesn't matter—you work for Death. I work for the Living."

She scowled, pointed her scepter at me. Blue fire crackled and hit my wall—rebounded, caught the hem of her queenie outfit on fire. Blue flames licked up her ankles. Aides rushed over and threw buckets of ice water on her from the knees down. She swished back to her cave in a royal frump worthy of a blueblood.

The squall descended out of the south. A sheer wall of water marched across the far-off ocean, and then, across the ridgetop. Took aim at our plateau, building in fury with each step toward the mountainside.

I pulled at my stakes. Softened mud released them. I stood, naked, facing the storm. I unknotted the ropes from around my wrists and ankles and walked to cliff's edge.

Streams from the hills above joined creeks from the surrounding plains. A brown, turgid river flowed over the cliff. Masses of squashed and now drowned army ants flowed downstream to join hogs and men in Disaster Bay.

I turned and walked back toward the mountain. Blue's gates into Dragon Mountain appeared to be open, but when I tried to step through, I hit another invisible wall and couldn't get in. I explored this new wall, one that felt different than the wall Jesus prayed for and Father had provided through Windy. Like it was an imitation of the real deal. I pressed all along the open gates, the full length of that space, pressing in with prayer—*Windy, help!*

Good, John, you're actively inquiring, seeking after Me. And, by the way, pick up your sheepskin and the lion's skin next to it. You'll need both of them shortly.

I looked around me and saw the skins. They'd blown against the mountain a little further down. I put both on. A good fit, both of them. A little weird, lion and lamb lying against my skin, but comfy.

Once warmed, I kept trying to get the hang of walking through walls. Pray 'n push, step back, push 'n pray. Light or hard pressure, thumping, stroking, clawing. Nothing seemed to work. I kept at it. And then, suddenly, when I had stepped back and was doing exactly nothing but praying, a big swoosh of frigid air blew through, from the inside out, and I stepped through on the other side.

Windy said, *Levites like you are always interested in walls, John. Boundaries between holy and profane. Some borders are seen clearly; others, not so easy. This essential training in clear seeing will continue.*

I walked into a deep cavern, complete with pointy, frozen rocks poking up from the floor and down from the ceiling. Snowdrifts had blown into the cavern. Close to the entrance, the flakes were like albino vultures' plumage. A few yards further in, climate change was more obvious. White feather-swoosh of snow had frozen rock hard. I began to shiver, even in my coats.

Blue's dais and the animals that supported her were a unit in the back of this cavern. They had positioned themselves close to another opening, a deeper and darker entryway into the dungeons beneath. Long icicles hung off these barred inner gates, and a tempest of freezing air howled through those bars. I bent over, wrapping lion and lamb tight around me. Approached the gates of hell. Once I did that, the winds reversed without warning. Now I was sucked toward hell with a pull as great as the push had been. I was spread-eagled against the gates of hell, unable to move, stuck solid against the iron bars. Blue's hell had frozen over and was killing me along with her. She sat still on her dais, covered in snow, smiling through her glares at my fate. She was still alive, but very still. Reaping-a-lifetime-of-coldness still.

I cried out to God, *you got me in this place. Now, please, get me out.*

A warmth, from the inside out, spread through my body. The shrieking winds from below luffed, ready to change direction again. At that moment, I dropped off those gates, released. I scooted away from Hell's Gates and approached Millie.

She stood quite still, a few yards away, in front of the other six beasts. Blue's dais remained on top of those beasts. I peered up into Millie's eyes. She blinked. A tear pushed out and froze immediately. I plucked it off her eyelid and tried patting her nose. The ice on her pelt cracked into tiny sparkles from the warmth of my fingers.

I mused, *Windy, Millie was the only female I've ever met that appeals to me, even if she's been locked inside a beast and is now covered in winter. Is this feeling something like sad?*

Windy said, *your courage and obedience have warmed your feeling heart, even in the dead of winter. And yes, what you feel for Millie is very sad indeed.*

I began to cry.

Windy whispered, *tears are good. Heartbreak shows you're human, on the journey from here to there of learning to care. Satan never cares. When he's done with Drusilla, he'll skate to another container. Human or fallen angel doesn't matter. His four-part strategy doesn't change: Invade, slow or quick. Seduce with power or pleasure. Vary fire with ice. Divide and conquer.*

A mound of hail piled up in front of Queenie. I snatched a push broom from a frozen handmaiden and swept the path from the outer cave entry on a gradual ramp up to her. I made the high places low. Windy made the low places high. Together we smoothed a highway for Cousin's arrival.[50]

I broomed Blue's face. Her smooth, translucent, blue-white skin had shriveled into a spiderweb of wrinkles.

I said, "Hail, Blue! The Chosen One comes. Prepare yourself."

Queenie glared at me, mouth struggling to shape a new curse, but the words froze as they left her lips. I broke them off, left her and her curses behind me.

54
LEAH

Sejanus' sailors had unfurled the sails and strapped them down when the storm struck—one moment, a cloud the size of a fist; the next, a swirling sea monster that ate water and spat out gale-force winds.

I had always wanted to see Windy paint her wordless witness of Father's might. Tonight, though, her painting was done with wind, wailing, and water. Much more muchy than what I'd prayed for. Rabbus lashed Gabe and me to the center mast and covered us with sail canvas. He also bound Jesus and Claudia side by side on the other side of the mast.

He yelled over the gale, "If the ship goes down, pull the end of this rope, and the knots will unravel. Hold onto the handles of those two barrels next to each of you. I'll be at my duty station with the emperor."

For the unbelieving, this typhoon was terrifying—our tiny ship, utterly lost in the raging ocean. We were beaten like a tiny, tin drum, driven backward to the north.

For the believing among us, God's passing storm had hitched Jesus to his appointed tasks. Windy would deliver us precisely and exactly at the right place and the right time. We were being airmailed, hurricane delivery. I prayed, *Father, guard the emperor from himself, the devil, and his own disobedience. Be gentle, please. We're all tucked inside your will, like baby chicks under a hen's wings.*

I heard a few words between Jesus and Claudia, but the storm snatched the whale's share of their conversation away from me. None would know these words spoken from his mouth to her ears. Windy's storm song, on the other hand, was public, irresistible, and triumphant.

Half a day, half a lifetime, passed. My crying toddler roused me, "Mama, go pee now?"

Okay, yes, me too. I undid our ropes, raised the canvas, and looked around—just in time. A monster wave slam-danced us directly toward jagged rocks. Scared the pee right outta me.

This cresting wave lifted a bloated warthog over the gunnels. The dead hog boarded the ship and knocked me back toward the center mast on its way in. I laid over Gabe, behind that thin, center stick, while a whole herd of warthogs followed—sea swine rising from the deep.

Ship lurched higher, higher, riding so high, and then the sea dropped us onto jagged limestone boulders. Thick outer hull timbers shattered into match sticks. Mast sheered in half, and the top half took flight. *Augustia* complained, groaned, crumbled. Rowers from below had spilled out of their hold and were smashed between ship and sea.

Augustia ground to a shuddering halt on the lower platform of an archer's tower that anchored to rock. Archer's tower and the front half of our ship were now one. Each rested in the other's arms, thrown together by a force far bigger than either of them alone.

We were still, and all was silent except for the sea and the rocks talking together. And then, even that stopped. A sovereign stillness took over. Inside this circle of quiet, a small moan, like Gabe's first cry in that dark cave under Eagle's Wings. Like Tiberius' last breath in that Jericho surgery before Windy raised him from the dead.

The cry came and went, journey's pause.

Tiberius broke the silence. He clambered down from the bridge. Rabbus followed. Jesus and Claudia rose from behind their protected spot in the storm. They jumped onto the tower's platform, held arms out to help us. We climbed onto that tower, then further, higher, up the cliff. Sejanus followed with the few surviving sailors.

Once on the cliff, we watched the sea steadily grind *Augustia* to bits—a ceaseless, joyful rhapsody, power at play. The massive redwood prow, now stuck in the tower, split in two. Augusta and her son finally split up.

I glanced over at the fatherless emperor whose eyes were now on the same split masthead. Both of his fathers, birth and adoptive, gone. And now, his mother cleaved from him.

A grim smile came on his face and went without a sound. *Grief or relief?*

Windy said, *yes, grief and relief, both. And more to come, in layers—not one and done.*

I said, *you teach me that over and over again—you serve your losses in thin layers so I can digest them.*

Claudia looked at her uncle. "During the storm, Jesus told me about Jonah. Inside the fish's guts, Jonah said, 'Praise Father in the storm with the sacrifice of thanksgiving.' [51]

"Jesus joined with the wind's chorus, Uncle, and I joined with him, loud as we could sing. I couldn't hear my voice in that blow—but I know I've never sounded that good."'

The drenched emperor stood with hands on hips, chin stuck out—ruler of one small cliff in enemy land. He fidgeted. I had the sense he was addled by the call to praise complication and loss. Perhaps he liked his religion served plain and raw, like a peeled onion. That way, you only had a wee weep now and again.

Claudia resumed talking to her uncle, "We praised his Father, and *He* saved you because of *this* man's obedience—in spite of you calling him a raving lunatic, Uncle."

Tiberius stood at the raw edge of himself. He looked past his and his mother's bashed in half-heads. Thousands of bloated warthogs drifted in the surge, lay on the shores, or were impaled on the barricades.

Tiberius sighed, "I knew our sunk armada was here in this bay, and I didn't want to return and look at it. Looking away from my losses was much easier."

Jesus replied, "In my small experience, Sire, we let go of the past only when we face it."

Tiberius stared at him askance, mute. He switched gears, "Perhaps. I'll file that thought, preferably in a remote warehouse. But back to your vision. What sunk me were the hogs. That was too crazy—a bay full of dead hogs?"

His face lit up. "But even so, you were wrong about one other thing. And that, in my mind, still discredits your good judgment."

Jesus looked at him, "Yes?"

"Ants. You said ships, sailors, hogs, *and ants* would be in the bay. Well, I guess three out of four isn't so bad, though, far as you seers go."

The words had barely left his lips when some upstream floodgate broke loose. A torrent of dead army ants sluiced over the ledge, covering the emperor head to toe. His red uniform was matted with mounds of black ants, and the excess flooded into the bay beyond.

Jesus raised both his hands skyward and then pasted them on his knees, bent over with hilarity at Windy's timing. Claudia fell on her knees, howling with glee. Sejanus looked confused but then grinned after Tiberius started to laugh; all of us gentled in the hands of a laughing God.

Relief wedded irony, and Jesus presided over the marriage. He scanned our faces and soberly offered a thought, "For the moment, you all believe."

His face fixed on Tiberius. "Your belief comes and goes, Sire. When you see fulfilled prophecy or miracles, you believe. But your faith fights daily with honest doubt. Neither scorn such doubt nor let it rule you. My doubt drives me further in my journey toward the Kingdom."

Tiberius stared at him through a veil of army ants that stuck to his face, clung to his beard, and dribbled off his chin. He turned his believing eyes on Jesus at a time when it was impossible not to believe.

Jesus looked directly at the emperor. "Father's unveilings sometimes reveal disaster. Other times, they're embodied in marriage.[52] Spirit swirls a thousand thousand veils that hide His face and Hers. Beyond the veils, find God's face, Sire, a face ablaze with beauty." [53]

He turned and looked up. A beam of sunlight switched off and on like a lighthouse between patches of nimbus. That focused sunbeam, in an instant, flicked the veil off his divinity. His was the most beautiful face I've ever seen, before or since.

Jesus glanced at the switchback trail leading up through the forest. He said to Tiberius, "Father's storm put us here for a purpose. John is waiting."

A sideways streak of sun velvet lit the forest canopy above. Kingfishers darted past, turquoise blue, skittering wild and free into patches of shade and light. I was knee-deep in wild goosegrass. I grabbed a handful of these emerald blades, sticky with sap, beaded with rain. Wildflowers loaded the field behind the barricades. Skylarks swooped in and out of golden broom. Swathes of parsley, primrose blues, sorrel reds, brilliant white poppies, umber chamomile, and orange marigolds splashed the meadow. *An artist's palate. My God, such outrageous colors! Breezes bent the field of flowers and then they popped up again. Windy took a bow.*

I stopped and gathered flowers from this field. My hands picked what my mind didn't know. But Windy knew. *Take plenty of poppy flowers and pods, Leah, dear. You're ignorant, my child, but not stupid. You can learn.*

From this brief meadow, darker evergreens fingered upwards, lingered all around, like unspoken hope hiding on the far side of danger. I walked into sun and shadow, light and dark, soothed by body in motion. Moving my body ticked my mind over. I seemed to hear God's voice better while I huffed along, Windy's breath energizing me. In this journey, She was the energy, Jesus was the road, and Father was the goal.

55
SLOW

Zacchaeus waddled out of the synagogue into Rahab's courtyard, deep in conversation with his half-brother. Rastus walked half-step ahead of Zac, slashing right hand down on left palm. He turned to stand on the balls of his feet to make his next point, as men condemned to smallness often do. Ruthless tax collector and semi-reformed murderer made an odd couple—short, fat, younger brother and skinny, even shorter reprobate. Both prodigals were observant, both lapsed. The older brother knew it; the other, not so much. Both smudged the boundary between law and outlaw.

The brothers' wives followed. They made even stranger friends. Esmeralda was tall and willowy; a Nubian bought by Zac from an African slave trader passing through town. Maltesa was a squatty, rich Jewess, as wide as she was tall.

Both women dressed to be seen. Esmeralda flowed like a Bengal tiger, lithe, in a form-fitting black and orange silk dress. She wore a tiger lily over her left ear. Maltesa wore a frilled, bright purple satin skirt under a sun-yellow, low-cut lace blouse. She'd braided her black hair in triple loops. These women obviously enjoyed each other. Both talked while interrupting, mouths and hands moving—each perfectly understanding what the other was saying, implying, and meant to say, but forgot.

Both couples were living examples of opposites repelling and attracting at the same time. Love and hate had never found such miserably happy bedfellows. Compared to Esmeralda's village-size, Zac looked like a city-state. Compared to Maltesa, Rastus was insignificant as a summer cough.

All four walked from the synagogue across the courtyard to our apartment. El Roi and his wife, Lydia, also joined us to celebrate Shabbat. *There, hanging low, two stars in the clear eastern sky—time to light the two Shabbat candles.*

I stood in the shadow of the entry's lintel. Hope and Michael were ready. They stood in front of Laz, father's arms around his children. All three stood at the head of our Shabbat table. Children jumped up and down with excitement.

Laz helped each child light the candles. Michael lit the "keep" candle. Hope lit the "remember" candle. The golden glow of candles' flickering dappled their faces with light. Laz's love painted their spirits with belonging—and both were beautiful to behold. I stood in the shadows and felt like a minor seraph—the one who throws out golden apples to any who visit her Father's temple.

Laz led us in singing Shalom Aleichem as we welcomed the angels of peace. El Roi recited the Kiddush prayer. Zac held up his wine glass, and we all followed with a sip of Kiddush wine. Lydia brought towels and a basin of water for us to wash our hands. Maltesa and I went to the kitchen together and removed three sweet, warm challah loaves from the oven, drizzling them with butter and honey. Maltesa took one of them and jammed half of it in her mouth.

I said, "Maltesa, please!"

She delicately burped, re-arranged her corset, and scraped crumbs off her top-shelf. We emerged from the kitchen and passed the remaining challah loaves around. Everyone tore off a warm piece of the sweet, braided bread. Another prayer of thanks to God, this time from Rastus, who ripped it out so fast it sounded like an extended burp.

Michael and Hope got bored with all the adult chatter. They crawled under the table like cats, rubbing against our ankles. Grown-up gossip and politics scattered around the table, along with laughter, lamb, and lentils. And the children's favorite for dessert, sticky-sweet baklava. Talk and laughter melted into one sound block. Now and then, a clear word floated to the listening angels' ears who hovered all around.

After the meal, Esmeralda cornered me in the kitchen while we were doing the dishes. "Let's be draggin' out washing-up long's we ken. Soon we goes home—Shabbat sex. Only good thing with fat boy, it be nice 'n short. He 'n me be flat-backin' to fill the law up. Shuck-shuck-de-buck, up 'n down, quick-like, whack-a-mole."

I slung back her slang, "Es, you be disrespectin' yo' lord and masta?"

Es rolled her eyes, shimmied her right hand skyward, "An, girlfriend, my praise, she go straight up and quick back down, jus' like Shabbat sex."

Es' face clouded over. She looked down, then asked, "Herod be braggin' ta Zac las' time he hauled tax gold up de hill. Herod lists all womens he dun. Den Zac brags 'bout girls off de back wall at Rahab's. Your name came up outta the scum-king's mouf, gurlfrien'."

My face burned. I shrugged and nodded.

Es said, "Zac done gone an' tol' his bro. Ras-de-knife gots ideas, you know, how to stick it to 'im."

Just then, Rastus sidled up. "Siren song of the wild-and-wooly avenger be singing in my ear, Slow."

I rolled my eyes, "Ras, get outta my kitchen. We're stoking the furnace with girl talk."

Rastus smiled his kinky grin, the one with his right eyebrow bouncing up and down. "Herod's headin' back to Jerusalem. Two days. I'm thinking he might have himself an accident. I got 'nuf time to get my rabble off the farm and do 'im proper."

I said, "Let God handle justice."

Inside, Cutter cried out, *let me plant the knife.*

Rastus said, "I told Laz his wife's honor was at stake. Told him a *real* man would pop that perp."

I raised my eyebrow. Laz hadn't mentioned this little chat.

"Know what he said? 'I'll pray over it.'"

Rastus ragged on. "I said, 'If ya can't run with the big dogs, get under the porch.' He didn't say crap to that. Got no dignity, letting his wife get the business."

Rastus spit on the floor, crossed his arms, threw his shoulders back.

"Rastus, a man doesn't keep his dignity. It keeps him. Go home."

Rastus did a dramatic eyebrow arch. "You two hold down the high-sounding side of the house. Say yur prayers while I'll slip out the back door and do deeds."

I got down on a knee, literally. "Don't save my ass, Ras—save yours. Jesus told you to put aside murdering, live right. You agreed."

"That was then—this is now. Milk-toast-Messiah be long gone. Says he's coming back. Right. Don't see hide nor hair of him. *Ain't right, ain't fit, ain't proper!* Deeds needs a- doin'."

"*Good* violence is a crock, Rastus. Killing bad people for good reasons? Still wrong."

Rastus grinned, "Don't forget the violence line-up, little lady. Wrong and wronger. Violence be wrong but he's in line back of Rape."

"Rastus, go home to Maltesa. Make *her* happy. I'm recovering in my own sweet 'n sour way. Besides, ya know what I really think?"

He took a knee, and his voice dripped drama, "Tell me, oh beauty queen, heart of my heart, longing of this lost soul."

I smiled at him, "Your affection is sweet, Ras, but misplaced—a boy's rescue fantasy stuck inside a middle-aged man. Avenging me is an excuse not to grow up."

Esmeralda had been watching and listening to this whole back 'n forth. She screeched, "My Gawd! She done laid you out, Ras! Get home, do d' wife."

Rastus flushed, "Maybe I am a kid trapped in a man's body—but I got one life, live or die. I probably overstayed my visit on earth anyway."

Es flashed a conspirator's grin, wide as a card shark's promise. She patted his bicep, slurred out her best slum-dog sleaze, "Sho 'nuf, Masser 'Venger, if you be a-wantin' to cash it *all* in, den we'll have us a good-bye party for ya."

Esmeralda winked at Rastus, hugged me, and headed out the torch-lit front gate.

I said, "Shabbat *Shalom*, 'Rastus."

"Shalom Shabbat, Slow." Rastus went out into the dark, alone.

Murder 'n song, rape 'n prayers. Happy times at Shabbat.

The night was too dark to think straight about such things. I found all my children, the ones outside and the ones inside. Put them all to bed. Found Laz, and we put our grown-up selves to bed. Only one thing remained. Shabbat sex. Mouth didn't need words during this time of the week. We surged and swelled, silent, eyes closed—skin without sin, saving and being saved from ourselves and my past.

Middle of the night, I woke with this dream. *I was lying on Ach's grave, weeping. I wasn't exactly on top of his grave. I'd slowed my way down into it, covered by dust halfway. A windy night, really windy. Only a strand of my hair, ash-white, showed—blowing wild in the night air.*

I tossed and turned, anxious for no good reason. Got up. Drank a cup of tea. Paced. Went back to bed next to my snoring husband. Dreamed, again.

Jesus was a combat soldier. He, El Roi, and Laz swirled a war dance around and over me, stomping and singing[54]*, pulling me out of a grave I'd sunk into with Herod, Ach, Cyn, and lots of others.*

Off in the distance, way out there, an angel, disguised as ass, with Maltesa's face and hair braids, dumped Rastus on the ground and sat on him—broke his legs—loud snapping sound.

I awoke, shocked at my mad dream-weaver. Laz roused, rolled over, and took me in his arms. He said, "You okay, sweetheart?"

I wiped away my tears. "Sleep, my husband. All manner of things will be good."

The next morning Laz looked at me over breakfast and said, "I must have been blind lately. When did that streak of white shoot through your hair?"

56

LEAH

This ridge above us on the path looked different. When I'd seen it from *Augustia*'s prow, bobbing about at anchor, it looked like a crumpled ribbon of fall colors, fat in the middle and narrow at both ends. Towering red trees bunched at the far end.

Now, closer, a feeling of enchantment swaddled me. Mist coiled and uncoiled, drifting from ridgetop toward the sea. I reached over my shoulders to pat Gabe's face. He was strapped to my back and busy sticking my hair in his mouth. I clambered up-trail, one handhold to another, grasping trunks of rain-slicked poplars, beech, and pine that misted out of the fog. Windy stooped me over, stretched out my hand to pick herbs now and again.

Yes, a few more of those white ones, thank you, and no, none of those purple.

Two owls darted in the shadows, shook their feathers in the sea-wind. Both were at home—only we humans struggled toward unknown, uncertain destinations.

I looked up to Jesus in front of me. He pulled upward, Claudia trailing behind him. I tripped, almost fell over a slippy root before I caught myself. Jesus slipped down a few steps past Claudia, took me by the shoulders. "Leah, look up, look down, back and forth, not too long either way. This journey requires total attention." [55]

He turned, and Claudia gave him her hand. She pulled. They kept climbing. I could barely see him, and he was only a few steps ahead of me. Forest branches bled fog—tricksical, moving down-slope. The mist fogged and fell like a wrapper, sliding down so steadily I wondered if I was falling up.

I shook some sense back into my body. A tree helped out, sticking a branch in my hand. Dense patches of purple hellebore and white oleander surrounded my feet and ankles. Both could be deadly if an open sore brushed against them. I walked carefully, sloshing through clusters of lavender jacarandas, then past a weeping pepper tree.

When I next squinted up, Jesus was directly in front of me. Or was that mist? I doubted my vision, even my sense of what was real—but when I tried to push through him, I couldn't. He was exactly himself, solid enough to steady me on my upward path. He leaned over me and smiled. In the mirror of his eyes, I saw myself taking shape. The shape I was meant to be—like a drawing of me being filled in, one color, one line, one at a time.

A few yards later, I spied a clump of shy asters twining with brazen goldenrod. Their purples and golds wound together. Such intimacy put me in mind of husband, who stood up ahead in a tangle of broom brambles at the mouth of a cave. Laurel sumac wove in and between the brambles, framing the entrance to that cave. A stream flowed out the cave's mouth, hit a ledge, and swirled down toward the sea.

My wary husband had stuck his short sword and stabbing *sica* into opposite sides of his belt. Leather breastplate and helmet thoroughly armored his head and chest. Tiberius stood behind and off to the right. Rabbus examined the cave's entrance—bird droppings and bigger scat as well. He deliberated, resting hands on hips—*an aviary for wild birds or a hiding place for predators? Crawl in or move on?*

Restless, I pushed ahead of Jesus, using his shoulder as a lever. As I approached husband, Gabe saw him and shouted, "Abba!"

Rabbus, surprised, reached for Gabe. In that moment of looking and reaching, a man-sized leopard screamed and leapt onto Rabbus back, sinking all four claws into his back and shoulders, ripping down with her hind feet, stripping his waist of meat below his chest armor. Her jaws angled, teeth seeking to rip open his throat. Three new cubs also spilled out of the cave, following their mother.

Rabbus hunched over, head tucked in to protect his throat, roaring. He quickly straightened, left and right hands flashing behind him, swords thrusting and slicing.

Leopard opened her mouth again to rip and roar, but no sound came. Her throat had been neatly cut. She flopped backward off his neck, gurgling out her life in the stream. Rabbus fell back with her, on top of her, twisting as he fell to face her. He held her down with his weight, knees pinning her hind legs. He worked his daggers deeper. She spasmed, fierce eyes glazing, hazing, gone. The three cubs scrambled onto their mother's back, mewling. From my view, it looked like one leopard with four heads, one big and three smaller ones poking up between her ears. [56]

I handed Gabe to Claudia and hurried to husband. I leaned my head in between husband and leopard, "Husband, how can I help you?"

Rabbus said, "Aw, back, sides… hurt, bad. Help."

This from a man who never asked for help.

He knelt before me, his eyes a pair of supplicants. I reached around his body with both arms, fingers fumbling, working his lacing through blooded eyelets. He let me slide it off him, careful, like he'd not let anyone else do.

Two sets of slashes ran down his back where the leather stopped, each stripe the width of the leopard's claws, each gouge having cut through heavy muscle to bone, a foot long. Two shorter sets of gouges ripped either side of his waist where he had no armor.

By his stripes, we were saved. By his call for help he was saved, from himself.

New scars furrowed over the old ones on his back, fresh blood streamed into rain's rivulet, mixing with leopard's blood. I screamed for Tiberius' physician, Hippo. We busied ourselves. I made a paste of herbs for his wounds. Hippo stitched husband up. Rabbus scrunched his eyes shut, shuddering out his pain.

I searched past people's knees and tunic fringes for my son. Yes, there! There he was with Claudia. The two of them sat beside the stream, cuddling newborn cubs. Gabe crawled around Claudia, leading the other cubs in a circle around their mother's still-warm body. [57]

Sound of branches breaking. I clutched husband tighter, looked up. Tiberius stood next to Sejanus over the cave, swords in their hands, scanning the woods, sniffing for the leopard's mate. Still around or gone?

I thought, *parent loss marks us all. Leopard or human didn't matter. Some fathers were seed donors, abandoning their mates and offspring once sated. Others stayed around to protect and bleed for you.*

I stroked husband's wounds, adoring my son's father. His blood swirled in the stream, down to the sea.

57
JESUS

Our trail topped out on a plateau. A parade ground stretched before us and ended in a towering bluff, covered with crimson trees bright with Father's glory. I could only gasp in wonder—nothing like this in Nazareth, for sure. A red kapok crowned these blazing maples and sycamores. The mountain itself looked alive, like a fire-breathing dragon, complete with cockscomb, head lifted warily.

Claudia took one look and said, "That dragon looks like she spilled fire on the mountainside."

I nodded, wondering, walking, almost tripping over a skinned, flattened bear who'd been left to hold its own leash. Army tents, clothing, supplies, and mounds of flattened anthills—chaos gone quiet.

Storm clouds had flown north, leaving a muggy heat behind. Humidity rose off the puddled ground like steam off a pot of boiling meat, the air like wet fire.

Sejanus and Tiberius picked their way through the mess, heading toward a stockade off to our right. Two legionnaires followed, carrying Rabbus' stretcher toward the enclosure. Leah walked beside him, one hand stroking his head, the other holding her son. Gabe saw me and struggled to get down.

I held out my arms for the toddler. He didn't seem to understand what had just happened to his father. All he saw was my backpack topped with leopard cubs. They seemed eager to play with him. I put him and them on the ground, and they raced around my legs, squandering their wiggles.

I turned my eyes back to the mountain, searching the bluff's base. Hm. What was that? Something peculiar—a veil of shimmering mist and ice. Snatches of deepening darkness moved behind the veil.

A lion broke through the veil, loping in our direction. I turned to run. Just then, the lion flicked his head back. John was under the lion's skin. He ran toward me, arms wide open, face breaking into a huge smile.

"Cousin, you found me here on Dragon's Ridge!"

I said, "Windy took matters into her own hands and blew us here. And, you've liberated a lion skin from its owner?"

John head-gestured over his left shoulder, "Blue took my clothes before she knocked the fig tree over with a lightning bolt. Then Windy came, put lion and lamb together, lying in layers on me." He unhitched his outer lion skin and showed us his inner, form-fitting lambskin tunic.

John continued, "Heads up. Over therein the stockade, Pontii and Julius are missing their chests, stomachs, and most of their thighs. Flayed. Ant-eaten. A real mess."

My skin turned to gooseflesh.

"That was before the soldiers turned to pigs, stampeded over the cliff, and hell froze over. Sort this out for me, Jesus."

Tiberius had walked up behind me and caught most of the conversation. The emperor said, "Strange and stranger things keep happening on my way to visit Gemellus."

I called to Claudia and Leah, "Hey, could you go over to the stockade along with Hippo? Men over there need your helping hands. John and I are headed over to that veil between us and the mountain."

John added a bit of insider knowledge, "Veil's the work of Drusilla, the Blue. She's a boarding house, renting her soul to Satan. She's not blue anymore, but white, so maybe that makes her the White witch. She has ten horned beasts, about two tons each, surrounding her—including someone who could have been my girlfriend, Millie. But she's frozen stiff too."

He shook his head. "I felt sad, really sad, Cousin. First real sad of my grown-up life. All those beasts harbor people inside who can't speak." He sighed, appeared to recover. "And of course," he said, "ten crowns hang on ten skulls stuck to ten spears planted in four-foot-thick ice blocks, one for each beast."

Claudia gave up. "Holy crap! Your sanity stampeded over the cliff with all those hogs."

John looked miffed. "It's all true, what I said. You two women do women's work at the stockade. And Claudia? Take your orders from Leah. Jesus and me will man-up and do the heavy lifting with all the demon stuff." He smacked one fist into the other open palm, bent his head and flexed, his shoulder muscles rippling under the lion's skin. Claudia turned away, rolled her eyes, and left for the stockade.

John and I walked toward the icy, white veil over a cave opening. When we got there, John ran to one side of the entrance. He returned with another pair of skins, lamb and bearskin. John said, "Put on the lambskin first. Then add the bearskin. Sperm belonged to Bato before he became a warthog, you know."

I stuck my hand through the sheets of cold steam and pulled it back out. An icicle had formed below my fingertip, an instant stalactite.

John stepped beyond the veil, dragging me after him. We walked into a blizzard wrapped in night. Cold and dark were frozen in time. I turned around in the inky cold, eyes wide with wonder. I pulled my skins tight around me. Yellow eyes, slitted ellipses, blinked at me. Hissing sounds echoed off the walls.

Tiberius stood behind us. He'd also crossed over, moving inwards with sword in hand, without asking or seeking permission. He said, "I saw you had coats. I borrowed Hippo's. I couldn't miss whatever was going to happen over here."

The three of us stood together in this frigid wonderland, thrumming with spookiness.

John had prepared a path before us. All around the tidied path were mounds of ice. We approached a figure, buried to the crown of its head in hail. Blue ice castles, complete with turrets, had frozen hard in the ice between the buried figure and gates behind. Ten sets of horns poked through the ice in a half-circle around this buried ice-person.

John dusted off the face. Inside, a frozen man was there, dressed up like a Pharisee, complete with a forehead phylactery. John touched the man's face, and it shattered into tiny shards.

John said, "Blue left a placeholder. I thought he'd been hollowed out, but this proves it. She somehow made her escape."

Windy's voice rustled between my ears. *Not all is as it seems. Our Archenemy is a master of the bait and switch, extreme climate change, hail in hell, freezing fear, dancing demons with yellow eyes, and Blue. The list goes on and on.*

I walked over to the inner barred gate. Tiberius followed. Once there, I shook the left side of this gate with both hands, seeing if I could shake it open. Tiberius grabbed the right gate, following my lead. Neither side budged. We peered down a dim, icy corridor. Howling noises echoed off the icy caverns.

I tried to remove my hands off the bars. They'd been there for only a few seconds, but I couldn't move either of them. I yanked hard. Hands came off but left skin behind—a perfect handprint on the bars. Blood seeped to the surface of my hands and froze. Skinless hands hurt like hell.

Tiberius saw what had happened to me and looked panicked. He too was unable to move his hands.

I said, "Sire, leave your skin. Take your life. *Pull now*!" He stayed stuck in place, frozen stiff. Whether from cold or fear or indecision, I don't know. I stood behind him, hands on his wrists, and said, "Together, now!" We yanked. Icy bars claimed his skin, but I had the man. For the moment, he was free of hell's lockdown.

Tiberius and I both shivered violently and beat a hasty retreat toward the outer veil. A glittering pair of blue eyes winked in the darkness amidst a bunch of smaller yellow eyes. All these eyes bounced around like a circus of hopped-up fireflies. I stopped, stared at the blue eyes.

Danger bells clanged inside me. Yet I inched into the darkness, deeper. Blue eyes flashed, tiny wedges of inverted radiance—a pulling, sticky suck. The suction was visceral, stretching my skinless hands out, moisture wicking out of me and dropping around my feet. I pried my right foot off the ice. My left sole stuck.

Blue eyes became an inbound tide, pulsing evil. Spiraling me further in, deeper down, beyond hell's foyer.

Windy yelled, *Trickster's at work—freezing you and Tiberius. Don't look at his bait—fool's gold, all.*

I pulled away. Left the ineluctable, inexorable. Left it behind. Headed toward the veil.

Windy counseled, *for now, in this preview of hell, keep moving. Later, you'll sit for three days beyond those gates. It's not time yet for them to open for you.*

I tried lifting my arms. Shoulders creaked like they'd rusted in place. Breath froze when it left my nostrils. Fear lulled my body, slowed my spirit. If I stayed longer, I wouldn't even know I was dead.

Sound of muffled screaming.

I worked my shoulders, slapped my sides. *Who was screaming?*

There, on veil's edge, Tiberius stood, sheered and screaming, stuck half in and half out of hell. Vision of *Augustia*'s prow split on the rocks, mother-face falling into the sea; man-face, flopping on the shore.

Black magic, spawned by Satan, had frozen Tiberius midway through his birthing passage, his skull neatly divided by fire and ice. Outside arm smoked and flapped. Inside arm had frozen in place. His eye inside the veil crusted with ice; the other eye, outside, rolled around, hot with terror. Half his scream had broken off and lay silent on the floor, encased in ice. Scream's other half rolled over the plateau, joining a racket of other sounds. Both hands were skinless.

Windy said, *don't waste a second. Lower your head. Run into him, full tilt. He's stuck in the birthing chute between boy and man. He runs hot and cold in spirit, moods, and sexual appetites for men and women. Reverent fear? It's beyond him, for now. He needs a rude rescue.*

I looked around. John stood behind me.

I said, "John, together, let's go!"

We bent forward and sprinted together right at Tiberius, gathering momentum as we went. We crashed headlong into him. Together we tumbled into the sun, dazed. My skinless hands skidded flat to a stop in the red dirt. We were surrounded by the screams of those who'd locked themselves inside the stockade. Also, other screams.

A pride of lions prowled between us and those gates, roaring, screaming. When John, Tiberius, and I sprawled onto the scene, they looked up with interest. *Hm, more meat.*

58
SLOW

Shabbat was now two days gone, and so was Rastus. Laz and I put Hope and Mike in Lydia's hands, under El Roi's eye. We rode Goodness and Kindness through rocky hills toward Rabbus farm. A few friends of mine, ex-whores like me, had married ex-murderers. They all worked the land while Rabbus and Leah were gone.

I'd told Laz about Rastus' heroic plans to take out Herod. Told him about my dream. Then I said, "Jesus told me I needed to practice what I believed. If I have a dream or vision, act on it."

"What does that mean now?"

"Bring a litter. We'll drag Rastus back after Maltesa breaks his legs."

Laz eyed my hair. "You have a new streak of faith in you, Slow."

"I'd hope so. Faith takes time to root—even down to the roots of my hair. You know what I believe, Laz? I'm accountable for every dream God gives me."

"I'll think about your words, wife. Spirits are living stones. All these stones scattered around us? Each has a seed inside.

Dream-soaks, when they're written down, meditated on, and acted on, crack those stones open."

I whipped my white shock of hair back and felt Windy seed my thoughts, courtesy of husband.

We took a shortcut along goat trails through the Judean hills. Faint paths required local knowledge. One misstep and you'd drop into a gopher hole, old salt mining pit, or through a thin crust into a bubbling sulfur sinkhole. Disappear. Or you might find Splittina's bones.

We were about halfway. Our mules ambled single file on the narrow path, down a Z-trail through a shady canyon. Inside this wadi, we allowed Goodness and Kindness to graze on an olive tree's leaves.

Laz fiddled with the bow he'd slung over his back. It had caught on the fletching of a quivered arrow. He spoke into the arid air, "I have a confession. When you told me Rastus was out to avenge you, I felt less than a man. *That was my job*, I told myself. But I changed my mind after I talked with Roy.'

"Yeah? What'd he say?"

"Roy said, 'Elders live close to the Flame. God's word rests heavier on them than the weight of the world. Lydia stills her looms. I pull back from the spinning wheel. You younger ones need your turn making glorious errors. How else can you learn success without moving from one failure to another without losing joy?'"

I said, "Seeds in those stones."

Laz nodded, "Yep. And I planted 'em. We'll harvest elders inside us one day. Right now, the path toward there is here, riding alongside you, not behind or in front of you. If I gallop ahead, I'd be rescuing me from Rastus' opinion. I don't care what he thinks of me. I don't care what I think of me. What Father thinks of me, well now, that's something else."

We kept moving out of that wadi and up-trail to a rocky pasture. We passed an empty grave, under an olive tree, beside an abandoned shepherd's hovel. His place was set on a hard-scrabble, dun-baked hill dotted with limestone boulders. A trickle of a stream ran through it into the wadi where we'd rested.

The shepherd's yard had gone to seed. No good crop to show for his life. Robbers had been at work, two and four-legged kinds. Men had looted and burned his hovel. Animals had routed his grave. Someone had started a marker stone but left it lying graveside, blank.

The grave itself was an open wound—corpse scattered, blowflies swarming his parts, rust-colored mites laying eggs the size of mustard seeds all over him. The ground around pulsed with life. Three crows pecked and tore at a burst lump of guts. Shiny red 'n green beetles seethed over his skull, a rippling blanket, cleaning his bones.

Laz stopped to look. I pulled my veil over my nose, clucked my tongue. Kindness and I passed by. I kept my ass moving to another olive tree. She foraged, yanking olive leaves off that tree with a pull and a twist.

I studied the prickly pear cactus dotting the whole slope before me, the ridge where our path would take us. Lydia had told me the flowers from this spikey-green flesh made a great cure for diarrhea. *Healing hid in a cactus, surrounded by stickles.*

Laz caught up with me. He said, "Empty grave reminded me of Jesus bringing me out of that old grave back in Sepphoris. And come to think, you've resurrected me too."

"Na, that's Jesus' specialty."

"Not what I meant. The man in me was addled, naïve. Your love raised me."

Some of my me's seeded that compliment. Soaked in it. We connected a bit more with each other these days. But still, we were sketchy, cobwebby.

We finally reached the steep defile that led out into Rabbus and Leah's homestead. Innocent-looking boulders, an army of sentinels, quietly watched our passage along both sides of the ravine. All were balanced on tipping points with make-weight levers. These thick sticks, hidden under brambles, were jammed in pivot points. A few well-placed whacks and down they'd come, burying whoever rode or walked where we were now. But it was a used trick. Rastus must have other caginess on call.

We stood now on a high plateau, mid-way up Mt. Gerizim, the Samaritan's Holy Mountain. Mt. Ebal shimmered, snow-covered, in the distance, towering over the city of Shechem. The sun edged down toward the horizon line.

Rabbus and Leah's homestead wasn't far. Cooked meat wafted on the wind. Snatches of speech drifted our way. We turned 'round the last wiggle in the trail before the farm.

Reprobates-on-the-mend sat in a circle out front. They were busy licking their fingers, crunching marrow out of roasted-goat bones, upending wineskins. Their mules were saddled, tied to the hitching post—all ready to follow their leader.

Rastus was talking. From what I caught, he should have been a rabbi.

Laz tied Goodness to the hitching post. I remembered her mate, Mercy, who'd bolted Leah under Eagle's wings and then died in the avalanche. Their offspring was my ride. I led Kindness into the circle of people. Their women left washing up to greet us. We'd been pottery mates not too long ago.

Laz said, "Hey, brothers. Your fields are white for harvest. It's that time of year. We're here to help you not get distracted from your *real* work by chasing stray foxes."

Rastus grumbled himself under an overhang. He looked stiff and tightly stuffed, like a minor civil servant. He must have seeded dark in stray patches of light 'cause shade was growing outta him.

He called over his shoulder. "Don't mess with us, Laz. We're about the noble business of resisting the occupation."

Laz spoke firm, loud. "Like misguided Crispus? Using a golden frame to hang murder's picture on your walls? Stoking men's loyalty with widow-maker rage?"

Rastus complained, "Lots of warriors in the scriptures—lots of vengeance."

Laz said, "You forgot Jesus' teaching on kindness, now haven't you? Waited till he was gone, so you could make him up as you go. But even if you mess up his memory, surely you remember our ancestor, David? He refused to kill King Saul. He had respect for the position of King, in spite of Saul hunting him down like a dog." [58]

Rastus' pit of madness was way beyond where words could travel. He walked my way, dodging reason. He forgot the proverb about wise men needing fear in three situations: in front of a tyrant, on every side of a fool, and in back of a mule.

He came up behind Kindness and me. An evening wind blew his hair in front of his eyes and my hair out of my eyes—the same Wind. I turned, looked at him, square on. He looked back at me, fright on his face.

He shouted, a high-pitched shriek, "Maltie, what are you here? You shouldn't have come!"

Kindness kicked, hind legs flying straight out behind her. A crunch, pop, and a scream—man down. Kindness reared up, knocked me over to the side, and lost her balance. Fell on Rastus. Another crunch.

I checked myself—dazed, but okay. I rushed to rescue my would-be savior. Pulled Kindness up by her bridle and handed her off to Esau-the-Dwarf. I bent over Rastus, my white shock of hair flying in the wind.

His eyes were wild, close to panic. "Maltie, why'd you do that to me? Legs are broke. I can't do nothing now." He broke down sobbing.

A seeded dream and an ass had obeyed a Voice, and I wasn't sure which one was me.

59

JESUS

The lions didn't wait long. The leader of the pride, a massive, maned warrior, charged. The others followed. Tiberius, John, and I laid on the ground, twenty yards away from the pride. The emperor scrambled to his feet, grabbed his sword from off the ground. His skinless hands spasmed. He screamed. His sword flipped up and out in an arc. It caught a flash of sun at its height, then landed on point, quivering.

Images flashed in my inner eye—a pride of lions stalking around the prophet Daniel in prison while he prayed.[59]

I said to Tiberius, "Stand still, Sire. Father's deliverance arrives, as I speak."

Tiberius, having no better options, obeyed. Together we faced the lions' charge. The lead lion was so close I could smell his breath. Between us, the Sword of the Spirit, closer than my missing hand-skin. Windy blasted glory-radiance, Himself a poised Sword. I shielded my eyes to keep the backs of my eyeballs from getting skinned.

The lead lion of the pride slid to a stop, reared high on his hind legs, and fell back in a heap on the others. All of them re-grouped, skittered backward. The pack circled, heads low, necks stretched out, gazing upward through squinted eyes—not at us, but Windy. Sword pointed right, toward a flock of feral goats on the ridgetop.

One of the goats bleated. These hapless creatures had snared themselves in brambles of unseen Mystery. The pride of lions shifted their attention and charged the goats. Re-directs are wonderful things. [60]

Windy vanished from view. Tiberius collapsed in a sand-swirl next to John and me. We sat, arms around each other's necks, giving and taking comfort—survivors of feral rage and divine Light.

Tiberius looked at John and me, searching our faces. He said, "Twice saved in less than an hour. I was caught between heat and ice, half of me freezing to death and the other half frying in a griddle. Both were magical, otherworldly.

"You two un-stuck me with your charge. Then I was frozen out here with fear and skinlessness, and you saved me from the lion's charge."

John said, "Don't look at me." He jerked his head toward me. "*He's* the Messiah."

Tiberius nodded, "The Hope god."

He looked at me. "You're more than a seer. Yes, you're a real magician who can serve me well."

"No, not a magician, Sire. Father's Spirit protected our lives so we can serve Him, the Emperor of all the worlds, seen and unseen. Time bears all earth's sons away. And these mountains around us will crumble. Yet his Spirit, Windy, remains immortal. His personal attendance today was *very* special. Father usually delegates a minor angel in such small matters."

Tiberias asked, "What? A spirit? Lions skidded to a stop and stared at *you*. You pointed, and they charged toward the goats. It had something to do with your words, 'Stand still. Perhaps lions can't see you if you're still?" The emperor looked all around him, face vexed, perplexed, searching for logical explanations.

He continued, "Now that I think of it, the lions squinted when they looked at some spot behind you. Hm. Reflected sun in their eyes, most likely. I'm no expert on lions, but the mix of heat and light together, off the frozen veil behind us. Yes, the combination might have dazzled them."

I said nothing to Tiberius. The three of us put arms around each other's shoulders, skinned hands dangling free. We walked toward the stockade, John to my right and Tiberius on my left. I winced when my raw palm touched the emperor's coat.

I looked at him as he limped along, haggard. This boy-man, almost four decades older than me, was on everyone's long journey—moving slowly from faith to faith by falling, failing, and rising again. *61*

We passed a large rock close to the stockade. Underneath the edge of that rock, I saw what appeared to be a transparent fluffy piece of almost nothing, lifting and then dropping in the wind. I bent down. Beneath the shelf of that rock, a black whipsnake lay molting. He'd wriggled out of his last skin and couldn't go back. His next skin wasn't yet ready. In the meanwhile, he was blind, vulnerable, skinless—betwixt and between on his journey. *Father, thanks for providing object lessons, but do you have to be so obvious?*

Father said, *did you notice? Neither Tiberius nor John saw the snake or got the lesson.*

The stockade doors flew open. Tiberius' Praetorian Guard spilled out into the open from their hiding place, swords all a-clutter. The guards surrounded their emperor with a fierce display of hyper-vigilance. I thought Tiberius might want to add these men to lions' lunch menu from the look on his face.

Tiberius ordered, "Sejanus, show me Pontii and Julius."

The two of us strode to where Claudia sat beside Pontii under a canvas pavilion. Claudia fanned the delirious legionnaire with one hand and wiped his fevered forehead with the other. I didn't look at Pontii. I looked at her. She seemed to draw sunbeams toward her, leaching the ground pale as chalk with her sky-blue eyes. My hands got clammy, and my heart pounded. *Father, why do you let a mere woman wreck me? I mean, is this fair after what I just went through?*

Father seemed amused. He said, *speak up. I couldn't quite hear you with all that heart-thudding.*

I walked to where Pontii lay, body blotched purple and black. He lay naked on his back, front of his body bare of skin and genitals; exposed guts going septic, stinking.

Hippo shook his head. "This man's not long for this world. Being flayed, emasculated, and chewed by army ants didn't agree with him. And the other one's not any better." He head-pointed toward Julius, a few yards away.

John piped up, "Both these men were brave. Neither cowered in the face of Bato's savagery. They howled when he carved them up—but anyone would have screamed while being skinned alive."

I knelt beside Claudia. Tiberius moved to examine Julius, laid out next to Rabbus. He wrinkled his nose at what he saw and smelled.

Leah sat nearby, rhythmically pounding away on something I couldn't see—*chocka, chocka, whap-de-dap.*

I said to Claudia, "First time attending a dying man?"

"Yes. Except for pathetic Postie, but he died because of my attending him. Pontii's worthier than Postie, but I'm not sure why. "

I said, "Each man and woman is made in Our image."

She replied, "If he's so precious, would it be too much to ask if you'd heal him? Not because he has any fondness for you." A coil of Pontii's intestines popped up, bluish purple. Claudia pushed them back inside his abdomen. Gas hissed out of a leak in that coil.

She looked at me, "In fact, Pontii hates your guts. And more, he propositioned me in our leaky tub on the way from Trimerus—right before he tried to kill me. When I said you came first in my heart, he tried to take my head off."

"True?"

She held her forefinger up, pointing heavenwards. "I do spice truth with lies most of the time—as befits a royal. This is not one of those times."

Pontii moaned pitifully, writhing in his delirium.

Claudia's eyes misted over. "I'm not asking for healing because of him, but because of another dream. The picture was all out of focus. A silver chalice was in his hand."

She leaned over and touched his right hand. "This hand hung over the chalice, dripping wet. The other hand pointed toward the shadows behind him, where I stood watching and burning inside. An unblemished white lamb had been staked out in front of him. He was about to sacrifice the lamb and wash his hands of it. No pity in him, no redemption, so why should I want you to save him?"

A shiver of terror rippled through me uncontrollably. I held my skinless right hand up, ready to reply.

Before I could answer her question, Claudia flinched. "What happened to you?"

Her uncle returned to my side. He showed her his hands too, "The same thing that happened to me. I followed him into hell."

He chin-pointed at his hands. "These *things* at our arms' ends got skinned. We'll heal, eventually. But now we must move forward and find Gemellus."

The emperor gave orders in clipped, preemptory snippets. No compassion. He looked down his nose at Pontii, jerked his head toward

Julius. "Both are dead men breathing. Put them out of their misery and bury them deep to keep the lions from scattering their bones. Uniforms go to others. Burial garments don't need pockets."

John walked over, unaware of the execution orders. "Hey, Jesus, I couldn't tell—was that an angel, or Another, impersonating the Sword out there?"

Claudia went nose-to-nose with John, "What are you talking about? Can't you see these men are dying and need Jesus' attention?"

I was confused. I did what I always do in moments like this—I dived inside for a Partner check. *Hey, Windy, what's next?*

60

WINDY

I tendered Jesus with my gaze. His inner eye and ear attended me. *Father and I are so proud of you. You weathered hell well and coped with the pride Satan sent.*

He replied, *I didn't know what I was doing.*

I said, your first tour in hell. You got to the entryway. Also, your first time with a pride of lions. In both cases, you trusted us. What a splendid example for Tiberius and John! You're learning to wait, listen, and breathe—particularly when you don't know what you're doing. I'm closer than the skin you have and don't have.

When I finished speaking, Jesus roused himself back into outer awareness. "Leah, how long have you been standing there?"

She smiled and offered a pot of paste. Jesus held his hands out to receive what was on offer.

Leah screamed when she saw his raw, bloody palms. "Your hands, Jesus!"

Tiberius edged around Jesus' back and showed her his hands as well.

"Oh, Emperor, you too—raw hands, but without those pools of blood leaking on the ground, like Jesus' hands! I was asking Windy to help heal Jesus."

Tiberius' gaze, emperesque, held her—*Here I am! Heal me.*

Leah continued, "Windy whispered to me on the path, before the leopard attack, 'pick that yarrow. Now get this dittany. Get more of the purple one, wound wart. You'll need them all. And over there, those pale stalks with white flowers and pods, poppies. Get a bunch of that.'

"I stuffed them all in my basket. Once we were here in the stockade, Windy told me, *sit in this corner on that stool. Reach under the ratty burlap bag there in the corner. Go ahead. Pull out a mortar and pestle from the bag.*

Put your flowers in the mortar, squeeze the juice from the poppy pods into the mix.

"I was only a little surprised to find the mortar and pestle in a bag. Once I sat, implements in front of me, bagged herbs at my feet, I did what she said, *Like this, Windy?*

"She said, *No, too much of the wound wart. Take a few leaves out. Okay, now grind the rest, two whacks down and a swoop in a circle, like this, chocka-chocka-swoosh. I'll say more later. We'll do a bit at a time. This way, you won't get flooded.*

"I did what she said. Didn't know what to do next. So, I gave it all to Jesus."

Tiberius breathed deep and looked directly up at my blue sky, making room for inspiration. "Was this the same voice that told you to lie on top of me and breathe into my mouth when I died?"

"Exactly, Sire."

Tiberius was fresh out of imperial edicts. He squeezed shut his eyes, blew on his palms, and waited. The white sun beat down. Pontii groaned in his delirium.

I instructed, *Son, hold your right hand over Leah's bowl. Wait a moment, not so fast. Okay. Add one drop of your blood to her paste. No more.*

Son held his hand over Leah's bowl. A drop of his blood hit the paste.

Leah stirred it into the mix.

I told her, *all right, Leah, Jesus' blood activated all the other gifts I've given you. Healing's now available for anyone wanting redemption.*

Leah said, *you're back to being male again, Windy—your voice got low.*

I squeezed a yes into her.

Tiberius had watched this whole operation—eyes squinted, chin on back of his right, loosely curled fist. He said, "Leah, I have roughly two billion, twelve million, eight hundred and fifty-eight thousand, nine hundred twenty-one sestertii in my treasury. At the moment. You, on the other hand, have *no* money. I'll give you a million sestertii to heal me, young woman."

She said, "Emperor, what healing I have is free from Jesus."

Guided by his pain, Tiberius opened his palms, but not his heart, to her. Both palms and insides of his fingers were red as ginseng berries. Leah fingered a thin layer of paste over his skin with her forefinger. Her finger passed over raw skin. Fresh skin was left behind, skin soft and pink as Gabe's bottom.

Tiberius' eyes brightened with something akin to entitlement. "Well, now! You could start a new religion with this stuff. Skin's arrived, finally. If you won't take money, I'll buy you and Rabbus a villa near mine on Rhodes."

I said to her, *Tiberius doesn't receive grace easily. Feels like he has to pay for all he gets.*

Leah boldened up, under my further instruction, "Excuse me, Sire, but perhaps you've forgotten something?"

"And what would that be?"

Leah got scared at her presumption. Almost balked. I nudged. She took a knee, bowed her head. "Gratitude, Sire. Not to me, but God. You were not *entitled* to healing, even though you be emperor. Healing's a gift from Jesus. You *might* want to say thanks, Sire, for the miracle he used me to provide. A mere suggestion, your Majestic-ness."

Tiberius, to his credit, looked abashed. He raised Leah to her feet, looked at Jesus, and grinned. "Thanks, Jesus. Pass it along to your Shareholders. Now, let's go. I have a war to fight."

Claudia said, "Uncle, wait a moment. Instead of mercy killing these two warriors, why not try a different form of mercy? Some pot paste from Leah, if it pleases you?"

He shrugged, disinterested now that he was healed.

She took a step toward Leah and motioned to the bowl. "May I?"

Leah was overcome with a new fit of uncertainty. The moment stretched. Her whitened fingers held tight the bowl. She breathed in my whisper, *let go, Leah. I'll handle this.*

Leah loosened her grip. Claudia took the bowl and a fingerful of paste, as she had seen Leah do. She looked into Son's eyes and fingered paste over his palm. The stigmata disappeared, and his palms skinned over. Claudia sucked in an "oh!" along with a whole new sense of self as a team player. *Healer of others, using Leah's obedience and Jesus' own blood.*

She fingered his other palm and watched it skin over. Then she moved two steps, sat on her haunches next to Pontii, and motioned with her hand for Jesus to join her. She dipped her finger in the bowl with his. Each got a fingerful. She said, "I'll start high and move down."

She looked at the empty spot where Pontii's penis and balls had been flayed off his body. "You do his thighs and *that* part. We'll meet in the middle."

They each did what I told them to do. Muscle and skin appeared where there had been none. A fresh, working penis, testicles, and scrotum, complete with epididymis, appeared when Jesus placed his hand over Pontii's bloody hole.

Pontii roused and looked at Claudia, reached to touch her face. "Am I dead, or did an angel rescue me?"

An invisible spiral saw corkscrewed in Jesus' heart. *Windy, is this jealousy? Maybe I should have let him die and changed my destiny.*

Father and I conferred and decided to let Son figure it out later.

Claudia said, "Yes, Pontii, God did come for you." She pushed his chin in my direction, "Pontii, meet God." He looked at Jesus and shut his eyes.

She and Son went to Leah and her paste-pot. Leah and Son attended Rabbus, then Claudia helped Jesus with Julius' healing, same as Pontii's.

Tiberius sulked in the only chair at the only table in the only pavilion in sight.

Morning crept past noon into the early afternoon. Rabbus' lay in the shade on his stomach, next to his napping son. The scars on his back had joined all his others, red ridges crisscrossing angry puckers. Gabe woke up and played with the leopard's cubs. Cubs chased boy, boy chased cubs—all four pouncing, rolling, and playing tug-of-war with Rabbus' shredded tunic.

Jesus crouched at Rabbus' pallet. Thick squares of gold sunlight beamed through a window, brightening the furrows of Rabbus' face.

Jesus said, "We're in the middle of enemy territory. This backcountry is chock-full of soldiers and demons. The emperor is set on finding his brother's grandson, Gemellus. What's your counsel?"

Rabbus replied, "Death has countless exits to let life out, but gods wrapped in skin are different. They want you, not foot soldiers like me, or even Tiberius. They may not know it, but if they get you, they get everything else."

I whispered to Son, *He's got that right. And, if they don't get you, they've got zip.*

Rabbus groaned, "Leah's paste was good. Thanks for adding your bit. My physical wounds healed, but the inside scars weigh me down, steal my joy, and fill me with sadness. When I force my mind off physical pain, my mind runs wide open. What heals that kind of pain?"

Before Jesus could answer, sound of infantry marching. He wondered, what comes our way, friend or fiend?

61

SLOW

Late afternoon. Laz sat with a scroll on his lap, opened to Isaiah. I worked in the kitchen, making dinner. Children wove in and out between his feet, playing with blocks, rolling them around like dice.

Their blocks brought back a memory of Cy visiting a few weeks back. He came in unannounced, sat down on the couch by the door. He'd barely survived getting ass-reamed and blinded by my pottery mates like I'd barely survived his violent rape years before that. The man kept getting better as his name got shorter—He'd gone from Cynico to Cyn to Cy.

Now he barely had any hair, just a couple of thin strands that caught breeze and moved about like dandelion fluff. Blue tubes in his temples pulsed. He dumped a bag on the floor in front of our son.

Michael tugged on his tunic and asked, "for me?"

Cy nodded.

Mike unloosed the bag's noose and dumped a pile of wooden blocks on the floor. He looked at them all, in wonder, wide-eyed—two-inch cubes, each one different than the next, gleaming with red, blue, and cream-colored pottery glaze. He ran over and jumped in Cy's lap, threw his arms around his neck.

Cy almost smiled. He said, "Always did have a wall 'round me, kid. Couldn't see it, being blind and all. Cyrena suggested I whittle my wall down, a bit at a time."

Mike put Cy's fingers on his own face, moving them around over his own eyes. "Fingers see me good. I love your Wall Whittle Bits! Thank you, lovely you, Uncle Cy."

Cy's blind eyes misted. He said, "Words don't work too good for me, but hands do. I couldn't talk a wall down, so I cut it into blocks. Maybe these hands can say sorry to your ma for days gone by. 'Sides, I wanted to give you some blocks to build what you want—walls, castles, maybe bridges to new places outta old ones. There's lots to choose from.'"

I let Cy's words compost inside me while I chopped beets into tiny bite-size blocks for dinner, frying them up with diced onions and shredded chicken. Beet trimmings, chicken bones, and yesterday's cantaloupe rinds ripened in a bag at my ankle, soon to bound for another kind of compost heap.

Our door opened, and Joanna walked in. She sat down in a chair at our table in the only puddle of light in the room. A lemon and an orange sat there in front of her, bright as a sunrise. She started to peel the orange with my paring knife I'd left on the table.

She said, "Long ride from Herodium. And, yes, thanks, I'll stay for dinner. What's cooking?"

I said, "Chicken. Since coming here, I've eaten so much chicken I've got a hen's wattle on my neck and pin feathers growing out my ankles. Dinner'll be a while, so plan on staying the night. Here's a cup of tea to go with that orange. Also, a pastry."

I got her a plate of pale pastries, the color and shape of newly hatched chicks that I'd bought for Hope. The pastries tasted like sawdust, but they were so pretty it didn't matter. Joanna bit the head off one and put the rest of it back, sipped her tea, and cut bits of orange off with Cutter's knife, popping them in her mouth. Her gray-streaked walnut hair caught all the afternoon light yet to be had.

I kept chopping beets. Looked sideways at her. The thin scar on her right cheek looked like it was on fire.

She whispered, loud enough for Laz and me to hear, "Herod was talking about you again, with that look in his eye. Probably in the next day or so, you might get a call…."

When Cutter heard the news, she wanted slip a sharp knife in either ear and bust both my eardrums. I held our hands to the cutting board.

Hope, our child with the jug ears, stopped her play underfoot and came over to me for a kiss. Her lips, held up for comfort, looked as red and vulnerable as a rose. Once my lips brushed hers, she held tight to my leg. My knees caught the trembling in her hands.

Laz piped up, "Joanna, on your way down from Herodium did you see that huge spice caravan camped outside of town? I hear it's headed south for Egypt tomorrow. Perhaps our family should melt into it, journey through your old home country, Slow. Those caravans go through Moab on the way to Alexandria."

Joanna reached out and popped Hope up on her lap, stacked up a few of Mike's blocks on the tabletop. "I did see that caravan on my way down here. But I thought you asked God what He wants on most stuff. And you might want to do that now."

She flicked the blocks, and they all fell down. "God will unblock your path if he wants you in Egypt."

My scalp began to tingle right where my hair had turned white. A patch of tingle. Like I was receiving signals from somewhere out there—or maybe one of my-me's inside.

Hope jumped down and ran to her abba, "Yes, Abba, yes. Can we go?" She didn't wait for an answer but immediately started putting Mike's blocks into his bag. She pulled the noose tight and said, "Okay, all ready to go now."

I laughed at her and then looked over at Laz. He been studying Isaiah nineteen all day. His finger pressed down on a verse—something about a highway to Egypt. [62]

Laz had pieces of scripture stockpiled for every possible occasion, but his finger on this verse seemed something more, beyond where his vision stopped.

God speaks out of an oh-so-ordinary day—husband's finger on a scripture, friend coming a long way for dinner, hair tingles with Hope's kiss, and compost ripening.

62

JESUS

Rome's four legions marched over the shoulder of Dragon Ridge. Gemellus and Caligula led the legions. Caligula jumped off his pony and ran as fast as his short frame could take him right into the arms of Tiberius.

These three men led us from Disaster Bay along the coastal marshlands north to the Buna River. From there, barges took us inland, east by northeast, to Castle Rozafa. This towering fortress, high on a bluff, overlooked the capital city of Scodra and the Kir, Buna, and Drin rivers. This triad of rivers fed Lake Scodra, north of the capital city.

Gemellus stayed to rule while Tiberius came and went to his villas on Rhodes and Capri with his covey of lovers, including Caligula. Rabbus always was with him, while Leah stayed with Gabe, John, and I in Scodra. Claudia also stayed, but by choice, not decree.

Whenever any of us left the castle to walk in the city, a detachment of Roman imperial guards accompanied us. We all learned yet another culture, another language. John and I formed a synagogue and taught Torah every day to the curious onlookers.

Claudia studied ancient Illyrian literature and formed a theatre troupe where she staged classic plays she had studied—and a few she had written. I attended all her performances, sat on the front row, hooted, and yelled with the rest of the audience. She was amazing, beautiful, and a gifted actress.

One late Friday afternoon, hot and sultry, she and I sat, together-apart as usual, on a balcony built for two on the castle's second story. Each of us had come from our separate wings in the castle to this courting porch for our one allowed weekly meet. We entered and exited this porch through separate doors and sat on separate sides of a lattice screen, as dictated by custom and Tiberius' decree.

A similar screen separated us from the view of merchants and buyers below in the castle's central courtyard. Stalls had been set up in this huge courtyard—produce on one side, meats and dairy on another, dry goods on a third side. Clothing, jewelry, and money changers took up the fourth side. Bedlam ruled during daylight hours, but the Romans squeezed out all the chaos at five o'clock every day.

I reclined on my couch. Claudia leaned against the lattice. She sat cross-legged in her flowing silk gown. She pulled off her veil and air-kissed me through the lattice. Her beauty had matured from an ordinary sort of pretty to stunning. I passed a bouquet of blue, love-in-a-mist through the lattice, one flower at a time.

She reached through the ragged hole in the lattice screen and stroked my arm. "All this apartness with a bare hour of divided togetherness—is it worth the angst?"

I replied, "Absolutely. But today, desire eats me up. I want you, but we can't have each other."

Claudia sulked. "I too am rotten with wanting. Anyone else in their right mind at my age would be married and have children. But us? We wait, paper to a flame that you refuse to spark."

I said, "I hold a flint within me, a flint with a heart of fire. I wait for Father's will to strike me."

Claudia rolled her eyes. "For God's sake, if you have a heart of fire, *marry me*! Better to marry than burn. But every time desire kindles you or me, you prove how little I matter compared to your Father. This thing you have going with him… ah, it's a little incestuous, if you ask me."

I said, "Father, Windy, and I are a unity. *My* desire is to have and hold you. They remind me that heartbreak is one crucial way they grow us both into maturity. Windy whispers, "unrequited love is the essence of being alive, of being on your journey from here to there."

Claudia said, "Who am I to argue with God? But for now, I hate heartbreak, hate unrequited love, hate this journey. Hate, hate, hate. And there you have it."

I waved my hands toward the mass of vendors and buyers milling around below us. "Everyone experiences these feelings. If I refuse, what good am I to you, or them? I suffer what everyone does, so you'll come to know Father. Many believe now. Millions will follow."

Claudia replied, "You blow my mind like a typhoon. I'm focused on us, here, now—trying to figure out how to get us married in the eyes of God and people. You sit above the circle of the earth watching a train of humans tromp through heaven's gates, starting with Adam and Eve."

I refused to speak what she couldn't hear, and I couldn't bear to say.

Claudia said, "We're both mid-twenties. People look at us like leftover birthday cakes. We should have married years ago. But you spend your time with John chin-wagging in the marketplace, arguing with pagan priests, whacking them about the head with Kingdom talk."

She tucked a stray strand of hair behind her ear. "Why don't we bamboozle each other into bed? Big castle, consenting adults, dim hallways. You know the rationales as well as me—we love each other, what's the harm, take the chariot for a spin before you buy it. Any or all of that. Besides, if we had sex, your conscience couldn't say no to marriage."

I said, "Ah, Claudia, don't think I haven't had the same thoughts. But we're fated to tangle spirits, not bodies. I'll never be your husband."

We both busted into tears of frustration. I held my head in one hand. I felt her two fingers on my arm. I grabbed her fingers and held on. A storm of desire swept over both of us like a forest fire.

63
WINDY

It was toward closing time. A wrinkled hag, dressed in a grunge-brown smock, slipped over Castle Rozafa's drawbridge. She was a covered woman, layered with dust and her lower face rag-wrapped. She shuffled along, facing outbound like everyone else in the people pack. But unlike all the others, one step shuffled forward and two steps backslid. Furthermore, hidden under her smock, one wooden shoe faced forward, and the other faced backward. No one noticed her slight of foot, not at all. What people expected to see, they saw. She slipped backward into the castle keep, her intent hidden in plain sight.

A slight stench arose from the canvas-wrapped package she hugged to her chest. She guarded her leaking package like she was carrying the Queen's jewels. The black, bloody drips behind her were trampled by people cutting and weaving, people in a hurry to get home.

The sergeant of the guard, hungry for dinner, didn't notice the old, shrouded hag. She arrived at the main square and sank into shade behind a pillar. A soft groan trickled from her lips. She gazed at Lover's Porch, where she knew Son was meeting with Claudia. She tucked a strand of blue-white hair back under her hijab. She sat and waited for shadows to lengthen.

She didn't have long to wait. Jesus had noticed the courtyard emptying out. Shabbat began in an hour or so. He and Claudia each departed their porch separately and met at the courtyard well. They unhooked the well's bucket, payed out the rope on its spinning spool. The weighted bucket clattered down into the castle's water supply. They waited for it to fill and then pulled the bucket up together. Claudia's eyes rested on Jesus, and she filled his eyes with her graceful, veiled movements.

Neither knew how close the Old Enemy had crept.

They filled their containers and turned to go, each heading for their separate rooms to prepare for the evening meal on this Day of Atonement.

The couple saw this old woman, head sagging to her side. She clutched what looked to be her only possession. Jesus approached. "Old woman, you look tired, and you have no bucket to draw water. Can we share our water with you?"

Her heavy brow held her eyes in shadow. "Yes, your lordship. I'm most thirsty."

Claudia moved in front of him, "Here, let me do this, Jesus."

She ladled water from her bucket for the old woman. Jesus stood behind her. The hag drank greedily, turned her head to the side, and let slip some spit back into Claudia's ladle. Claudia put the ladle back in her bucket.

Claudia suddenly remembered kneeling before Satan at Sepphoris well. She remembered feeling fried with desire. She shook off the memory, forgot about Satan's shape-shifting genius.

She whispered to Jesus, "This woman creeps me out. Let's go. Our good deed's done."

Jesus twanged a memory trace—*this woman's pupils are freaky weird, unnatural. And those blue irises, yellowed whites, dancing in the dark beneath her cowl. Where have I seen that?*

The hag pulled her cape over her whole face and hid the boils on her cheek and chin. Her filthy smock covered all the others.

She lowered her eyes, "Thank you, m' lord 'n lady. I'll bother you no more."

Claudia pulled on Jesus' arm, murmured in his ear, "Please, let's leave. *Now.*"

They moved into the castle corridor. On the way, I said, *Son, you've seen these eyes before—in another dark place. Remember?*

Jesus replied, *My body remembers, Windy, but my brain is a mind of little memory. Where, when? I can't place it.*

I blew his memory back inside Dragon Ridge, eyes blinking in the dark, and let his imagination out for a wander. *Minimal steerage on my part best sharpened his discernment.*

Jesus couldn't grab the memory. That memory played in the corner of his mind but wouldn't come out of hiding. He bid the woman goodbye, "Shalom Aleichem, old woman."

Drusilla said, "And to you as well, master." She whispered the return greeting in her native tongue, "Aleichem Salam." She watched the two go arm in arm into the castle's interior, turning into opposite halls.

Night fell, a soft black net, suffocating any remaining light.

Alone with Satan, Drusilla unwrapped the high priest. She'd cut the Druid high priest in twelve pieces after they'd last had sex. She'd only brought his head with her, but it bubbled with pus-drenched poxy buboes. Satan, inhabiting her, cackled, "Justice is served!"[63]

A guttural hacking came from Drusilla's mouth. This was the closest thing to a laugh that Satan could flog from inside her dying body. Drusilla-the-Witch had spun down a titch. Well, no matter. No one had seen her drop off the rest of her divided house. He'd been well distributed. One hand in this well, a foot in another. On her way into Scodra, she'd left a leg in the Buna River, an arm in the Drin River, guts in the mouth of Lake Scodra—all the town's freshwater supplies. A poxed priest and priestess had been well used for the greater evil.

Satan used Drusilla's hands to pull out the high priest's severed head, plant a rock in his mouth, and drop it in the well.

Satan steadied Drusilla's tottering frame. He wandered among the vendor's stalls and hawked bloody wads of phlegm on the wooden tabletops. Little pox deposits, waiting to be paid forward. *Unsuspecting imbeciles, these humans. They'd carry this pandemic far and wide.*

Satan moved the worn-out Blue Queen to the main sewage tunnel that flowed under the castle walls. He slipped out of her body and stood next to her, a shadowed form in a black thawab. He carried her to an open sewer grate, dropped her like excrement into the hole.

He slipped down after her, straddling the current, bent over, held her head under the sewage. Once she'd kicked around a bit, she stopped breathing. Her spirit departed for Hades. A slow-moving current of raw sewage trapped her body against the sewer grate. Her arms and legs flopped about, mimicking life in death as she had before she'd died.

Satan was now truly alone. He thought, *Blue played her part. Strutted across the stage, full of sound and bombast. My armies will arrive soon, and the siege will start. We'll see how well Jesus handles this plague in a month or two once his converts start eating their childr*en.

Satan, full of hatred for all things human, howled into the night.

DISCUSSION QUESTIONS FOR GROUPS

This third novel in *Jesus' Silent Years* has many intense moments—Jesus' roughest ride of all four volumes, the lowest point in his journey to maturity. Below are some questions for you to process your journey.

You might want to do this with others in a small group. Remember the old Swahili saying, "if you want to go fast, go alone. If you want to go far, go together."

1. *Journey* has given a new meaning to silence in *Jesus' Silent Years.* In chapter nine, Jesus is shamed into silence by prison, starvation, deprivation, poverty, and sexual abuse. Windy tells Jesus, *Shame had squashed you into silence. Your silent years....* Marginalized people, racial minorities, people of color—Jesus joins with all these groups in his life experience. In what ways has life silenced *your* voice? How, like Slow, have you been fractured into No-Speak? Or, like Leah, silenced by depression? Or reduced to spouting ideas without emotion, like John?
2. The hero's journey always takes that person down. The hero begins with an ordinary life, suffers lower and lower, and then rises to an extraordinary plateau of life. What distinguishes a hero from a non-hero in your mind?
3. Cannibalism is a gruesome part of this book. "Eat my body, drink my blood." These words Jesus spoke were misinterpreted by early Roman rulers. Isaiah said, "If you're generous with the hungry and start giving yourselves to the down and out, your lives will begin to glow in the darkness, your shadowed lives will be bathed with sunlight." (58:10) How do you feed the hungry with your time, money, and energy? Bato, in chapter 46, said to Julius: "You're no different than the rest of his followers. Jesus is far more food for thought than what you can

stomach." Discuss one scene in this book that moves an interesting *idea* to *nourishment* in your body and community.

4. Jesus experienced a long recovery from abuse while in a garden. He dragged and doubted. He had no energy. Today we would prescribe an antidepressant and get him into cognitive behavior therapy. Instead, Father and Windy let him sit and soak in grief, sent Leah to rub his feet, put him to work pulling weeds, helped him dig up reminders of the abuse in their presence, and allowed Satan to tempt him in a cemetery. They sat silently with him, cried with him. What takeaway lessons for responding to loss did you glean?
5. We're all exiled in different ways. Some from a home country, from close friends, and many from their true selves. Mary, in chapter one, identified with fellow Jews during the Holocaust on her personal night of "broken glass." What in your life has been thrown down, crunched, shattered, lost—reflecting your status as an 'exile'? How have you experienced a personal exile, similar to Claudia, where you were forced to develop new life skills?
6. Rites of passage have an essential place in life. Some are traditional, like a teen leaving home, or a senior living with adult children, or in an assisted living environment. Emperor Tiberius was a middle-aged adolescent. He'd delayed leaving "home" till his mid-50's; he'd grown older without growing up. Discuss a rite of passage—leaving home, committing to a life partner, retiring, moving to a new place) you've experienced or avoided in your life. Perhaps, if there are no words, draw or sculpt or dance or listen to a song on your device that captures the emotion of this challenge.
7. We observe character formation in the names of certain characters. For example, Cynico, Cyn, and Cy are names that mirror one man's maturation as a person. How have you claimed or rejected the names given to you, based on your maturation process?

Preview the last volume in this series, scheduled for release, Fall, 2021:

Jesus' Silent Years, Homecoming:

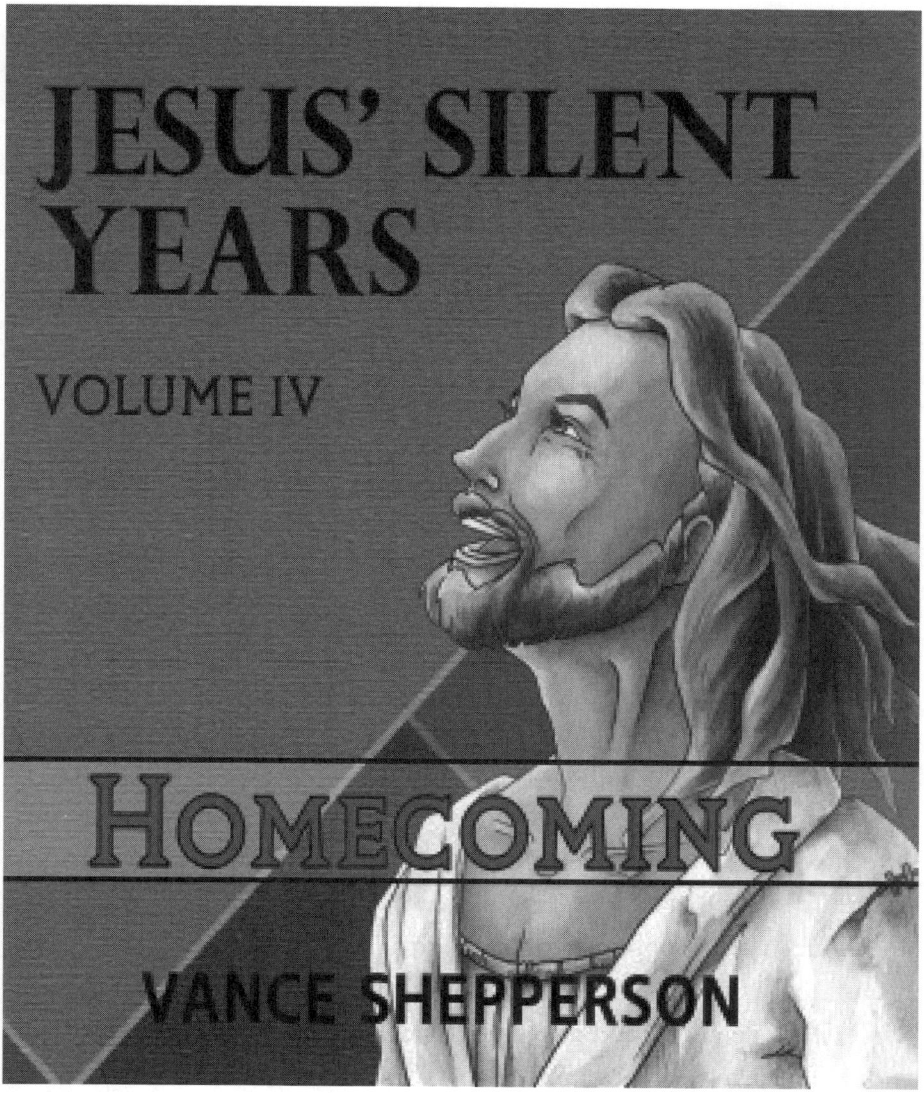

1

WINDY

The head catapulted over the fortress' wall. It landed between the emperor's feet. He looked down at the drained face of his brother's grandson, Gemellus, lying on the courtyard's cobblestones.

Father's Son, Jesus bar Joseph, stood at Caesar Tiberius' right hand. Claudia, the emperor's niece, stood behind Jesus, and Caligula, the emperor's nephew, stood under a shadowed overhang at a distance. A smile played at the corners of Caligula's mouth. When he turned away it hung in the air, like the afterglow of some evil presence.

Tiberius knelt and stroked his heir's hair. The atmosphere was still and stale as if inside a capped jar. A mindless light filled his eyes like you might see in a crushed dog who'd just been run down. He clenched his jaw, refusing to register yet another loss.

Jesus, on the other hand, was available and responsive to Father's voice delivered with my breath. When I blew, he consciously took my wind in his lungs—in and out sixteen times a minute, syncing my breath with his, Father's heartbeat with his own. Claudia, the friend Jesus loved, also responded to my prompting. She too was teachable and because of that, reachable for kingdom purposes. What moved Son, moved her.

The night before this execution, Gemellus lived. He'd reclined at table with his Uncle Tiberius. Servants brought the meal, their slippers shush-shushing into the cavernous banquet hall.

Gemellus had looked at what they'd placed in front of him—a hot, open-faced ham and onion sandwich, dripping with horseradish garnish, a side of deviled eggs, and a Caesars salad. Iced herb tea, sweetened with honey and garnished with mint leaves, was to the right of his plate.

He blinked. What remained on the table before him was a bowl of thin gruel with a lonely carrot peel floating on the top. Everyone else's place setting held a similar bowl, the same soup.

Decades of incense, pregnant in the heavy wall tapestries, served to soften the stink of unwashed bodies. The stone fireplace, smudged by many fires, was big enough to baste a brace of boars, or alternately, a good-sized giraffe with his head up the flue. Now it was dark and empty.

Gemellus sipped his soup from a silver spoon. He re-capped, "the siege has already lasted a year. Pox and battle have chopped off two-thirds of our army. The only remaining meat inside the castle is human. And these corpses are worthless—eating poxed people poxes people. So, we burn them. We live with the smell of roasted flesh in the air. Our stomachs remind us daily that living dogs are better than dead lions."

Tiberius had also lost a third of his body weight during the last year. He said, "I'd never thought I'd eat my citizens. But now I'm melting to sticks. I've taken to hoping a non-poxed Roman will die so we can roast him and stay alive another day."

Gemellus made a careful study of his shoes. "Let me lead a sortie through the sewage tunnel tonight. It's a new moon, dark. We can slip their knot. I'll inform Grandmother. I'm sure she'll crush this rebellion."

Tiberius thought, *no chance of success there. Mother is punishing me for leaving her. She knows exactly what she's doing. 'This is what you get, Tibbie, for not following my directions. See where this new Seer had led you?'*

He said, "I can't let you do that. What you suggest is too dangerous. Your father, Drusus, would agree—we can afford to loser lesser people, but you're unique."

Gemellus replied, "Unique means alone, Uncle."

Tiberius shook his head. "Our enemies crouch at the door like a pack of hyenas, waiting to devour us."

Gemellus agreed. "All we do is catapult our poxed dead over the wall, and our enemies do the same. Weaponized corpses fly by each other, going opposite ways. Meanwhile, we starve and our enemies feast. They'll come over the walls on the ramp they're building. Only the dead will greet them. I wonder, Uncle, why hasn't Grandmother sent reinforcements from

Rome?" Before the emperor could craft yet another lie, Gemellus abruptly stood and strode out the door into a shadowy hallway.

Caligula had been reclining back of a screen that was positioned behind Tiberius. His protection from those still recovering from plague. He'd positioned himself well with his uncle as boy toy and practiced, adroit admirer—a potent mix of youth, sex, and clever imitation.

Cal excused himself. He trotted away through a shadowy doorway, different from the one Gemellus had taken. He needed a water closet, quick. Preserved from pox, he'd been plagued by an irritable bowel. His ambition strained north. His body drained south.

He glided in and out of shadows, one wall torch to the next. Squatting over the toilet hole, he multi-tasked. Released his bowels and scribbled a note. Tied it to a rock.

Once finished, he hurried on, quick-quick; made his way alone along a balustrade, into a curtain of rain pouring at a diagonal across the marshlands below. Lightning forked down and rolled across the gassy swamp in a ball before splintering into white-hot whips, then nothing more.

Cal flicked a glance at the banquet room above, checking for prying eyes. Creamy light poured out the lunettes but no curious eyes stared down at him.

He tossed the rock over the wall toward an old growth cypress tree. *Rock rolled downhill. Sound of scampering feet briefly hushed the tree frogs and cicadas. Rushlight flared, extinguished.*

Back in the ballroom, three people huddled around as many candles—Tiberius, Jesus, and Claudia. The emperor's bodyguard stalked the room's perimeter, looking behind draperies, popping open doors, hand on his dagger. Rabbus had become almost mute after cholera claimed his toddler son. Gabe's body had been sent to the kitchen. Rabbus *understood* that all non-plague corpses were to be used to feed the living. But after the idea was made flesh in his own family, Rabbus entered a sad, silent year, situated between grief and denial.

While silent Rabbus guarded himself from sadness, the inner circle huddled over dim puddles of light at table. Candles' flickering flames danced in contrary breezes.

Tiberius said, "God-man, it's only a matter of days before these savages are up and over the wall. Now or never, Seer. Tell me what to do."[1]

I hovered around, over, and within Son. Could he remain One with Father and I, or would he dither into rescues not given him for him to do? I brooded like a mother hen, nesting love and limits into him. Jesus was tempted to engage with the emperor. I nudged a 'no' into him. *Do not let his panic infect you.*

He said, "Sire, I've not yet recovered from the plague.If it pleases you, I'll consult Father in the night hours and we'll talk in the morning."

Jesus and Claudia left the room, leaning on each other, heading for the infirmary. Jesus had followed my instructions and passed this test. But could he keep his mind and heart on point? The emperor's pressured presence, a short sword of desperation; Claudia, a net of longing and love. We'd provided both as a gauntlet to train our growing Messiah into maturity.

Tiberius remained with Rabbus alone. He grumped, examined the empty platters in front of him. He wiped the last bit of gravy smear from Jesus' plate and sucked it off his finger. Truth was, he was famished for a seared steak, medium rare. *Such a hungry muscle—his beating, beaten heart.*

ENDNOTES

[1]Isaiah 64:4 *Since before time began no one has ever imagined, no ear heard, no eye seen, a God like you who works for those who wait for him.*

[2]This is an oblique reference to a more recent persecution on November 9th, 1938. See this reference for photos of that pogram. https://www.history.com/news/kristallnacht-photos-pogrom-1938-hitler.

[3]2 Chronicles 32:31, "God left him [Hezekiah] to test him and to know everything that was in his heart."

[4]*My God, don't turn a deaf ear.... Liars are pouring out invective on me; Their lying tongues are like a pack of dogs out to get me, barking their hate, nipping my heels—and for no reason! Psalm 109:1-2, MSG*

[5]Reminiscent of the prophet Elijah in I Kings 17:1-7.

[6]Isaiah 41:15-16, *I'm transforming you from worm to harrow, from insect to iron. As a sharp-toothed harrow you'll smooth out the mountains, turn those tough old hills into loamy soil. You'll open the rough ground... to the blasts of sun and wind and rain—MSG*

[7]Abbate, Carolyn, *In Search of Opera*, Princeton University Press, Princeton, NJ. 2001

[8]https://www.ancient.eu/Romulus_and_Remus/

[9]See Psalm 23.

[10]*Bulfinch, Thomas (2016). Bulfinch's mythology. Digireads.com Publishing. ISBN: 978420953046.*

[11]James 1:21, "... In simple humility, let our gardener, God, landscape you with the Word, making a salvation garden of your life." *MSG*

[12]https://positivepsychology.com/what-is-peak-end-theory/

[13]Job 2:13, "So they sat down with him on the ground seven days and seven nights, and no one spoke a word to him, for they saw that *his* grief was very great." *NKJV*

[14]Revelation 20: 8-9; see also https://www.christianity.com/wiki/end-times/what-are-gog-and-magog.html

[15]John 14:6

[16]Isaiah 27:1, depicts as a demon serpent any powerful political system that works to displace or replace God's kingdom: "In that day the Lord with His severe sword, great and strong, will punish Leviathan the fleeing serpent, Leviathan that twisted serpent; And He will slay the reptile that *is* in the sea."

[17]John 13:36, *Jesus answered, "You can't now follow me where I'm going. You will follow later."*

[18]Revelation 5:6, vision of the coming King as a lamb, "Then I saw a Lamb, looking as if it had been slain, standing at the center of the throne, encircled by the four living creatures and the elders. The Lamb had seven horns and seven eyes, which are the seven spirits of God sent out into all the earth." *NIV*

[19]Micah 6:8

[20]Matthew 27:26, *Then he released Barabbas to them. But he had Jesus flogged, and handed him over to be crucified."*

[21]Psalm 8:2, "*Gurgling infants sing choruses about you. Toddlers shout the songs that drown out enemy talk, silence atheist babble." MSG*

[22]Ancient Jewish wedding rituals included a negotiation between fathers for the bride's price, symbolized in a cup of wine. The groom observed the proceedings. When a demand for payment was made by the bride's father, the groom could say, "Let this cup pass from me, Father, but not my will—your will be done." *The father would judge if the relationship was worth the cost.* If the cost was too much, the son would not drink. If the relationship was worth the cost, his son would drink the full cup of wine. Toller, Mathew; *Grace Undone*, 2018, p. 77.

[23]Deuteronomy 8:15

[24]See Joshua 9 for a story of how the Gibeonites pulled this same ruse with Israel.

[25]Hosea 10:8, *They will say to the mountains, "Cover us!" and to the hills, "Fall on us!"*

[26]2 Chronicles 20:21-22, "Jehoshaphat appointed men to sing to the Lord and to praise him for the splendor of his holiness as they went out at the head of the army, saying: "Give thanks to the Lord, for his love endures forever." As they began to sing and praise, the Lord set ambushes against

the men of Ammon and Moab and Mount Seir who were invading Judah, and they were defeated."

[27]Josephus Flavius, War 1, 31, 10, *Antiquities XIV*, 323-325.

[28]Psalm 139:15 *MSG*

[29]Roman quinqueremes carried a total crew of 420—300 rowers, and the rest marines. The quinquereme would have 90 oars in each side, and 30-strong files of oarsmen. The fully decked quinquereme could also carry a marine detachment of 70 to 120, giving a total complement of about 400. Coates, John F. (2004). "The Naval Architecture and Oar Systems of Ancient Galleys". In Gardiner, Robert (ed.). *Age of the Galley: Mediterranean Oared Vessels since pre-Classical Times*. Conway Maritime Press. pp. 127–141.

[30]*Senex*, the Latin word for 'seventy,' signifies old age with some mix of wisdom and crotchetiness. *Puer*, Latin for 'youth,' signifies the immature male with cheery optimism and/or naivete. In Jungian psychology, the archetype known as the 'puer-senex' complex, indicates a balance between the two energies within a person.

[31]John 17:3, "*You put him in charge of everything human so he might give real and eternal life to all in his charge." MSG*

[32]Revelation 19:11, *"Then I saw Heaven open wide—and oh! a white horse and its Rider. The Rider, named Faithful and True, judges and makes war in pure righteousness."*

[33]John 17:11-12, "Holy Father, guard them as they pursue this life … so they can be one heart and mind as we are one heart and mind."—Jesus, *MSG*

[34]Egg-eater snakes symbolize the act of killing off life before it begins, like the massacre of the innocents in Bethlehem. They are ancient archetypes of potential devoured; what is possible, engorged.

[35]Slow's story is typical of many Dissociative Identity Disorder (DID) folks. See: Maldonado, JR; Spiegel D (2008). "Dissociative disorders — Dissociative identity disorder (Multiple personality disorder)". In Hales RE; Yudofsky SC; Gabbard GO (eds.). *The American Psychiatric Publishing textbook of psychiatry* (5th ed.). Washington, DC: American Psychiatric Pub. pp. 681–710. ISBN 978-1-58562-257-3.

DID is a spectrum disorder. Some of us have only a thin veil between ego states—we're aware of other parts of ourself. Others require a nice, thick protective wall between their parts. But regardless of where you are on this continuum, you can take hope from Jesus' comment to his Father: *(One day) they'll be as unified and together as we are—I in them and you in me. Then they'll be mature in this oneness.* John 17:23—*MSG*

[36]Romans 8:26, *God's Spirit is right alongside helping us along. If we don't know how or what to pray, it doesn't matter. He does our praying in and for us, making prayer out of our wordless sighs, our aching groans. He knows us far better than we know ourselves, knows our pregnant condition, and keeps us present before God—MSG*

[37]Matthew 25:4, The foolish ones took their lamps but did not take any oil with them. The wise ones, however, took oil in jars along with their lamps—*NIV*

[38]Evil's power often mirrors the forces of goodness. Here we see a darker mirror of Ephesians 3:20—*God can do anything, you know—far more than you could ever imagine or guess or request in your wildest dreams!*

[39]See Luke 1:39-40.

[40]See Matthew 5:21-22, *You're familiar with the command to the ancients, 'Do not murder.' I'm telling you that anyone who is so much as angry with a brother or sister is guilty of murder.*

[41]Man was created on the sixth day of creation (Genesis 1:27). When repeated three times, 666 becomes known as the mark of the Beast (Revelation 13:18). Bato, in this parable, prefigures the Beast.

[42]Daniel 7:7, *A fourth animal appeared in my dream. This one was a grisly horror—hideous. It had huge iron teeth. It crunched and swallowed its victims.*

[43]Cannibalism was commonly practiced among some Illyrians of that day—eat your enemies' strength and weaken them with terror. Many Romans also viewed early Christians as cannibals—see *Ancient Rome* by William E. Dunstan 2010, page 293. John 6:51-57 references Jesus' comments about the Eucharist. His comment about the mystical union of believers "in Christ" was widely misunderstood, then and now, not as a parable but as a literal command to engage in cannibalism.

[44]Revelation 12:3, "And then another sign alongside the first: a huge and fiery dragon. It had seven heads and ten horns, a crown on each of the seven heads…." Another symbol, prefiguring days to come.

[45]Isaiah 21:11, "“*Night watchman! How long till daybreak? How long will this night last?" The night watchman calls back, "Morning's coming, But for now it's still night.—MSG*

[46]Song of Solomon 1:12-14, "*My fragrance filled the room. His head rested between my breasts. The head of my lover was a sachet of sweet myrrh." MSG*

[47]Daniel 11:36, "Meanwhile the king of the north will do whatever he pleases. He'll puff himself up and posture himself as greater than any god. He will even dare to brag in defiance of the God of gods. And he'll get by with it for a while….""

[48]Psalm 2:7-10, "You're my Son, and today is your birthday. What do you want? Name it: nations as a present? Continents as a prize? You can command them all to dance for you or throw them out with tomorrow's trash." *MSG*

[49]I Kings 18:44-45, "The servant reported, 'A cloud as small as a man's hand is arising from the sea. So Elijah said, Go tell Ahab, 'Hitch up your chariot and go down before the rain stops you.' Meanwhile the sky grew black with clouds, the wind rose, and a heavy rain started falling."

[50]Isaiah 40:3-5, "…Prepare for God's arrival! Make the road straight and smooth, a highway fit for our God. Fill in the valleys, level off the hills, smooth out the ruts, clear out the rocks. Then God's glory will shine and everyone will see it. yes. Just as God has said." *MSG*

[51]Jonah 2: 9,10—"But I, with shouts of grateful praise, will sacrifice to you. What I have vowed I will make good. I will say, 'Salvation comes from the Lord.' And the Lord commanded the fish, and it vomited Jonah onto dry land." *NIV*

[52]Jesus refers to the Greek *apokalupsis*, from the root words: *apo*, to remove, and *kalupsis*, a veil. At a wedding, separation ends; bride and groom are unveiled and see each other naked, without shame.

[53]Matthew 6:13, *You're in charge! You can do anything you want! You're ablaze in beauty!—MSG*

[54]Zephaniah 3:17, "The Lord your God is in your midst, a Warrior who saves, He will rejoice over you with joy, He will be quiet in his Love (making no mention of your past sins), He will rejoice over you with shouts of joy." *Amplified*

[55]Matthew 7:14, "The way to life—to God! —is vigorous and requires total attention." *MSG*

[56]Daniel 7:6, *"Next I saw another animal. This one looked like a panther... with four heads...."*

[57]Isaiah 11:6-9, *"The wolf romp with the lamb, the leopard sleep with the kid. Calf and lion will eat from the same trough, and a little child shall lead them." MSG*

[58]I Kings 24:12-13, "God may avenge me, but it is in His hands, not mine... be assured that my hand won't touch you, Saul." *—MSG*

[59]Daniel 6: 19-22, "At daybreak the king got up and hurried to the lions' den. As he approached the den, he called out anxiously, "Daniel, servant of the living God, has your God, whom you serve so loyally, saved you from the lions?" "O king, live forever!" said Daniel. "My God sent his angel, who closed the mouths of the lions so that they would not hurt me."

[60]Genesis 22: 12-13, "Don't lay a hand on that boy! Don't touch him! Now I know how fearlessly you fear God; you didn't hesitate to place your son, your dear son, on the altar for me." Abraham looked up. He saw a ram caught by its horns in the thicket. Abraham took the ram and sacrificed it as a burnt offering instead of his son."-*MSG*

[61]Romans 1:17, "The righteousness of God is revealed from faith to faith, as it is written the just shall live by faith." *NKJV*

[62]Isaiah 19:23, In that day there will be a highway from Egypt to Assyria. The Assyrians will go to Egypt and the Egyptians to Assyria. The Egyptians and Assyrians will worship together. In that day Israel will be the third, along with Egypt and Assyria, a blessing on the earth. The Lord Almighty will bless them, saying, "Blessed be Egypt my people, Assyria my handiwork, and Israel my inheritance."

[63]See Judges 19:29 for a similar story about using a cut-up body to send a message of revenge.